ALSO BY BETTE PESETSKY

Stories Up to a Point

Author from a Savage People

DIGS

DIGS

BY BETTE PESETSKY

ALFRED A. KNOPF   NEW YORK   1984

Library of Congress Cataloging in Publication Data

Pesetsky, Bette. [date]   Digs.

  I. Title.
PS3566.E738D5   1985   813'.54   84-47850
ISBN 0-394-53932-X

Manufactured in the United States of America

FIRST EDITION

Who would have undertaken such great works, continued through so many years—have spent such large means out of his fortune—have dug through layers of debris heaped one on the other in a series that seemed almost endless, down to the deep-lying virgin soil—except a man who was penetrated with an assured, nay, an enthusiastic conviction? The Burnt City would still have lain to this day hidden in the earth, had not imagination guided the spade.

—Dr. Rudolf Virchow
in defense of Heinrich Schliemann

DIGS

notes made by m. conlon, county sheriff's office

August 21—Called to Bayley Farm House on Oglethorpe Road, now occupied by W. and S. Simon, because of flashlights and noise in yard behind house. Warned by Mrs. Simon to watch out for hole. Found two women in backyard digging with shovels in large hole (excavation). When questioned, the women (Jane Doe and Jane Doe) stated that they were looking for Captain Kidd's buried treasure. Females about mid-forties. Parked on the road across from Bayley Farm House was Dodge sedan with New York dealer plates.

September 4—Called to Bayley Farm House on Oglethorpe Road, now occupied by W. and S. Simon, because of screaming man on lawn. Found man naked except for greenish loincloth running around the outside of house shouting that it was his. Heard the word *Indians*. Man identified from cards in pocket of coat discarded by tree as a C. Meinhard of East Twelfth Street, NYC, no house number given.

September 6—Called to Bayley Farm House on Oglethorpe Road, now occupied by W. and S. Simon, because of complaint from Mr. K. Marley of 10 Oglethorpe Road about cars filled with noisy or shouting men down the road by Bayley Farm House. Arrived at Bayley Farm House but automobiles had left. Mrs. S. Simon had not obtained license numbers.

September 12—Delivered citation to W. Simon of Bayley Farm House, Oglethorpe Road, for dumping unauthorized soil in County Landfill #1325.

Note to Jerry: Know what you think, but on speaking to them, the Simons do not seem peculiar. Will speak to Mr. Castleberry.

DIGS

October 10—Called to Bayley Farm House on Oglethorpe Road, now occupied by W. and S. Simon, because of people in white robes or sheets sighted at back of property. Arrived at 11 p.m. and found two women, two men, dressed in sheets (Jane Doe, Jane Doe, John Smith, and John Smith). First Jane Doe said she had vision that God would appear to her from "bowels of earth" at excavation. No identification on parties, appeared to have walked to Bayley Farm House from the highway.

Note to Jerry: Wait until next town meeting—all hell will break loose.

sara

notes for conlon

I am in a state of shock, and no one is asking me any direct questions.

But listen, Conlon, I would be glad to tell you anything I know.

My son Alexander said to you, She does not remember.

Not so, Conlon.

Of course, I remember.

Now this whole thing was not about money.

And my Walter was—is—not berserk.

I mean I saw that in the newspapers too.

I went downstairs for breakfast one day.

BUSINESSMAN GOES BERSERK.

I read that. Catchy phrase on page 1, story cont'd on page 4. Never mind, Conlon. What do they know? I could outline it for you. Start with the hypothesis: What has happened? A) Accident; B) Occurrence of unknown origin; C) Illegal activity.

What have I omitted? Mystery? Death?

By the way, Conlon, I appreciate your concern for my welfare.

How do I feel?

Actually, my flesh is healing.

What I'm left with is a scab shaped like a crescent running knee to thigh. Also, there is a tattoo of bruises, purple to grey.

I am writing this, Conlon, on bits of paper, backs of envelopes, anything I can find in the dresser drawers. I never had a desk in this room.

Afterwards I will stuff the papers under my mattress.

No one turns mattresses anymore.

I am being tranquilized, systematically. Valium, Elavil, you name it.

I'm not being held prisoner.

I'm being soothed.

By both my sons—Alexander and Norman.

A most difficult time in her life, I overheard.

Who said that? The kids? The doctor?

The worst moments.

How can they be certain?

Conlon, this is in response to the questions you asked outside my door.

I would like, you said, your mother's eyewitness report of what happened.

Now at that moment I would have gotten up and opened the door, but you understand I was not able to do that. My legs and arms felt wired together. I was hot, I was perspiring, water dripped from my arms like saliva.

Alexander, my baby, stood guard.

My mother, he said, is unable to speak right now.

Truth.

But you, Conlon, I must say, you were certainly very nice about it.

But then we were always on very friendly terms.

I figure you must have a file on us already. You are not coming into this cold. Refer here to the outline, Conlon.

But nevertheless, you only know the flashier moments.

You were always polite, Conlon. If there is anyone to whom I should write a letter of commendation, just tell me.

I will give you an eyewitness account.

How?

I love Walter, Conlon. Even now, when I find that I am not thinking about him as often. It's true. Walter whom I love but have ceased to think about. Believe me, it is absolutely true that there is nothing that I wouldn't do for Walter. But my mind, my mind is saturated with color. I am an artist, you know. And right now color rules. Vermillion, blue, dull brown, copper, transparent black. Yes, my mind is saturated with these hues. I feel a contentment.

Yesterday, Conlon, I heard you inquire about my health.

You sounded sincere.

Thank you.

Eyewitness account. I believe that you should know the details.

I will do for you some pivotal scenes.

The question is where—or what—shall I start with?

Yes, pivotal scenes.

Better that way than I should pour my life out for you.

What shall I tell you first? About the Hole itself? Why it happened? The Historical Society?

A decision, Conlon. Yes, a decision.

I will tell it to you as I wish.

Eyewitness account.

one

"Rascals," the old man said, poking me in the leg with one of his canes. When he poked you, it hurt. "Scoundrels! Conscience—they have no conscience. Responsibilities end with my generation. Who will carry on here? Who? My nephews, paltry souls. Who will care?"

I didn't answer. I wasn't supposed to answer. Was I a match for the old man? I was five-feet-eleven, a strong woman. More muscular than I looked. Sometimes that led me to do dumb things. A man pushed me once on the subway platform. I was waiting for the number 6 train. It was a deliberate shove. "Cunt," he said. He came just past my shoulder. I punched him, my fist into his jaw that was hard and boney and at the same time warm and covered with real skin. He fell down and immediately everyone moved back from us, making a half-circle of dead air space. "She's crazy," the man on the concrete platform said, but he didn't get right up. The train came into the station and I got on. Afterwards Walter said that I was out of my mind. What *that* man could have done to me, Walter said. He held me close.

The old man's cheeks were flushed. His grip on the canes was tight. He suffered from chronic infections of the tear ducts, and his moist eyes were less clear than earlier, but then the business of the day was over. Was freedom possible? No, he could bully me. I knew that. Age can bully you, also money and power. The old man had drunk three maybe four glasses of champagne. It didn't help his wobbling walk, both arms leaning heavily on the handholds of the aluminum canes. He looked well, though. All afternoon at the annual meeting of the DeLeuce Foundation people had remarked how well he looked. Eighty-five, they said, and still going strong.

He had trapped me, made a China Wall of his canes. The backs of my thighs pressed against the carved edge of the tabletop. I felt the branding of rosettes and lozenges. The raised rubber tips of the canes threatened my ankles. The old man had me, I was singled out. This had happened before. That was just one problem with being tall, a prime disadvantage. He had seen me. The old man was slightly drunk, he was about to become nostalgic.

"Shall I find a chair for you, Mr. DeLeuce?" I thought he was going to fall down.

He shook his head with its silver flow of hair. "Two chairs," he said. "Chairs for us."

One finger gripped my sleeve as I steered the way past the conference table which held the buffet, most platters still intact and edged with fluted radishes. They always ordered too much food. Even with the wives of the Board members, we were only twenty.

"Eric DeLeuce," Mrs. Jack T. Petersborough said, waving her plate, her fork, her arm. "I haven't seen you since last spring."

"'Til next spring then," the old man said and hauled his body past her to the chairs against the wall. "Woman's built like a sack of hay," he said to me. He motioned to the caterer's waitress. "More," he called. She brought two glasses of champagne.

I looked at the clock across the room. It was four-fifteen. I couldn't escape. No chance. I was under his dominion, his subjugation. I was an employee of the DeLeuce Foundation. We had two Program Officers. I was one of them. The old man was the Director. Fanny his wife was the Treasurer.

"I know a secret," Eric DeLeuce said. The left eyelid already drooping, fell the rest of the way. It was a wink.

"Secret?"

"Painting."

"Painting?" I kept my tone even, but I was suddenly frightened. If you have a secret life, you're frightened.

"The room, pudding," he said. "You painted your room."

That. It was just that.

"Yes," I said. "I did."

"Why? It was just done—hardly dry."

It had been a dumb fool gesture. I'd painted my office because I didn't like the color. Color was everything. The room was supposed to be painted white. *Crystal White* was printed on the label on the can. They painted every four years. When the paint dried, it was pale yellow. The pukingest of pale yellows. Old yeller. It had jaundiced the reflections from the windows, hepatitized the glow on the furniture. I hated it. I knew what had happened. I guessed what had happened. Fanny had done it. Fanny who loved yellow. I imagined her sneaking over to the painters, bribing them. Crazy old loon, they must have thought. But fifty bucks was fifty bucks. A touch of yellow pigment. Lookeehere, grandma? How's this? And Fanny, the disturber, would croon her contentment. What to do? I had come into the office on a Saturday with a can of Sherwin-Williams, with plastic dropcloths and a roller. It had been hard. It had been terrible. Walter wouldn't help. You don't live there for God's sake, he had said. I had to move all the furniture myself. The DeLeuce Foundation was housed in a brownstone, the ceilings were twelve feet high.

"I hate yellow walls," I said.

"I brought it up at the executive session," the old man said.

"Brought up the *walls*?"

"Yep. Good sign—sign of commitment."

I smiled. Commitment was everything.

The old man finished his glass, tilting it far back. "More," he said.

"Good meeting," I tried, but he wouldn't be distracted.

"The hell with the meeting. Do you know how many annual meetings I've been to? First one I went to was in 1916. We were into Women's Suffrage, hot topic. Anna Howard spoke. Ugly woman, needed a better corset. But I knew my duty. I let her speak. Duty is everything."

"Yes," I said. "Was Fanny upset?"

"About the walls?—hell yes. Did I ever tell you how I met Fanny?"

I closed my eyes. "Yes," I said.

"I met her in 1926 or maybe 1927. I met her at a party. She was drunk. She was falling-down, half-dead drunk. I took her out to my car, and I raped her. Can you imagine doing a goddamn thing like that—raping Fanny? Insipid little snip, not even pretty in 1926 or 1927. Did they say 'rape' then? I think they said 'took advantage of.' Then I married her—it was a society shotgun wedding. Too bad she had money—you can't pay off someone with money."

The old man sighed, overcome with regrets. I looked around the room. No one would rescue me.

"You're interested in history," the old man said.

"Art history."

"History is history. Take Columbus, for instance. I've always rather enjoyed the idea that Columbus brought syphilis back to Europe with him," the old man said. "Think about all those microorganisms curling up inside those warm sailor bodies. It's true, you know, a genuine theory. Myself, though, I got it in Europe in 1916. Yes, it was probably 1916. Who was it? The girls, my dear Sara, the girls. The Annes, Margarets, Ninas, Maries, Bessies, Laras. Where could it have been? Such a young man I was. A bare eighteen at the time—quite bare. Such a hunger, such priapic thoughts. Now it was either on my trip west of Lake Gorda—girls, fourteen, fifteen. A lovely child, one, that frail look of flower, black silk hair. Or perhaps it was in Copenhagen with somebody named Emilie or something like that.

"I was just a boy, I paid no attention, I was immortal. Then came the first chancre, a firm sore. Yet it was painless, my dear, infectious but painless. No pain until the relapses. It was arsenic treatment then. But you do know that the infectious period passes?"

"Yes," I said. "Passes."

The rubber tip of one cane moved across my ankle and up the calf. "Still," he said, "it got my legs. *Tabes dorsalis.* Yes, it got my legs. Worth it, though."

I was staring straight ahead. I was looking very serious. That was lucky. That was what must have brought Dennys across the room. He was carrying a plate with a piece of cake. We always had a sheet cake, white frosting with blue letters: *DeLeuce Foundation Annual Meeting.* The cake was awful.

Dennys was the new Program Officer. He was jealous. I smiled at the old man. I touched his sleeve. Dennys excused himself from his conversation with Mrs. Jack T. Petersborough. I smiled more. Dennys couldn't get across the room fast enough.

"Mr. DeLeuce," he said, pulling close, ignoring me. "I've wanted to talk to you about a few projects I've become interested in—an expansion of our imperatives."

"Here," I said, "take my chair."

I got up. Tall people can be very agile. Dennys was just in time for the full description of the arsenic treatment, then there was the sanitarium in Gstaad, later the Austrian nurse.

"Sara!" the old man called, but champagne had slowed his speech. I was already through the doorway. Who could say that I had heard him?

After Women's Suffrage was phased out, the DeLeuce Foundation went into Homes for Unwed Mothers. Afterwards they went looking for something that would last. There are plenty of *big* foundations that can do the causes, Eric DeLeuce said. The foundation went looking for something else. Let's stick close to home, he said. We were small but solid.

They were funding state projects when they hired me. Small art museums, Indian artifact collections, historical societies. I was perfect, the hiring committee from the Board said. I came to them directly from Ford. I was a non-practicing artist. Right background, they said. They hired me.

Non-practicing artist—those were Eric DeLeuce's words. I lied. I was an artist, my secret life. A practicing artist—although blocked.

Each spring right after the annual meeting I went on my site visits, my tour of the projects that were my responsibility. I went just before the checks were sent for the renewals. I rented a car for the trip. It didn't pay to keep a car in the city, Walter said. Our building didn't have a garage, and he hated the idea of chasing around for a parking space. Anyway, the Foundation paid for the rental. It was a perk, a benefit.

"I can make it the twelfth," Walter said on the telephone, "or the fourteenth, then skip to the twentieth or the twenty-fifth."

I checked my calendar. "The fourteenth then," I said. "Now that's definite, isn't it? I have to make the appointments."

"Right," Walter said. "I'll set it up for the fourteenth. Do we need any liquor for tonight? I forgot to look."

"No," I said. "We have enough."

"Okay," Walter said. "Got to go now."

I hung up. Whenever he could, Walter went with me on my site visits. We made a day of it. If the weather was right, I packed a lunch. We would stop someplace, pull off the road, be alone. It was great.

I buzzed Maddy, the Foundation secretary. There were only four paid employees. "Set up the visits for the fourteenth," I said. "Follow that list—I won't need more than one hour each. End with Castleberry. Remember about the food."

"Yeah," she said.

The food stipulation was important. No luncheons, no food. I would be visiting four projects that we funded. If they weren't told in advance, each group would set up food. And still, there was always coffee and pastries.

I paid a lot of attention to detail. Should an artist behave with abandon? No, I didn't believe that was necessary.

I was planning the trip. I was planning for the fourteenth of April. There were no premonitions, no soot-covered cat pouncing across my path. No neon-lit calendar to point out that April 14th would be my last happy day in New York. And I was worrying about pastries and coffee and food. But that's how it was. Actually, that's how it is for everyone, I believe. I mean on pivotal days— unexpected pivotal days—we behave in ordinary domestic ways. I should not have planned to make this trip with Walter. The schedule should not have been possible. Sorry, Walter, I must go on the fifteenth. But all I did was to reflect how good it had been last year. We'd driven upstate along Route 9, along the Hudson, turning west past Poughkeepsie. A good day, warm. We'd spread a blanket in a field and had a small feast. Afterwards Walter had made love to me. When someone yelled, "Hey you!"

Walter had thrown the blanket across me and gone to meet the man.

"I'm married," Walter had explained calmly. "This is a tryst with another woman, an assignation—better than a motel."

The man—the owner of the meadow—had laughed. "Go to it," he had said.

I didn't know if we could find the same meadow this year.

TWO

They were coming to dinner. But first when I got home I thumb-tacked a note to the back of the kitchen door. April 14th. I wanted to remember to double-check with Walter. Then I started the dinner. I was marinating the strawberries in wine when Walter came home. Walter stood five-feet-ten. His jacket and trousers were rumpled, his tie loosened. Walter once complained that a man in a shoe store had called him "Teach." Why? he demanded of me. How the hell does it show? Your sleeve, I told him. Chalk dust.

"Rotten day," Walter said and kissed me. "How was the annual spaniel?"

"Fine meeting, successful, soporific. April fourteenth?"

"Set." Walter leaned against the counter, frowning.

"Spill it," I said and stopped slicing strawberries.

"Nothing really. Just heard that Eileen is in California."

"In California?"

"Yes. Probably wrong. I'll go clean up."

Did bad news come in threes or twos? Eileen was our Norman's ex-wife. We had a son with an ex-wife. I'm going to California, Norman had said a year ago, and clear my head. Now Eileen was there. Had she followed him? Or vice versa? So there was either one more bad thing coming—or two.

"Shit," I said and mashed two berries.

These were Walter's friends coming to dinner. I mean I knew them, but they were Walter's friends. People after all have different tastes. Who was coming to dinner? Jay and Arthur and their wives.

Walter, Arthur, and Jay graduated from the Bronx High School of Science in 1948. They hadn't gone to that big school reunion that was held a few years ago. They had talked about it, about going as a group, with wives, but they hadn't gone. Who wanted to see a bunch of men turned into suits marked stout? But when that article appeared in *The New York Times*, they were sorry that they had missed it. Next time, they said to each other. Next time, they'd go.

Listen, they would have split up at that reunion even if they had gone as a group. Walter and Jay and Arthur would have moved off in different directions to greet their own particular friends. In high school they hadn't been so close. And that would have left us together, the wives. Marilyn, Louise, and me. We saw a lot of each other, and we had acquired a community of memories. We did things together. I wouldn't say we were friends, though. Jay was the only one who had a previous wife. I never knew her. Her name was Ellie, and one day she became sick with a disease that made her feet elongate and then her forehead seemed to grow upward. Her whole body changed until she died. I used to look at Jay from time to time, searching for sorrow. I believed that I saw it too. I've seen her pictures, Marilyn once said. Ellie was beautiful.

How did we all get together? Serendipity. When we came back to New York from our journeys in the Midwest, Walter met Jay and Arthur at one of those large community parties held to benefit the campaign of Eugene McCarthy. They were popular, the kind of event where everyone gave a donation to be admitted into a stranger's rooms for sherry and deviled eggs and then another pledge. I hadn't gone that evening. Come on, Walter said. Hell, I said, I want to paint. Give a check in my name. I had stayed home. But Walter told me about it. I ran into those friends, he said, you know, those guys from high school. One meeting led to another. Walking our dog, Chaminade, in Riverside Park one Saturday morning Walter saw Arthur again. Arthur's wife Louise called me up. I guess she called up Jay's wife too, and all of us went to Chinatown for dim sum. The following week we all stood in line for a Third Avenue movie.

We were forced on each other, Marilyn, Louise, and I. The men acted as if they had always hung around together. The differences that existed between them seemed less pronounced than the differences that existed between us, the wives. I was at Ford at the time, and Walter was teaching in Queens. Personal tastes and interests differed—and then there was financial reality. At no time could Walter come home and say, Hey baby love, we are off to warm places.

Jay was a chemist at a pharmaceutical house, already at the level where he got cloth napkins in the dining room. Arthur with an earned doctorate—maybe in sociology—was a full partner in his family's chain of discount hardware stores. There was no comparison between how we added up our monthly receipts and they did. I didn't mind, not really—no, not at all. Walter and I had a rent-controlled apartment, not as nice as the others, but not bad. Walter's friends came over to our house as often as we went to theirs. We sat and talked. Given those particular times when we first met, the men usually sat together at the living room side and the women remained around the dining room table among the scraps of food at the other end of the L-shaped room. Our children were grown, our exposed complaints similar, our exchanged anecdotes casual. Bit by bit the men dug deeper into their lives. But at the dining room end, we were very careful. We never said anything that couldn't be overheard. I believed that Marilyn and Louise led a private social life together, but I didn't pursue that.

Marilyn and Jay arrived first. Marilyn didn't believe in skin cancer. She kept her tan all year—I use a reflector, she always said. Her mother was always tan too—look how old her mother was. Marilyn was fond of remarking that she laid it right on the line. How tall are you? she had asked me the first time we met. Five-eleven, I told her. In stocking feet? she asked. Yes.

Arthur and Louise were always last. Arthur was happy, he looked happy as soon as Walter opened the door. "I need a drink," he said. Walter was ready. He gave Arthur a glass. "I'm celebrating," Arthur announced. "New store. Family opposed. I said, Don't pass up the mall location. Who today passes up a mall? I was right."

"So you were right," Louise said. "So your brothers aren't speaking to you."

"Take Louise's coat," I said.

Under her coat Louise wore black. Black sets off white skin.

"Louise is afraid that I'll make her move," Arthur said. "I've got ideas for expansion, more expansion on the Island. Louise is afraid to move. Twenty years in the same place."

"Move?" Walter said and poured more drinks. He knew what everyone wanted. "You people don't know about moving. Move two blocks and right away you don't know where the subway is. Move was my middle name. We moved from Milwaukee in 1939. We packed up everything to go, almost everything. My mother threw away a lot. No more old toys, she said. If you don't play with it, it goes. We can't afford to ship that much. I lost many future antiques that way. We moved to Springfield, Illinois, near the fairgrounds. I hated that. No hill on the corner, no boarded-up house to throw bottles at—there was nothing.

"The furniture doesn't fit, my mother told her sister Lea. Everything is too big, too old. I never should have shipped it. It's enough to say that our father stayed in Milwaukee. We were absolutely certain that he would come after a while. He did. In 1941 we moved to Chicago. Windy City, here we come, my mother said and nudged me. That move didn't bother me. It bothers you more when you're very little. I could start school anywhere. So long, old pal o' mine, my father said and vanished that very first night in Chicago. He'll come back, my mother said. You can bet your boots on that. He did.

"We sold the old furniture, wine-colored brocade and a grey chair with prickly loops. Blonde wood, my mother said. Hooray for the new, she said. We didn't take along any old curtains or a geranium plant for remembrance.

"One day the blonde wood was scratched up, and the veneer loose at the corners. We'll scuttle the ship, my mother said. Back to the old hometown. In fall when the leaves dried up, we moved to NYC. Grand Concourse, my mother said. Now doesn't that have a ring."

"To know where to put a new store," Arthur said, "that's an art. My brother Harold is always saying, What did you learn in college. College, he says, is not where the bottom line is. About new stores—I learned nothing. What I learned, I tell him, is how to apply my senses."

All this I heard as I moved from kitchen to dining room table. The men spoke out loud. I thought Marilyn and Louise were whispering.

"I'm going to a meeting in Houston next week," Jay said. "I'm taking Marilyn. Over there on the wall, Walter, your frame is hanging at an angle."

"Yeah," Walter said, "I'll straighten it. Can't have a high school diploma hanging crooked. Did I ever tell you where I was while you guys marched to *Pomp and Circumstance?*"

"Yes," I said and put a bowl down on the table.

"When the rest of you guys were high-stepping down that aisle, I wasn't there. Where was I? Locked in my bedroom, that's where. My mother screaming her head off. Get out of there, she was shouting. I swear I'll have the super come saw that door down. Did she reach me with her pleas? I vowed never to come out. What had happened? My cousin—same last name, my father's brother's son—had been arrested for stealing from Klein's basement. Why was this newsworthy? Hell, the bastard started to wreck the place when they grabbed him. A picture—a picture of this guy in the *News*. I died. I was disgraced. I was certain that everyone knew we were kin."

"Why did he do it?" Arthur asked. "The cousin?"

"I don't know," Walter said. "He had money. He had a job. I think his family sent him afterwards to a psychiatrist—he wasn't a kid—he was twenty-eight, twenty-nine at the time. He lives, I think, in Sarasota now. A grandfather."

"Eat," I said. "Let's eat."

I led the way, everyone followed.

At the table Arthur started talking about money—big money. I thought it was more of their favorite routine, the act I called *coarse* middle-class. They loved it—pretending they never read a book. Give me some of that chopped liver, Jay will say to the man behind the counter at Zabar's, pointing to the pâté de foie gras with truffles at sixty-six ninety-five a pound. Or the way Walter will wear that Hawaiian shirt with the purple-blue jacaranda down the front that Arthur brought back for him. I thought this talk was part of that—a new part.

"With the right idea," Walter was saying, "you can make big bucks, real mazoola. Then you can do something, you know— then you can create your dreams."

"Oh the call of the wild," said Arthur.

"What a man needs," Walter said that night to his friends, "is a little backing."

"A rich uncle," Arthur said and gestured at his wife. "Get me a little more chicken, sweetheart."

"Who has a rich uncle?" Walter said. "My only uncle was the father of that thief who stole from me my high school graduation."

"An idea," Arthur said. "The Ah-mer-i-can dream. Bubbala, you can have ideas from here to the end of the world."

"No," Walter said. "With the right idea, money can still be made, if you want it enough. One of life's strongest forces is wanting things."

I heard that. I should have perked up, paid attention. I knew about wanting things. It was a game I had played. It was a game invented on my street. What do you want? one little girl would say. I want, said the other, to be a great movie star. I want to be like Dorothy Lamour. Somebody else wanted to be a nurse, and somebody wanted to be married. And that made everyone giggle. Guess who she loves?

"And I want," said little Sara, "to be a great painter."

Wanting things was a first-rate game. I remember also wanting my cousin Leo. In 1942 my cousin Leo was inducted into the army and sent to Fort Leonard Wood. He kissed me goodbye before he left and said, "You be sure and wait for me, sweetheart." He patted my behind, but not under the dress. I was eight years old and already five-feet-three. Leo was five-feet-seven. We put a star in our window for Leo. In a family that ran to girls, he was the only one to go to war. I heard what happened to Leo. Leo met a girl in the USO in St. Louis and got married. Our Leo, everyone said. Leo was ugly. Not a great brain either, I heard.

"Should I still wait for him?" I asked my mother.

"How stupid can you be?" my mother said.

By 1953 it had all changed. I brought Walter home to meet my father. Veronica, my father's second wife, made a company dinner with roast beef, mashed potatoes, dill pickles. My father took Walter aside for a talk. Then my father called me into the kitchen. "So you're going to get married," he said.

I nodded.

"He's not a bad-looking man," my father said.

"No Leo," I said.

"What?"

"Never mind."

"My cards are on the table, Sara. I'll tell you as I see it. You want to marry him because he wants to marry you. He's not a go-getter. Maybe not a hard worker—but I don't want to condemn. He works with papers, with stray numbers. The man needs a product. Something firm. Something you can feel and squeeze. If for instance he was to inherit my chain of four dress stores, I can see they would go poof. So right off the bat, I tell you he won't inherit."

I retasted Veronica's roast beef. "I didn't come here for an inheritance. I came here to introduce him."

"I'll tell you how it is—a grown girl about to get married," my father said. "You look in the mirror—who do you look like? Like your blessed mother? Like me? A big tall girl—you don't look like anyone I know. Did I ever bring this up to your mother? I never did. Now I'm not saying anything, Sara. I raised you to be my daughter and daughter you'll be. But for instance look at my boys—Veronica's boys. Cyril and Cyrus are the spitting image of

me—already at ages four and five. And truth is truth, I must
provide for them."

"Yeah, Pa," I said. I went into the living room where Walter
was trying to resist Veronica as she urged him to have a choc-
olate-covered caramel.

"Thanks for the food, Veronica," I said. "Let's go, Walter."

I closed their apartment door tightly. What I wished on my
father from his Cyril and Cyrus was endless *tsurus*—a euphon-
ious curse.

I mean I never went around saying that I wanted money. I
don't remember Walter ever going around saying that he wanted
money. So that's why I wasn't really listening. They were full of
good food. Those men sitting there. They were at my house.
I had made fillet of sole à la vénitienne, I had made chicken
à la portugaise. We had three bottles of good domestic wine.
I had made my special hazelnut chocolate cake with soft
frosting.

At what point should I have jumped into the conversation? I
mean suddenly I knew where it was going. It was going in the
direction of the Book of Good Ideas. I should have suggested a
movie—wasn't I the hostess? Let's go to a movie, I should have
said. They're doing a revival of *Scenes from a Marriage*. Let's
walk down the street and pretend to be tourists—Walter can wear
his hunter-green polyester jacket with the snags.

But tired from my day, I sat back on my chair at the dining
room table and relaxed. I heard the hum of Louise's voice. "I said
to the bastard, don't tell me that was cut to order. You were
supposed to have measured the damn windows."

I was hearing the story of the windows when I should have
stopped the money story.

"Five thousand," Arthur said. "I'll give five thousand."

Louise at that dining room table immediately forgot the curtains.

"Ditto," Jay said.

"Hey," I said and jumped up too fast for a tall woman. "What's this?"

"A business investment," Walter said. His face was flushed.

"A business investment," I said. I did the laugh, I did the light tones. "No business investments at dinner."

My father had always said, "Two people not to do business with are friends and family."

Behind me at that cluttered dining room table was total silence.

"Discuss it all again in the morning," I said.

"What business?" Marilyn said.

"Who knows?" her husband said.

In the morning it should have ended. It was Saturday morning. We were all middle-aged people, our children were grown, we were set upon our paths. The only variables I could think of facing in our lives began with d—divorce, disaster, death.

I told Walter that he should be ashamed of himself. He was certainly not going to take money from his friends. Walter did not feel good. He took an Alka-Seltzer, he took my strongest coffee, he took some Fernet Banca.

What went on while I sat in my apartment, sat in the room that had once been shared by my sons, sat there and faced my morning sheet of D'Arcy cold-pressed paper and tried to paint— I didn't know. I was an artist. It was April, the ground was late to thaw. I walked Chaminade. The air was pungent.

I didn't believe anything was going to happen. I read to Walter an article from the newspaper. *"I have a lot of options in life," said the sixty-five-year-old grandmother of three on her graduation day.* There was a picture of the grandmother in her white gown and pasteboard cap. She was the valedictorian of her class at the Penwha Community College. Grade-point average was three-point-eight-nine. Being photographed with the graduate were her husband, her daughter, and slightly behind and to the left, her son-in-law. According to the article there was a party in the backyard of the class valedictorian. The family came and neighbors for baked ham and potato salad and three frosted coconut cakes. *The valedictorian, the article continued, was tired by the end of her exciting day. She had cooked the entire feast. What will she do next? "With that education," said her husband, "she can do anything. Still, that's a good job she has at Smellen and Thaser Lumber."*

"Imagine," I said to Walter. "What do you think she'll do?"

"She'll go back to work on Monday doing what she always did," Walter said. "She'll be congratulated. There'll be envy, annoyance, a who-does-she-think-she-is-anyway attitude from her co-workers."

When had they met? Those three men? I had visions of Walter, Arthur, and Jay in an envelope of fog on a street corner at dawn before the coffee shop neon sign went on. An exchange of envelopes. It had happened, and Louise became cool, then Marilyn. Two certified checks for five thousand each turned up in my account. My checking account balance was ten thousand, two hundred, and seventy-three dollars.

Walter was sitting at the dining room table grading papers. "This kid," he was saying, "this kid is brainless. I'm telling his mother that he cannot spell algebra much less start it—he cannot do long division. And she, obese charmer that she is, is telling me that he's a genius. The kid is standing right there and he's smirking. I'm thinking of wiping his nose off and pinning it to the bulletin board."

"Walter," I whispered, "return the money."

"My father," Walter said, "is sending me the Book of Good Ideas by registered mail."

I argued that night, I went to the couch dragging my quilt with me. The *d* for disaster loomed there on the wall more fearsome than other letters.

Walter had telephoned his father in Phoenix. Walter was fond of saying that his father had retired there. Not exactly. His father

had married Marybeth who lived there, and that's how he happened to be in that particular land of sunshine. My father, Walter
had said to me, is a man of contradictions. So I wasn't surprised
when I first saw Walter's father. He was handsome, he was not
growing old, he was paused somewhere—a set piece with wide
lapels, the man I imagined to whom Norma Shearer eternally
held out her arms. He was slim, he had silver hair. "How did you
two meet?" Walter asked the bride-to-be at the pre-nuptial dinner
given by Marybeth's sister. Marybeth laughed, a great laugh that
heaved the depths of her breasts upward from the scoop-necked
dress. "In the aisles of Walgreen's on Broadway," she said and
winked. "I was checking out Band-Aids, and he picked out the
right box for me."

Marybeth was fat, but not loose fat—she was solid, her body
sculpted. Her face had high color, alternating bands of pink and
white. Her eyes were colder though than the smile, those eyes
glistened, and sometimes she spoke sharply to Walter's father.
"Hush!" she said.

We were invited to the wedding held in her sister's apartment.
After the ceremony Marybeth said to Walter, "Son, I'm going to
give you a wedding present in reverse." She handed him a slip
of paper. "My broker's name," she said, "and a tip."

Walter stuffed the paper into his pocket. He shifted his glass
from hand to hand. "Thanks," he said, and his damp fingers
clasped hers. "Thanks."

That night Walter couldn't find the piece of paper. "I must
have lost it," he said. "Damn! Maybe I could ask her for another
one."

"You're kidding," I said.

Marybeth owned a restaurant supply business in Phoenix.
What happened there, we never knew.

Walter's father was proud of his ideas. He wrote them down
as they occurred. "I get them everywhere," he said to me one
day on the telephone. We were in Chicago. "There are one

hundred forty-five in the book. I find them everywhere—you name it—one came to me on the john, one came to me when I was smacked by a wave at Key Biscayne, one I got while reading Kahlil Gibran. When I die, children, the richest thing I will leave to you will be this notebook. Meanwhile, whenever I can, I try a few of the ideas."

I think that was the year we sent him three hundred dollars. It was after the bankruptcy, I believe. "I'm sick of the hardware store, anyway," he said on the telephone. "I spit on the hardware store. Bring Walter back to the Big Time, Sara. I'll let him work on the next idea with me. I owe it to him."

"We'll think about," I said. We were floating through a parade of places at the time. We had just left Cleveland.

"I don't understand," Walter's father said, "how he expects to make it from jobs with papers. I have no taste for papers with numbers—who knows what they mean?"

The Book of Good Ideas arrived by registered mail. I'm the one who answered the door, greeted the mailman, signed my name. The thing to do was to have destroyed the book. I knew that. Was it impressive? I took it out of the wrappings. It was in a box from a department store, a Christmas box. I had never actually seen it before. It was a spiral notebook, adhesive tape on the cover. Written in black ink on the tape, *Book of Good Ideas— property of R. L. Simon.* A thick notebook, blue covers, built-in separators. Kids could keep notes for several classes in that notebook.

I left the whole package on the table—notebook, wrappings, string. Walter saw it when he came home. I wasn't making dinner for him. He brought home a bag from the deli—salami on rye. He took a cold beer from the refrigerator.

I was sitting in the living room. I was pretending to read a magazine, turning the pages, making each page slap against the next.

"Sara," Walter said. "Accept it—I'm going to take the money."

"Walter," I said, "you are not a yahoo, you are not a jerk. Your father never made a dime in his life. Are you forgetting that he moved out of your house—out of your life—when you were twelve years old."

"It was a disagreement," Walter said. "Never mind what my mother told you. He moved in with another woman, didn't he? It must have been sexual."

"Sexual, hell," I said. "Who supported you? Him? And when did you hear from him again, huh? From age twelve to age twenty-six—not a word. He calls *us* up one day—he's stone-broke. And after that, God knows why, he's been your papa ever since. You forgive."

"I forgive," Walter says.

At that moment, I was reminded of Walter's sweet nature.

"You'll lose it all," I said. "Walter, the money of two friends. Kaput! You'll lose their friendship. Kaput!"

Walter shook his head. "Whatever I go into," he said, "we'll do it right. We'll get a lawyer. They'll get equal shares."

The light stayed on in the living room after I went to bed. Walter stayed up reading the Book of Good Ideas. I got up once for a drink of water. He was making notes. Go to sleep, I wanted to say. You have to go to work tomorrow and pin some kid's nose to the wall.

On the twelfth of April, Walter woke up and turned to me. It was a Tuesday. "Madness," he said. "What was I thinking about? What can you do with ten thousand dollars? Along with money, I need time. If you are going to be a success, you can't just jump into it. You need to reflect."

He returned the money.

Maybe this wasn't the right time. Maybe this wasn't the big opportunity. Reality, you see, isn't that strong. A thin strap.

THree

How did the site visits go? The site visits went as they always did. We weren't touching anything controversial. They were friendly, everything was *pro forma*. I picked up a nice compact car from Avis. I packed a picnic lunch. We'd nibble cold chicken and drink wine, and Walter would make jokes about his wife's tough job. The ride was always wonderful. Upstate a Technicolor contrast to the city. We drove past all the old river towns.

"A potentially great day," Walter said. "Where to first, lady?"

I unfolded the map and pointed. "This one," I said.

We sang in the car. We sang "Row, Row, Row Your Boat," we sang "I've Been Working on the Railroad."

We had four stops. All day the sunlight had been intermittent, the air chilly. But the sun returned to glow steadily as we headed for my last appointment. "Here," I said and pointed on the map.

It was early in the blooming season—the forsythia was beginning to turn brown, but there were still enough bushes with yellow fire to attract attention. I hadn't been to this area before. Twice, I gave Walter the wrong directions. But the surroundings were pleasant, not too heavily built up.

"We are definitely off the tourist track," Walter said. "No strips."

"Next left turn," I said. "Yes, we're on the right track." How did I know? There was a sign. We were four miles to Shilton, population six thousand within the incorporated limits. We were two and a half hours from New York City.

Castleberry was waiting for us. He was waiting for us outside the library, pacing back and forth. All my correspondence on this project was with him. He wrote these formal letters, his signature right off the Declaration of Independence. I thought he was an old man— I assumed he was an old man. He wasn't. He was perhaps in his mid-thirties. This was my first visit to the Shilton Historical Society. Castleberry wasn't the Society's President, he was the Secretary-Treasurer. A Mrs. Adele Stopwood was the President.

We paused in front of the library, and at once Castleberry motioned us to a parking spot. Parking was not a problem. But the man insisted on guiding us—he motioned Walter to turn this way, then that. He wore a jacket from some discarded uniform that I couldn't identify, on one shoulder a tattoo of holes where an insignia had been removed.

"Probably an ex-MP," Walter said.

The man was ready to open my car door, with both bow and flourish. "Hello, hello," Castleberry said. "Greetings, greetings."

"God!" Walter whispered.

I poked Walter. "Mr. Castleberry?" I said and offered my hand.

"Mrs. Simon?"

"My husband."

"Mr. Simon! Come into our home. Come into our home, please."

We followed the man into the town library building, the Society was housed in the basement.

"We'll be put out," Castleberry said, "if the library ever expands. But finances these days—yes, finances."

The lower floor had street-level windows, and the two rooms were bright and sunny. There were boxes along one wall, shelves with papers wildly stacked, pictures dropped everywhere, dangling from windowsills. A handful of frames had been hung on one wall. The room looked like a hidden closet, a forgotten storeroom, the aftermath of a disaster. Nothing existed here not coated with dust. I checked my folder. The name of this project was "Retaining the Architectural Past of Shilton and Environs." A modest budget, so small in fact that the site visit was not necessary, but Shilton could fit into the driving half-circle for that day. I had decided—why not go.

"Mrs. Stopwood," Castleberry was calling. "Our visitors."

A woman came out of the back room. A short, thin woman with grey hair. She wore an apron and smelled of library paste. We all shook hands.

"Mrs. Stopwood has a job here," Castleberry said. "A part-time job. She catalogues and repairs books." Castleberry made a gesture. Like an exercise, I thought, called Swinging the Arms. "Look around, please. This is the beginning of our work, our dream."

"Yes," I said. I took a deep breath. "Perhaps you might give a brief description of your plans?" I didn't know whether to look at him or at the Society President.

"Man's search," Castleberry said. "Man's search is everything. My great-grandfather lived here. My father's father unfortunately went west. When the time came to seek a suitable homestead for my *own* children, three, I returned here. *Returned* is the wrong word—I came here. A primal urge, you might say, but after the spawning not before."

I could hear Walter choking. I could hear Walter turning his laughter into a cough.

"Look around you, what do you see? This town is nondescript. Yes, nondescript," Castleberry said. "No architectural wonders here. Our Mrs. Stopwood's family—part Iroquois on her great-grandmother's side—used to live in the second oldest house in Shilton. Gone, all gone. But the past can be recreated. Yes, I believe that. Recreate the past for the future. Photographs. Paintings."

We looked at Mrs. Stopwood. She was looking at Castleberry.

"Come," Castleberry said and half-bowed, "come into Mrs. Stopwood's office."

We had no choice. I was horrified when I saw the card table set up there. He was going to *feed* us? "Mr. Castleberry," I said firmly, "did my secretary forget to tell you that on these visits I prefer that food not be served."

"Yes," he said. "Indeed, she did. Coffee, she said. How many visits on a day? I asked. Four, she said. Then I imagined four urns of coffee, four plates of Danish, straw dough, eruptions of frostings. What we have here, Mrs. Simon, is not a meal. What we have here is my homemade split pea soup, made myself, with a ham bone from Freom's butcher shop. He saves the best for me. Normally, I would offer with this collation garlic bread with the faintest topping of grilled parmesan cheese. Delightful. But I felt that under the circumstances I would dispense with the garlic bread and just do soup."

This time I could distinctly hear Walter snickering.

"I always make this huge, this overwhelming pot," Castleberry said.

The overwhelming pot stood steaming on a hot plate. The whole thing, I assumed, carted in from elsewhere. There was nothing for it, but Walter and I must sit down. Walter, with exaggerated formality, pulled out the folding chair for me. Castleberry immediately began ladling the thick soup into four brown dull-glazed bowls.

The soup was good. No, it was superb. I caught just one glimpse of the look in Castleberry's eyes. He knew.

"Excellent," Walter said first.

"Thank you," Castleberry said. He sat down and proceeded to sip his soup, making a slight gulping sound.

I put my spoon down. "How is the collection of photographs coming along?" I looked at Mrs. Stopwood sitting across from me.

Castleberry sighed. "Slowly, Mrs. Simon. Slowly. The town itself, that is the incorporated town, exists only in old photographs. Fire here in 1879 took it all. Then there was the 1926 storm that did in the remainder. Yet, prior to that fire, prime architecture. Really prime. The Jedlin place, for instance. Descriptions vary, but early colonial. Early, early. Stone walls, thick. One painting, two photographs. In the town—oldest place dates to the Depression. Modern is what they crave around here. Modern as in new.

"How many old families are still here? Already we are exurbia. Without a past, this area will become just another piece of countryside, trees, new houses. We who are left have a responsibility.

I believe in this town. Did I mention that I own the Ode Bookstore and the Castle Cheese Shoppe near the railroad station? Perhaps you saw the Castle Cheese Shoppe?"

"No," I said. "We must have entered town from the other direction. At least we didn't pass the railroad station."

"We have some commuters," Castleberry said. "We are not inconvenient."

He turned to Walter. "Soon, Mr. Simon, there will be a total exhibit. Photographs, paintings. The past."

"Sounds encouraging," Walter said.

"Can you imagine—one woman, one woman now residing in Brooklyn, actually offered to *sell* us her photographs—her ancestry." Castleberry shook his head. "Six photographs for one hundred dollars. Pictures of Covern Hill in 1902, pictures of the twin houses built for Captain Covern. Inexcusable."

"Tough," Walter said.

"I purchased them—with Mrs. Stopwood's concurrence, of course. Yes, our hands were tied. She had the pictures. On loan, I first wrote her. No dice, she wrote back. So I purchased them. Listed in our financial report."

I nodded.

"Know what you can see from the top of Covern Hill?" Castleberry said. "You can see the distant Catskills. Know what the Indians called them?"

"*On-ti-oras*," Walter said.

Castleberry stared at him. Castleberry looked interested, I thought. "Come, Mr. Simon," he said. "I would like your opinion of the beginning of our exhibit—there on the north wall."

Walter winked at me and stood up. "Sure thing," he said.

Castleberry took Walter's arm and steered him to the handful of pictures that were dangling from wires on the wall.

"Look," Castleberry said. "Prime examples. I've put these up side by side like a street—not true, of course—these buildings were everywhere and separated by time too. But here, Mr. Simon, they are a street, a community. I have made them come together, never mind what might have happened in these houses—deaths, drownings, fierce shadows."

Castleberry's plump fingers tapped the glass of each frame. From where I sat, the pictures looked similar.

"Here, for instance," Castleberry said. His fingers had landed on one frame. "This house revealed here in fading tones of grey and black—can't you see the life within? Don't we see the children playing on this veranda, the voices shrill, high-pitched, husband and wife cozily upstairs."

Castleberry's index finger slid to a tiny window. "In this very bedroom, I see them, behind the curtain, the husband and wife beneath a quilt in midafternoon."

"Time!" I said and stood up. "Time to be going." The man was bats, nuts, bonkers. I should have been more careful—hadn't Castleberry's correspondence been a touch strange? Jottings of the deranged. Thank goodness, the grant was for peanuts. I might have given that man real money.

Castleberry nodded formally. "A pleasure, Mr. and Mrs. Simon," he said. "And I hope I have the pleasure of your company again."

He followed us to the sidewalk. "Wait," he said, "I've something for you." He ran back into the building.

"Under a quilt," Walter whispered.

"Midafternoon," I said softly.

Castleberry reappeared slightly breathless and presented us with a stapled sheaf of papers. "My list," he said. "My list of native trees and vegetation. It's mimeo and a little smudged. But next to each species I have traced from an appropriate book a sketch either of tree or leaf or flower. This will make your trip home more worthwhile."

Just a touch of Castleberry was all we had that day, like the first encounter at Plymouth Rock, and potentially just as dangerous.

"*On-ti-oras*," we said to each other and giggled.

"Here," Walter said, "past that clump of trees."

"Check the vegetation chart," I said.
"Shut up."
"Isn't it too cold?"
"No, I have a blanket. It's not cold."

notes to conlon

I could take the old man, Conlon. I could even take Fanny. True, I could not take yellow walls. But we all have our problems. Through it all, I had my painting, my art. My feelings about color, about line, about rhythms. Didn't Walter have dreams? Of course, Walter had his dreams too.

Disorientation? They must have said that three or four times. I heard them through the wall. What were they talking about? Hell, moving from NYC, that's all, leaving the city. Someone sure as shooting will go on about the effects of environment on behavior. As if that applied. Prior to their leaving the apartment in NYC—who said that?—how long had they resided there? Christ, Conlon, you ought to be ashamed of yourself. You never spoke to me like that. Resided there for eighteen years, and *prior* to that resided elsewhere for five or six years and *prior* to that resided in a lot of elsewheres due to Walter trying his wings as a management trainee. In short, Conlon, Walter could not keep a job.

I could end your research, Conlon, if my boys would let me speak to you. She's in shock, they said again. I presume that is somewhat true. I do hurt. I mean I do ache. I took my pulse. A cool seventy.

So there I am, Conlon. Flat on my back, and there you are looking for that eyewitness account. An account that covers all time. The truth, the accurate truth.

So be it, Conlon. I will continue to write it out for you as best I can. What we have here today in the way of writing implementia is one ball-point pen that writes real well. On the side of said pen the inscription *Smellen & Thaser.* Who? Or what? Never you mind. Why I never put a desk in this room, I don't know. For paper today, one envelope standard size with slit seams and flattened down, plus the backs of three calendar pages for the soon to be months of Oct., Nov., and Dec. Ditto the back of a sheet of washing instructions for a sweater. Next time I go downstairs

I'll cop something else. Now this is my house, and I am not being held a prisoner, not at all. No siree. But let's face it, Norman and Alexander do not want me to talk to you. She is not composed, she is not herself, they say. Partially true.

They are afraid, Conlon. Afraid of what happened—the accident, the occurrence of unknown origin, the possibility of illegal activity. They are scared stiff.

You were in on some of what happened, Conlon. I mean you don't have a complete blank waiting for the fill-in. No, you have a file on us. Don't you have a file on us?

Walter decided to become a teacher one afternoon, Conlon. We were living in St. Louis at the time on DeBaleviere Avenue. It was a moist summer afternoon, and one window fan pulled the hot air in, and the other pulled it out. Walter was in a management trainee program. We throw a lot of paper clips, he said. I can hit the wastebasket three times out of four, he said. I didn't believe him. I figured he was going to be canned. His heart wasn't in it. He mumbled in his sleep.

Our Norman and Alexander were little boys. Walter was an aging trainee. He had been a trainee in Cleveland, in Duluth, in Milwaukee. We were in a state of flux, mobile, transient. I had four sets of curtains in different sizes.

I've been thinking, Walter said, about going back into teaching. I mean I wouldn't make such a decision without your approval. I had long hair at the time. What I did was to twist it up and pin it to the top of my head, never mind appearances. It was hot. Then I took a tissue and wiped my neck and the moisture between my breasts. Walter was staring past me and out the window where the traffic moved just as if it weren't above ninety and midday on a Saturday. Where can they be going? he said. There isn't any beach around here. That's it, Sara, we're going east. Let's go.

Did this work out? We packed up and went back to NYC. This worked out just fine. We found an apartment on Riverside

Drive. I gave away all the curtains, none fit. I bought new. Walter became a seventh-grade mathematics teacher. I was then as always an artist. Three days a week I went out to different places as a Girl Friday. You can get away with being called something like that if your typing is only middling. I had my problems with the artistic life, and once in a while Walter thought about business. One day I got a full-time job.

What I think about the ability to make money is this: It's in the blood, a genetic programming, an alteration of the nucleus. Not that I despise money. I just never thought about it as important. I am an artist. Walter didn't despise money either. But his mother also never made much of it. She was a flat-breasted woman, she read poetry. It wouldn't have mattered to her if Walter ended up as a seventh-grade teacher of mathematics. Why not? It used the brain.

FOUr

This explains how we ended up on a country road. It was the fourth month of the marriage of Walter's father to Marybeth. We received a letter. It was written on Marybeth's stationery. Creamy-colored paper with a large scrolled lavender *M*.

The union, Walter's father wrote, *is in a state of civil war. Marybeth has got a body of lava. The woman never sleeps. What I need, Walter, is a small advance of money, either air or bus fare. I cannot put together two dimes here. That woman even counts the change from the grocery store. I could be an asset to her business, Walter. I'll help, I tell her. She stares at me. Hands off, buster, she says. I'm puking here, Walter.*

This was probably true. Let him, I said to Walter. But Walter was planning to send the money. Next paycheck, Walter said. But then one night Marybeth had a yearning for a cup of soft ice cream. We know for a fact that she was wearing her pale green plastic curlers and a khaki-colored caftan. Had she roused Walter's father? Did she say, Get up! She took him with her in her blue Camaro. There are twenty-four-hour places for those cursed with the desire for soft ice cream at three in the morning. The young man who sold her two cones, large-size chocolate, later described the scene. The fat lady, he said, made a bet with these two guys how her Camaro could beat the hell out of their Camaro. You're on, one guy said. These guys bought vanilla, regular size.

The cars collided in the ring of an intersection with a neat flattening of hoods. By the time the hospital located Walter it was over. To his beloved son, Walter's father left all. Marybeth died first by an hour. Her will left everything to her sister in NYC with a bequest of twenty percent of her estate to her husband of record at the time of her death. Walter's father was husband number four. First, Marybeth's sister seemed inclined to dispute the will. The bastard, she said, wasn't even in the family long enough to spit. But then she found out how much there was. What the hell, she said.

"We're not rich," Walter told me, "but certainly something can be done."

He said that to me when I came home and found him sitting in the living room with the lights off. The certified check was in his hands. "Some business," he said. "This could buy time."

I'm always reading these stories about how people report that from their earliest days they always knew what they wanted to do—Dürer at thirteen, Saint Simon at twelve, Mozart at eight. All right for some, yes. But for others? Was it hindsight—did they really want this—a straight line through life? Perhaps. It was never so clear for me, yearning as I did for popular life, disputative, bad-tempered, always expecting.

Listen, I thought a lot about Ginger Rogers. I could have danced. I'm certain I could have danced. I did imitations for the family. I did "Shirley Temple singing *The Good Ship Lollipop*" and Mae West inviting you to come up and see her some time. What for? I didn't know. I was only nine. I went from this, though. I went from this straight to Amelia Earhart.

Did someone save my early drawings? There was a doorstop made in kindergarten as a Mother's Day present. It was green with a flower painted on one end. A present, my mother would say, my baby made it for me. I had Crayolas—forty-eight colors—coloring books, I stayed within the lines. Was I culture deprived? My mother stood me up against the wall and drew a line for height. Tall for a Jewish girl. It was 1940. A child, the neighbors said, she'll stop growing soon. I didn't. We had an apartment off Kings Highway. It was pleasant, there were green cloth awnings put up every summer by the janitor. There was no doorman, though. Later, my mother said there was. But there never was one there.

We went one summer to a bungalow by Lake Wintucket. I had a set of No. 12 Watermark watercolors. Go paint, my mother said. I took a canvas folding chair to the beach and practiced trying to paint the way sand looked on my paper.

The child, someone asked my mother, is *stumm?* All day she fills paper with tan paint. Always a disgrace, my mother cried.

Did I really want to be an artist? I didn't go to museums at every opportunity. I displayed no precocious talent. Yet I began to draw. Began to want to draw, to paint. We moved to Manhattan, to Washington Heights. I was tall for a Jewish teenager. No one would want me. No one, God forbid, will ever marry me. I should wear nothing but ballet slippers, my mother said. Wear Capezios. You think height doesn't matter, she said. Slouch, she said.

I bought a set of watercolors. No. 347 Mastersons. I did not look good in ruffles, in pleats, nor when I said coyly, *Who me?* My father made money from the dress stores that now specialized in ladies' uniforms.

My father never said to me, What do you want? You think there isn't a difference between that and—*What do you want from my life?*

First of all my mother was wrong. Not only didn't every girl on that block get married, but I did. My mother however didn't live to see it. One year after we unveiled her stone in that cemetery on Long Island, my father married Veronica. I want you to call me Ma, she said. I called her Veronica, but she was basically nice. She played a lot of Perry Como records. It was Veronica who taught me how to dance. It matters, she said, when I protested. When you are finally asked—what will you say? I don't know how. For such a big girl, you got small feet.

Art was an elective. I elected it. Everyone those days wanted to get married. Hardly anyone wanted anything else.

Being an artist was expensive. What I did with my allowance was my business, my father said that plain and clear. So I spent all of it on art supplies. Veronica sneaked from the household money and bought me Maybelline mascara, anonymous tubes of lipstick, and stockings. I said that I wanted to go to college and study art. Veronica asked my father, Do you think it's a good idea? Why not? my father said. She'll be able to make a living. There's advertisements. Posters.

I decided to go to Buffalo. I didn't know one place from another. The woman who taught art in high school was surprised. I don't remember your work, she said. Show me what you've done.

I went to Buffalo with a trunk filled with white cotton blouses and plaid skirts. Avoid ruffles and lace, Veronica said. On tall girls and also on older women they look foolish.

I also looked foolish dancing.

I met Walter in Buffalo. He was in a training program, he was an industrial intern, it did not pay a living wage.

They had assigned roommates at Buffalo. I got a brunette from Ithaca. "From New York?" she said to me. "Why'd you come here from New York?"

Her name was Malka, and she looked good as an artist. She wore tight black pants and a loose grey sweater. "Have a cigarette," she said. "The hell with unpacking. Let's reconnoiter."

But I thought how hard it would be to iron all those wrinkled cotton blouses if they endured another hour in that stuffed trunk. I let her reconnoiter by herself.

"Art," Malka said to me one day, "is like anything else—you have to stand out, you have to have connections."

Another day I came back to our room, and it smelled peculiar. "Like ammonia," I said.

"Right," Malka said. "On my hair with peroxide. I'm going blonde."

Malka made Joseph L. Atkins' master art class.

"Babe," she said, "you try for it too."

But I knew better, Malka had real training. "Babe," Malka said, "the atmosphere there is great. Try."

What I did at that time were pictures of streets all in one color, just shades of one color, like sand. Maybe there would be figures, two figures walking away. I left three pictures for Atkins to see, not even matted, just paper rolled up and held together by rubberbands.

I made Atkins' master class. I could work in the back of the room. No one ever bothered me. You see, I wore these white cotton blouses and plaid skirts—Malka said it was remarked that I looked like I was baking for Home Ec. Malka was elected that year to be Queen of the Beaux Arts Ball.

Did I care? Of course.

I didn't hang around with anyone. Come on, Malka would say. But I never did. I drew, I painted, I studied.

It was Malka who came into our room one night and pushed my shoulder. "Wake up," she said. "Hey Sara, wake up."

"What?" I was startled. "What?"

"We went to Land's Tavern," Malka said. "A bunch of us. We'd been drinking all evening, but we ran out of bottles so we went to Land's. You know what Atkins said there? You won't guess."

"Atkins was there?"

"Sure he was. You know what he said—like out of the blue, like that. He said—and this is a direct quote—Sara Bromfield has more talent than all of you, than every single person at this table, in this whole place, in the whole damn school. Sara Bromfield is an artist."

What could I do knowing that? I painted the whole weekend. I thought that I could work forever.

It was Malka who talked me into going with her to a party. It wasn't hard—it was Saturday night, my back ached from standing all day, it was spring, there was dogwood blossoming. I put on the dirndl skirt, the three petticoats, the Capezios.

"You look," Malka said, "like choir practice." She shook her head. "Never mind, what the hell. Let's go."

Now at this party held in someone's apartment whose name I never heard, there was plenty of smoke, plenty of cheap wine, a punch made from purloined lab alcohol. I sat down on a couch, seated I didn't look so tall. I had some wine, I had something else in a glass. It became very crowded. I recognized several people. I recognized three former blind dates. Someone yelled, "Let's play Malka's game. Let's play Life."

I believe that I may have yelled, "Yeah!"

Lots of people were playing.

What you had here was an early version of an orgy. I had more to drink. Perhaps I drank several more. I was no longer on the couch. Someone else was on the couch. I was on the rug, several people were on cushions. I was being unbuttoned, the elastic bands of my petticoats were being pulled down, there was a pink rubbery pattern around my waist. I believe I had someone to the left of me and someone to the right of me. The one on the left was down to my last petticoat and ready for the garter belt. "Tomorrow," I said or maybe thought I said, "tomorrow, I'll try to paint a portrait. Yes, I will."

Were my eyes closed? I opened them. It was Walter. Wasn't he one of the blind dates?

"Hi there, Selena," he said.

"Sara," I said.

"Yes, Sara."

I looked up at Walter. "Are you thinking of me?" I said.

Walter was squeezing my breasts, but also he was looking around the room. Around us were pretty girls. He was distracted.

I considered the situation. My Capezios were lost. I was shrinking my length—even drunk—with knees bent on the floor. My purple lipstick was almost gone. I was tall.

"Walter," I said, "I want to celebrate. I am an artist."

He turned back to me. The room was shadowy. I thought it was lit by candles. I used unsuspected gymnastic ability. My knees pushed against the porcupine-sticking rug. I went down on Walter.

I was going to quit college. Let's get married, Walter said. Atkins had a fit. "You are stupid," he said. "You can get married anytime—maybe you'll never get married—who cares?—but these are the years for you to paint. Are you pregnant?"

I shook my head.

"Painting," Walter said to me, "can be done anywhere."

Veronica sent me one of those trick postcards. Held in a certain way the brunette in a sarong winked at you. In the space for a message Veronica had written—*I told you so!*

Walter and I left for Cleveland in June. It was a new management training program. Veronica forwarded the letter to me in Cleveland. I had been awarded the college's Dexter Art Prize for 1950. It was a check for two hundred and fifty dollars.

Walter has always supported me in my painting. He has had faith in me. Why do I destroy all my work? Ego.

Did Walter go to sleep the night the check from Marybeth's estate arrived? All night he sat up. In the morning I found him sitting in the living room next to a crowded ashtray. He still smoked then. He had been reading the Book of Good Ideas. The early entries in the notebook were dated from forty years ago.

"Some," Walter said, "my father tried. Health food drive-ins, buying cloth in Singapore, running social clubs. Some aren't half-bad."

I made coffee. What I believed in was the philosophical Walter. The Walter who dreamed—but sensibly.

"What do you think?" Walter said. "Alexander and me—we could go into something together. Father and son. Norman—Norman would never go for it."

I began to get upset. I thought he was crazy, I decided it was from lack of sleep. "Leave them alone," I said, not kindly.

"Alexander," Walter said.

"He's happy," I said. "He likes what he's doing."

"A librarian, for Christ's sake. He makes peanuts."

"Happy," I said. "Our Alexander is happy."

"Brains," Walter said. "He has a mountain of brains."

The following week, Walter gave Alexander five thousand dollars. He sent five thousand dollars to Norman in California.

"I want to move," Walter said.

"Good God, why?"

"I gave it much consideration," Walter said. "It would be stupid to just jump in and invest the money in a business."

"Right," I said.

"So first we'll move. I believe that we would have a better chance out of the city. The city is essentially taken. I'll look into it."

I let Walter look into it. I assumed it might take forever.

It didn't.

Walter called me at the office. "Dinner," he said, "is on me."

"You want to go out? It's only Tuesday."

"Absolutely. I'll pick you up after work."

"All right," I said. "Where are we going?"

"I'll decide," he said. "As a matter of fact I've already chosen the restaurant—a surprise."

What I did after the telephone call was to check the calendar. Both of us usually had trouble remembering birthdays, anniversaries, that kind of thing. What had I forgotten? I was nervous.

At six o'clock, I put on more lipstick, I combed my hair, I did an overall spray with the desk bottle of cologne.

"It's romantic," Maddy said as she covered her typewriter.

"It's my husband," I said.

Yes, Walter looked excited. His face was flushed. "Come on, sweetheart," he said and held my arm.

The restaurant was French, dark, a suggestion of passion in the style. "A gourmet's delight," Walter whispered.

"Maybe," I said. In fact, the food was only fair, but the wine was excellent.

"I'm waiting," I said finally.

Walter nodded. "I've been considering for weeks—you have to admit I didn't just announce a one-two-three decision. I want us to leave the city, Sara."

"I know," I said. I twirled the half-empty wine glass, accidentally made a small tidal pool of red on the tablecloth. "You said that before."

"I mean I want to go now, Sara darling. You'll resign, I'll resign."

I felt choked, but I was certain that I could keep it out of my voice. "We have to think this through, Walter. What will support us?"

"The Marybeth money at first. We'll use up some capital but just a little."

I reached for Walter's hand, only my fingers were cold. "We're settled," I said. "My work, your work."

"Look," Walter said, "think about your painting, Sara. The hell with the work. I mean when will you have the time for painting. This is it—right now, kiddo—these are the years for painting. Can you pass this up?"

Suddenly, I visualized an endless circle of time—just me and my paint. "Is there really enough?" I asked. "Enough money for this—for this dumb-fool thing?"

"You bet," Walter said.

"Perhaps I could take a leave of absence," I said. "I wonder if the old man would give me a leave of absence?"

Walter smiled. He leaned over and kissed my earlobe. "Bull's-eye," he said.

My father had a co-op on Seventy-second Street. Veronica never lived to see it. Son Cyril ran a couple of the stores. No one knew what happened to Cyrus. "I don't understand," my father said to me on the telephone. "Two grown adults leaving the city. How far from the city?"

"Two hours—a one-hundred-twenty-minute drive. Maybe a little more when the traffic is heavy," I said.

"Why would two grown adults leave the city?" my father persisted.

"Walter wants to go into business," I said. "Walter is going into a business upstate."

"A business upstate is nuts," my father said. "Walter knows nothing about business. Walter reads. Tell me, does he still read?"

"Yes."

"See!"

Jay called me. "I hear that Walter is going into business up-state?"

"Yes. Maybe."

"What kind?"

"He doesn't know."

"What do you mean he doesn't know? Has he *forgotten* his friends? His one-time partners?"

"He's for the time being buying a farmhouse."

"A what?"

"A farmhouse."

How had we ended up on a country road? We had come out blind. Walter had stopped the car on a street between here and no place, I thought, and walked into a real estate office. Steiglitz from behind his desk quizzed us about our needs. He thought we had been referred by someone. A country house, Walter had told him, as primary residence. We were willing to cover a wide area of the county. Walter pulled out a map on which he had made a big circle with pencil. The sight of the map chilled me. Could we really be doing this?

"Inside this circle," Walter said. "Anywhere inside this circle."

I bent over and looked at the map. I squinted. "Isn't this near whatchamacallit—that Shilton town?"

"General vicinity," Walter said. "Nice country."

Steiglitz nodded and took his listings and drove us every-where—contemporaries, old houses, handyman specials. We were hard to please. Sunday after Sunday, Steiglitz took us around. He took us to a house on Oglethorpe Road. A farm-style house with twelve acres. The house had been painted white the previous year and had a wide porch that ran three-quarters around its girth. In truth, it had never been a farmhouse, just built to look like one.

"The Bayley Farm House," Steiglitz said and drove on.

"I've seen it before," Walter said and looked at me.

"I haven't," I said.

"Yes," Walter said. "Now I remember. On the wall. This house was in one of the pictures on the wall of that library. You know— one of the Castleberry pictures."

Steiglitz grew more enthusiastic. He smiled more. His fillings were brown-toned. "You know our Mr. Castleberry? A very civic-minded man."

"Why?" I said to Walter. "Why would this house have been on the wall? It's not historic. Mr. Steiglitz said it was built in 1940."

"On the wall," Walter said firmly. "That's it—I liked that pic-ture. If the house checks out, that's it." He looked at me.

I shrugged.

It was at that point that Steiglitz took us for very serious. "Listen," he said, "these are modern times and there are Jews like us all around here, maybe thirty to thirty-five percent. But of all the places I've taken you—take for instance that stylish new cedar and glass job on Monroe Road. On Monroe we have a Jewish doctor and a dentist. Or maybe we should go for one of those new babies on Huntington or Pearlville?"

Did we say anything? No.

Steiglitz sighed. We were not his idea of the perfect couple. "I'm a judge of people," he said, "it's my business." He stared at us, two perfectly carved rows appearing on his forehead. Steiglitz looked at me. "No schools?"

"Yes," I said. "Grown children."

Steiglitz slowly nodded. I thought that we had at last fitted into one of his customer profiles. Middle-aged couple about to satisfy that yearning for a country home, leaving the city behind.

Walter smiled—he looked benign, he looked angelic. He was wearing his Sunday-look-at-houses tweed jacket with the big patch pockets and his grey slacks. Steiglitz took him for a rube, a house hick. "Let's go take another look at the Oglethorpe Road house," Walter said.

Steiglitz checked his pockets for keys. Current house owner was Myra McConigle, a widow who had left for Tampa against Steiglitz's advice, he told us. Hang around, he had said. An empty house after all suggested an anxious owner. She hadn't listened.

All the way to Oglethorpe Road, Steiglitz spoke about the glories of awakening in the country. Once he looked over his shoulder directly at me. "The produce," he said, "you wouldn't believe. The canning is fabulous."

I smiled back at Steiglitz.

At the house Walter pulled out an awl from his pocket to test the beams for solidity, searching for termite-softened wood. He went to work on the wiring. "The electric board," he told Steiglitz, "less than one hundred amperes." I held Walter's jacket as he pulled out his notebook and humming softly vanished into a crawl space, banging at pipes.

I tried to accept what I could not change by arguments or tears or common sense. This move might be beneficial. For years I had used the odd corner of a bedroom as my studio. Once when we lived in Duluth in a duplex, I had an entire room to myself. Maybe here I could paint. I wandered out into the yard, half cultivated, half in woods. It looked neglected. It was nice, though. I would learn the names of trees.

Walter had made innumerable calculations in his notebook.

"The widow," Steiglitz said, "is not in a hurry. She is well situated."

"That's all right," Walter said. "If not here, then elsewhere."

notes to conlon

We moved out here, Conlon, out here in the middle of nowhere. We moved on the twenty-eighth of December. City people. How had I permitted it to happen?

Walter had seduced me into moving. It hadn't been hard, not after he found the right line. "Resign," he kept whispering in my ear. "Think, Sara, you could paint all the time."

I began dreaming then in swirls of color.

We moved into the house on Oglethorpe Road. "We've arrived," Walter shouted that first night. "Honest, honey, did you ever think we'd own such a place—a genuine, woodsy house?"

My Walter glowed, his face reddened by unseasonal rushes of blood. He wanted that night to make love five different ways. But first we must tape the uncurtained windows with newspaper. There could be someone out there—I didn't believe in the innocence of country life. Walter taped the newspapers in place with Scotch tape, masking tape, electrical tape, parcel-post tape that curled unwillingly against the glass. We did it five different ways.

Walter bought cans of white paint, great galvanized buckets, and expandable ladders. I bought a feather duster with a collapsible pole and a certificate that the feathers were genuine ostrich. I would help him, his partner in these efforts. The rooms were large, square. Steiglitz had pointed out the generosity of the previous owner in leaving for us a cabinet that covered one wall of the dining room. I tried to push it—a huge mahogany armoire. It wouldn't budge. It was a relic—a place to keep bones. "We got taken," I called out to Walter. "The damn thing weighs a ton."

I climbed onto a chair to investigate another legacy—an elk's head with cross-eyed glassy stare that was nailed to a wooden plaque and hung on the wall near the door to greet visitors. I rubbed the tiny brass plate embedded in the wood. "Pointchern Hotel, 1937," I read out loud. "Think the elk was stolen?"

"No," Walter said. "Hardly fit in a suitcase, would it?"

"You mean they *bought* it?"

Walter kept on painting. On the wallpapered walls, lattices climbed ever upward. I discovered window seats, alcoves. On the blue-grey slate roof an unreliable weather vane with rooster shape proclaimed an east which was west. I scrubbed the grey fireplace stones stippled with dark streaks. "Mouse droppings," Walter said.

What was in the basement? Trough-shaped laundry tubs with tobacco-colored veins of rust. If there were any house ghosts, they certainly would have to be down there. I could see the ghost laundress, in fact, doomed to wash and iron in primitive fashion. "Not in 1940," Walter said. "The tubs were probably never used—a jot of ancient life, for atmosphere."

One day ants invaded the kitchen like a well-trained army—not guerrillas—marched up the walls in columns four abreast. A water bug, black and shiny and the size of a campaign button, sat next to a yellow ceramic pitcher. All this I saw. I was fascinated. I would paint now.

Walter was rattling around. Walter was going out to look for a suitable business, put the rest of the money to work. No hurry, Walter said. In March, fat purple hyacinths appeared in sturdy rows beneath the kitchen window. Walter bought *The Audubon Guide to Wild Flowers, The Guide to Birds of the Northeast, The Guide to Trees of the Northeast.*

Me, I was busy practicing my arts.

One Saturday a thick brown envelope was stuffed into our large country mailbox. The envelope was addressed to Walter Simon. Upper left-hand corner it said *Castleberry*. No stamps—put into the mailbox—a clear violation of the law. "Here," I said to Walter.

"For me?" he said and opened the envelope.

What was it? A framed photograph. "Look," Walter said smiling. "I'll be damned. This is the picture that was on the wall in that library. See—I told you this was the house."

I stared at the photograph. Our house looked older in that picture—stiff, alone in its space. I disagreed with Castleberry. In this picture, the house looked unpeopled.

"I'll be damned," Walter kept saying.

I left him in the kitchen looking at the photograph.

Castleberry figures in this, Conlon. Castleberry figures in this a lot. Wasn't it Castleberry who persuaded Walter to join the Historical Society? Mangy people.

This is another Castleberry incident. Castleberry smiled at me. I didn't like that. My arms were full from Stop & Shop. "I ran into your husband," he said, "just the other day. In my cheese store. Fontina, Danish Port Salut. Oh yes, I do tie my people into their purchases. I recognized him right away. Come down next Sunday, I told him, and see our exhibit. There are some pictures, I told him, that will surprise you."

I noted that Castleberry did not invite me. Did I care? Actually not.

Two days later Castleberry sent Walter an official invitation to join the Shilton Historical Society. "Why not?" Walter said. "I'll send my dues. It can't hurt."

"The Shilton Historical Society!" I laughed and pushed Walter's arm. "You must be kidding. Why not join the Grange or maybe the Farmer's Cooperative or the ILGWU?"

Walter went to the exhibit. He went to the opening on a Friday evening. They served coffee and Danish. He woke me up when he came home.

"You'll never guess, Sara," he said, "what I found."

"No," I said.

"They had all the photographs up on the walls—there in the basement. All that junk we saw was cleaned up. Admission was

three dollars. I was walking around, Sara, being polite and looking at the photographs in those black wooden Woolworth-type
frames. Beneath each picture was a hand-printed caption pinned
to the wall. An Amateur Hour exhibit."

Where had the money from the DeLeuce Foundation gone?
I wondered.

"Then," Walter continued, "on the wall where it makes a
sharp bend to box a pipe, I made my discovery." He paused.

"What?" I said.

"There was a picture on the wall, not a photograph but a kind
of fanciful architectural drawing. I looked more closely, I examined the map beneath the picture. What I had found, Sara,
was the following: Our property was the original site of Shilton
Court."

"What the hell is Shilton Court?"

"An apartment house."

"My God, Walter," I said. "Let me go back to sleep."

"On our property, Sara. There's a pamphlet about it—a rural
retreat, a dream influenced by the architect's travels. The dream,
the courtyard, the stone fountain. By 1912 the building was gone,
destroyed. Gone, you see, burned down or razed. No record. Castleberry came up then. So you found it, he said. He's going to
give me copies of the drawings, the map."

I love Walter, Conlon. Never mind what you have heard. I believe
that you deserve to know the details. Conlon, every family divides
itself. Two groups, the rich relatives and the poor. The norm is
variable. In my family—mother, father, etc.—we were on the
rich side. Walter was not. Now what rich meant was only that
we did not live either above the store or behind it. Although
later it got much better.

This however is not about money. It is about love. I love Walter. And as he slips away from me, I feel it stronger.

. . .

DIGS

Yesterday afternoon, Conlon, you spoke to Norman about the Hole. Wrong son. What the hell do I know? Norman said.

The Hole.

Walter picked up that obsession like he had caught a cold, one of those bad ones that linger on and on and won't end, and people say be patient, wait until the weather changes.

In March, Walter began getting up early in the morning to do exercises. Push-ups. Sit-ups. Weightlifting. I thought right away a girl.

"What the hell are you doing?" I asked.

"I'm getting into condition," Walter said. "I'm flabby. It's for a project. You need stamina for physical activity."

In March, Walter tested the soil. "Still frozen," he reported.

In April, Walter began to dig. He had a Hansen No. 2 shovel, blunt nose. He put two little wooden stakes in the ground, tied a string to each stake and began to turn over soil along the line.

"Hey Farmer Brown," I yelled out the back door. "I swear the vegetables will be cheaper if we buy them at the market."

Walter smiled.

How was I to know? And even so—what could I have done at that point? Told the children that their father was digging in the backyard?

When did Mr. Simon start the Hole (you said "commence the digging")?

I know when it began, Conlon. It began in spring. With the thaws. Eleven months ago, before the trouble, before we moved away from the city, before the changes that cannot be reversed, I would get up every morning and perform certain routine functions. I didn't put on makeup, I just washed, brushed my hair, dressed, and walked one block to buy two hot bagels and *The New York Times*. Then I went back to our apartment where I ground coffee beans fresh, made the coffee, ate a bagel, and read the newspaper, starting for no particular reason with the Metropolitan Section. After a time, Walter would come in, drink some of the coffee, eat the other bagel, then he would go. We never had any formula leavetaking. Like have a good day, dear. No, we did not speak much in the morning, not from any lack of interest in each other, but just from not wanting to speak too much in the morning. This was how it was. Now I knew that I would eventually enter the subway in the morning and go where I wanted. I tell you these things, Conlon, to emphasize the effects of environment upon behavior. There in the city we were all right, we were well-adapted city péople. We were not trapped by disorders of the spirit.

When did Mr. Simon commence the digging?

I know.

Do I blame Castleberry?

Yes.

What I believe, Conlon, is that the Hole could have been kept secret. Alexander believed that. Wait, he told me, just wait until the weather changes. Wait until winter. Can you dig in winter?

But the Hole went public, Conlon.

The Hole went public in the local edition of the Gannett newspaper.

MAN DIGS HOLE

A week earlier, inclining to a rumor, a photographer came out. But I stopped him. That's why there was no photograph that first time. Walter hadn't been home when the photographer came. Walter would have led the man around to the land in the back, shown, explained, described. Walter would have been charming. Have a drink, Walter would have said. Not me.

I put Chaminade on a leash and went outside. "You get off my property," I yelled. "You get the hell away from here."

I was effective—I think I was effective. The barking dog, the sun lighting up the ends of my hair making it look flame-licked. I had a branch in my hand, held it like a spear. I was trying for savagery.

"Going, lady," the man said. "You hold tight to that dog."

I told Walter.

"I want a rifle," I said.

Walter stared. "A rifle? *You?* We don't believe in that."

"I do," I said. "You can just bet I do."

"Come on, sweetheart," Walter said. "Cut the crap."

That newspaper article brought four telephone calls. One from a laughing woman who said, "Tell me, do the people in China really walk upside down?"

I hung up.

notes to conlon

For a wedding present, Conlon, my father sent a certified check for one thousand dollars. I never told Walter. I folded that check and put it in the bottom of my wooden junk-jewelry box. It's still there. The ink turned the color of copper.

One day Walter buttered his toast and said to me, "I am about to make my move. I am going to buy a motel."

I was stunned. What had gone wrong? I wondered. Were we still following advice from the grave?

"The Book of Good Ideas," I whispered.

Walter shook his head. "No," he said. "I really couldn't find anything suitable. I've been checking out this motel—casing it, you might say."

"*Which motel?*" I was afraid that I knew.

"The Stopwood Motel," said my Walter, my sweet Walter.

"The one owned by Adele Stopwood's stepson?" I said.

"He doesn't own it," Walter said. "The entire family does. He runs it. He wants to go west. Tells me that he has California on his mind."

"Shit, Walter," I said. "What do you know about motels? The damn thing is half-empty most of the time. We are *not* on the tourist trail. We are not!"

"I am not a fool," Walter said. His face was flushed.

I was doing this all wrong. I had been lost upstairs, lost in my atelier. I had left Walter too much alone. To wander everywhere.

"Walter," I said, calming my voice, dropping the tone, "I don't think that we can afford it."

"With a business loan," Walter said, "after the down payment. The Stopwood boy—he said that he would stay and run the place for a time until I got the hang of it."

I bet he did.

. . .

I never thought about art in terms of money. I am plagued with this huge, this impenetrable block. I thought that out here in the country I would be able to work again—that a theme, a vision would come back to me. In the city I would sit and make pictures. Then I would rip the paper into eighths and throw it away. I have to give Walter credit. He never asked for an explanation. He never asked me why.

Now there I was looking for my theme, my vision. How could I stop Walter when he began the Hole? No, I didn't really think that I could. But then I didn't try. Was it part jealousy? Part respect? Had Walter come into his own—while I was still looking?

Can you imagine, Conlon, the flak that everyone threw at me for not stopping Walter from digging? But at the beginning, I couldn't stop him. I mean—was it right to stop him? He's a great reader, Walter. He should have been a philosopher. Let me relate to you an incident with Arthur and Jay in the city.

Walter said, "The philosopher has a moral responsibility. And it is one that I would have welcomed."

"For God's sake," Jay said, "why didn't you become one then?"

"Yeah," Arthur said.

Walter smiled. "No money in it."

They roared. They liked that.

This morning, Conlon, I discovered that Norman is putting together a folder about the Hole. Discovered this by accident. I went downstairs for breakfast. If you don't eat, Norman said to me, Waddington will have to put you in a hospital. Norman was scrambling some eggs for me. I went to the refrigerator to get milk. I saw the folder then, Conlon. A manila folder on top of the refrigerator. Norman had his back to me, so I opened the cover. Clippings inside and notes. I had less than a second, not enough time to examine them thoroughly. But I grabbed a piece of paper and stuffed it into my bathrobe pocket. Later, I will try for more.

Couldn't wait to get back to my room to see what I had snatched. This is it, Conlon. This is a description of the Hole. An early interview. Norman did not identify the newspaper.

Walter Simon, former schoolteacher, has dug what may be one of the country's largest holes dug by one man with limited power tools. The only use of power that Mr. Simon admits to is a pump to remove water from his huge hole when it rains. What is he digging for? Buried treasure? Indian ruins? Maybe a swimming pool? No, indeed. Walter Simon is digging up an apartment house. That's right—an apartment house that according to Mr. Simon was built on the site of his home in 1910—to be more precise in his backyard.

"What I found," says Mr. Simon, a muscular fiftyish man, "was that my property was the site of Shilton Court. An apartment house designed by a man named Lazarre. A visionary who planned a series of two-story buildings with connecting courtyards. Rooms of great beauty with strange configurations, some five-, some six-sided. A rural community life not based on any defined community rules—just beauty. This Lazarre built the first apartment building on my site— there are drawings of it. Beautiful, the garden, a fine stone fountain. A small building, just ten units. The building seems to have vanished one year later in 1911 or 1912—gone, razed, burned down."

"And you are looking for this apartment building?"

"Yes," says Walter Simon.

A man in search of his own lost Atlantis. Good luck, Walter!

All right, Conlon, Walter was digging up an apartment house.

The clean and pure parts I can accept.

One day Walter said to me, "I paid my dues, I'm a card-carrying member of the town Historical Society."

"Yes," I said. Sure. Why not? I was thinking shades of blue, you see. I misunderstood his meaning—I was thinking we'd get some kind of Society bulletin—the *National Geographic*.

Did I tell you, Conlon, that the Shilton Historical Society began meeting in our house. Walter should have warned me in advance, but he didn't. I opened the door one afternoon and there they were—twelve of them. "Good afternoon, Mrs. Simon," Castleberry said. "We have come for our meeting."

What could I do? I let them in. I made coffee, I served scones and jelly.

The people who really went to the Historical Society meetings weren't town newcomers. There was a cadre of party workers. Sometimes I would sit in the kitchen and listen to their meetings. After all, it wasn't a secret society. One man reminded me of Fatty Arbuckle. Castleberry ran the meetings, never mind Mrs. Stopwood. They talked and gossiped at the meetings, they told stories about the Shilton High School baseball team and about their own schooldays there. Only Castleberry and Walter had not attended the Shilton High School. I don't think anyone noticed. One day someone proposed that Walter should be made a retroactive native-born Shilton citizen. The motion was seconded and unanimously passed. Fatty Arbuckle put his finger between his lips and blew a whistle sound.

"Walter," Castleberry said, "you belong."

Much of the blame was Castleberry's. The troubles that followed were his. What did the Society want from Walter?—plenty. We're talking donations, Conlon. Not fifty cents, not I-gave-at-the-office, not five dollars slipped into an envelope. We're talking money.

Somewhere, Conlon, although probably not in this room, is my first letter from Eric DeLeuce. After I took my leave of absence.

He sent it from Milan. He said the Foundation was in desperate need of me. His exact words. *Sara*, he wrote. *Give up your crazy notions of being an artist. Come back, Liebchen.*

I am an artist.

Then he sent a second letter, also from Milan. *What I have in mind*, he wrote, *what I have always had in mind—my dear Sara—is marriage. I will marry you. Fanny is not well, Sara. She is definitely on the way. I will marry you then, Sara.*

I didn't show that letter to Walter. I didn't show that written proposal to him. I didn't show that letter to Walter because it arrived at a period when I had stopped speaking to Walter. Can you blame me, Conlon?

Yesterday, I received another letter. From Rome. I have it here. Blue aerogram.

> *Dear Sara,*
>   *I know what's going on. I have my ways. Fanny, bless her soul, is in a clinic. What she has left in her—who knows?*
>   *Love,*
>   *Eric DeLeuce*

Conlon, I find myself with a marriage proposal from an eighty-five-year-old syphilitic man with a very despotic temper.

I have an excavation in my backyard marked off in grids.

And Walter is gone.

Five

Walter said that he didn't dream anymore.

He said it in calm tones, no agitation. Clearly it didn't bother him. We were in our kitchen. We were in our *new* kitchen on Oglethorpe Road. Walter was cooking breakfast. Several weeks ago he had begun cooking his own breakfasts. He made big breakfasts for the physical labor ahead. That morning he was making an omelet. On the cutting board he had chopped ham, onions, and one sweet red pepper. It didn't bother him to cook for me.

I set the table. I'll go that far these mornings. "About the dreams," I began. "You don't stop dreaming. You always dream. What you mean is that you don't remember. It's different just not remembering dreaming."

"I don't dream anymore," Walter said and started the butter sizzling.

He fell asleep fast because of all the work he did, but I wouldn't mention that. Before I left his bed and moved to the room down the hall, I used to be awake after Walter fell asleep, and sometimes I would bounce around to try and wake him but he just slept on, with heavy breathing and once in a while a snort or two. Sometimes, I'd get up and just sit by the window looking out. On Oglethorpe Road there were no streetlights. Hard to get used to for real city people. At first I never saw anything out that window. It was just one big soft black marshmallow. But after a bit, night vision took over, and the road turned grey and the wire fence across the road gave off a sequin sparkle. Did it soothe me—that country view? The longer I sat there, the angrier I became. If it was impossible to fall asleep, I'd go downstairs and turn on the television set that was hooked up to cable and watch one of those late night blue movies. Some man pumping away. Astonishing how you could see both faces and neither of them looked bad.

Walter and I used to make love. What kind of a substitute

was digging? Once I got so mad that I ran right back upstairs and took aim at Walter's humped rear end and kicked it. Walter just rolled over, opened his eyes, said one loud, clear "Hell!" and went right off to sleep again.

Sometimes he was my Walter—the man whom I truly loved, but he had fallen into that Hole, as if he had waited for it forever, the fit was so tight.

After I moved out of our bedroom and down the hall into the other room I started sleeping again myself. The insomnia went just like that. But the first two weeks I fixed myself up before turning in, a spray of perfume, brushed hair, either that new white gown or the old nothing-at-all. I said to myself that he would come padding down the hall. Walter was a man of appetites. But never once did he come, not one single time. You would have thought that my sleeping down the hall was his idea. For a time I left my clothes, everything in the closet in the other bedroom, my stuff on top of the dresser, but that became tiresome so I moved it all to my new room. It was Alexander's wife snooping around who noticed the change first time she went upstairs to use the bathroom.

"Mother," Alexander said to me, "you've got to be patient. Dad is just going through an experience. It will pass—you know that."

Alexander looks just like me, but he has Walter's build. He's like Walter too, he's kind and thinks the best. I think the other way.

"Wait until winter," Alexander said.

Walter divided the egg neatly into two even portions. By rights I should have taken less, should have generously pushed the greater amount towards him, but I didn't. Walter poured the coffee, put the toast on the table. I didn't have to ask Walter what he was going to do today. I knew full well what he was going to do today.

It was half-past five and no shard of light in the sky anywhere. I believed that there was not one single other person awake on

Oglethorpe Road, just us sitting there in that kitchen under fluorescent light. Walter in his overalls and me in a faded green bathrobe. There ought to be a sign outside the window that blinked on and off and said *Cafe*, only the Interstate was five miles away, and we were in the kitchen of an authentic reproduction of a farmhouse.

"I'm giving an interview today," Walter said. "Don't forget. The man will be here at two o'clock."

"An interview." I put down my coffee cup and held up my hands in mock alarm. "Hold the presses!"

"Stop it," Walter said.

I looked at him. But he was not really annoyed. Was it because I wasn't there? At least not in any way that was important? Hey, let's leave. I would say that. We could leave.

"I should have done that right from the start," Walter said. "I should have given a simple explanation—the reason for the Hole. Everyone would have understood."

"What the hell would you have said?" I shouted. "What *reason?*"

"Sara," Walter said softly, "I would have told them that I was digging up an apartment building."

That was as close as he came to a reproof. That was for me because I had kept that first reporter away. And just last week I had seen another man, a short skinny man slipping along the windbreak of spruce like a divorce-case lawyer. He wore a wool jacket and had a camera hanging around his neck. I had picked up a stick. We had plenty of branches lying around since the lawn service became unnecessary. I did the mowing in the front myself. "Yeoow!" I had yelled and charged. That man took one look at me, height and all. I chased him the length of the driveway, ran him off, but that wasn't the end.

I stopped that particular man, but could I catch the others? Could I stay home forever? We were public already.

I might have missed that first published account—the one in the Gannett newspaper—but Mrs. Sorley from Number 8 Oglethorpe Road came over. Mrs. Sorley was past seventy. She was one of our few speaking neighbors. "Look," she said and passed me the folded newspaper open to the right page. "Hell of a lot of trouble," she said.

It was just two paragraphs, just an oddity, just a man-eats-goldfish type of news. "Nothing," I said to Mrs. Sorley. We were on my front path. "It's nothing."

"Remind me to tell you the story of Minna Howard's canes one day," Mrs. Sorley said. "Just you wait."

The man in the wool jacket with the camera came back with an officer from the county police. I was digging in the small rock garden by the dining room window. I wore rubber boots, the soil was soft and muddy. I lifted my shovel, small garden shovel, and cracked it downward into clods of dirt. I stood with my feet widely spaced, my swing was smooth.

"Hallo," the officer called. No use creeping up on me. The dog in the house was already barking.

I turned around. "What?" I said.

"You ran Mr. Argo off," the man in the uniform said. "Threatened him."

"A stranger," I said, "sneaking across my land."

"I rang the doorbell," Mr. Argo said, his voice less angry than whining. "She didn't wait to see my identification. I've a right," he said. "There's been a complaint."

"I was here alone," I said. "I must defend myself. Complaint about what?"

"Construction," the officer said, "without a permit."

"I see," I said. What construction? Who had complained? I pulled off my black gloves. Did Walter have permits for whatever he was doing? I never thought he could be gotten that way.

"Construction," Mr. Argo said. "Behind your house."

"Is he authorized to go there?"

"Yes," the officer said.

I thought about the possible benefits. "All right," I said and leaned the shovel against the side of the house. "You want to see back there."

The two men followed me, trying to stay on the randomly

spaced stone path, well-trained countrymen protecting the plantings, if there were any. I looked at the little man's face. One violation, he was thinking, and he'd throw the book at us, damn new people. It occurred to me that I could deny permission—that I could call the lawyer, Jack R. V. Haight, I could call Alexander. But if I did that, was I protecting Walter or me? I did not want to protect Walter.

There were sharp aches of memory. Ever since the move into my own bedroom I'd been keeping a journal. A listing of everything that Walter had ever done to hurt me. The time he confessed how as a boy he had slept with his cousin, a homely puss of a girl. That day Pearl Gray gave a party. I had gone for a walk in Pearl's garden, such an orderly garden. Then opening the door that led to the mud room I had seen Walter with Pearl. He had her blouse open and was sucking her breast. I had closed that door. Drunk, Walter had said later. Hell, I was drunk.

Around the side of the house past the all-glass enclosed sunroom, the men came upon the Hole.

"Christ almighty!" the officer said.

"Like a Grand Canyon," Mr. Argo spluttered. "Look at that—biggest pisshole I've ever seen."

It was dawn when I saw the two women in the yard. They were dressed like skiers. They had shovels or maybe pickaxes. "Heave ho," one of them kept shouting.

I opened the window. "What are you doing out there?"

"Don't worry," one woman shouted, "there's plenty for everyone. This is where Captain Kidd stashed his loot. My daughter's boyfriend read about it."

I called the police.

Conlon came.

. . .

I spent more time with my pencils, graphite No. 2. I was drawing trees, the grass. Figures had left my work years ago. I did the fence across the road. Deliberately I tried to put in Mr. Petrie, the mailman, but when I finished that picture—the mailman wasn't in it. I saw country lightning flare in the sky one summer evening, and I hurried upstairs directly from the dinner table to put it down on paper. All that blackness and the saw-toothed edges of white streaks, the stump of a tree. I could see mountains from my windows. I tried mountains, made frost silver the lower hills. At the end of each day I took all the torn-up bits of paper downstairs to the trash to avoid the possibility of fire hazard.

You don't have to tell people that you're an artist, if you really are one. You don't need any artistic touches. An artist is there. I was an artist, if blocked. I never blamed my failures on my babies, my children. Did I ever beat my breast and shout, You stole my life. Some excuse that would have been. Also, I never ran away from home.

Does an artist destroy every single picture she painted? This one did. One picture, my father said, I can't have one picture. Your mother may she rest in peace never understood. You're an artist without portfolio. But do I care?—wife and mother is enough.

Walter never asked to see my work. Never. Usually the way I began was to take a sheet of paper and with my thumb I made a blue-grey smudge blending the grey into the blue. I would lean back and squint at the paper. I used to be able to look at these smudges and see the possibilities, the hidden shapes. But now I saw only a bruise of color. With a black pen I began a line but it ended in a doodle. A sky with a doodle. Then I tore up the sheet of paper.

From my third-floor window I looked down to the top of Walter's head.

"Hey Walter," I called. "You want to eat dinner?"

He looked up, leaned on his shovel. "No," he said. "I'll work with the light."

That's how it was. I was an artist and he was a digger and
he was going to work with the light. And I didn't care a bit about
the light. Maybe I ought to take classes.

My back hurt. I rubbed it, twisting my arm around. The chair
was good, though, also the table. Everything was the right height.
But my back still hurt and Walter bless him would come into the
house at twilight as fit as ever. Feel good, he would say. His body
was hard. Like sleeping with a jock, like some high school football
star, legs, calves, thighs. Nothing like that about to happen
though.

I cleaned my brushes, cleaned up everything. My studio was
the attic, a finished room with kid glove smooth plaster walls
once white now turned to the color of curdled cream. I had a
bathroom up there, the one shared by two tiny bedrooms. Real
rooms without slanted ceilings. I had taken the attic by choice.
No one used those bedrooms. Empty with old wallpapered walls
with faded ribbon designs. I tried a couple of deep kneebends. I
decided to make an easy dinner. I'd make ham sandwiches. Cook
of my dreams, Walter used to call me.

I went downstairs. Walter was digging near the kitchen windows. He had knotted a red bandana around his forehead for a
sweatband. He worked that hard. He looked like a member of a
road crew out there. I could make something of that.

SIX

The man wearing only an aquamarine leather loincloth was leaping across our front lawn. How did I know someone was there? The dog. It was eleven o'clock at night. Chaminade's ears flattened, and she began a growl without any accompanying throaty whines, so I figured it wasn't just a raccoon. On that lawn inherited from the previous owner was one of those wrought iron shoulder-high lanterns, English charm for the countryside. I turned the switch in the hall. "Oh God," I said. The man stopped his leaping, pulled apart the loincloth, and began urinating. I opened a living room window. "Get away from here," I yelled.

The man turned to stare at me, not stopping the flow of fluid. He held his head at an angle—I thought that he might be squinting in the poor light. I picked up something, it was a glass tumbler. I threw it through the open window. I have good aim. I meant for it to hit the iron pole holding up the lantern. It did, and crashed and splintered there. Was it stupidity that kept the man from jumping back? I was certain that he grimaced at me. I screamed again. It was then that Walter appeared behind me. All of this occurring in the tenth month of my sorrow.

"Damn, he's pissing on our property," Walter said and grabbed the broom from the back of the hall closet. He unlocked the front door. We had a simple lock on the door, we were not afraid.

"No," I said, but too late. Walter was running towards the man.

"Get the hell off, you creep!" Walter shouted and waved the broom. Walter was a strong man. If he attacked, if he declared war, the younger man wouldn't have a chance. But Walter was not of a violent nature, and the broom only cut through the air.

"All this is mine," the night visitor said and leaped away. I thought he might be a dancer. "I have my rights—my ancestral burial ground. Everything found here is mine." The man did a pas de cheval followed by a fouetté en tournant.

"Walter, come back," I called. "I'll telephone the police."

Which I did. Walter sat down in the living room, still holding the broom. "I can take him," he said.

The young man doing his dance on the lawn did not look particularly threatening.

"You don't move," I said to Walter.

I kept looking out the window and within fifteen minutes I saw the black car with the gold emblem painted on the door appear. It was the second appearance of Conlon. I liked him— he wasn't a native, he was from somewhere farther upstate. He grabbed the arm of the man whose loincloth was once again in place. It didn't seem to me that the leaping stag protested, but he did point in the direction of our spruce. The two men walked over there. And when they came back, Conlon had some clothes over his arm. Actually I didn't see how that man could have made it all the way to our place and down the length of Oglethorpe Road wearing just an aquamarine leather loincloth.

Conlon called us from the station house. "The trespasser is a C. Meinhard from Avenue A and East Twelfth Street, New York City. The man says he's an Indian," he said. "Says you are disturbing his ancestral burial ground. Says whatever you've found is his."

Finders keepers, I wanted to say. But we'll make an exception. It's all yours, I wanted to say. I envisioned a parade of dump trucks moving in stately procession down Twelfth Street and turning onto Avenue A and dropping truckload after truckload of dirt at his doorstep. This is what we found, I would say. I admit the truth, it's yours. Sift through it.

"Send him back to the city, please," I said.

Conlon was really nice about the whole business.

I made a note in that journal I was keeping. It started out to be about Walter, but wasn't always. *The source of all art is tragedy*, I wrote. The next day I wouldn't speak to Walter. But I left him a letter on the kitchen table. *The Hole*, I wrote, *the goddamn*

Hole is big enough. What have you found? A handful of bricks.
The Historical Society is no longer welcome in my house. You
cannot make a living from a twenty-four-unit motel on a back
road.
All this I wrote and left for Walter.
Sometimes I spoke to Alexander on the telephone.
"Wait for winter," Alexander said to me, "wait."

What did they want from my life?
There I was at four a.m. playing the radio. Twiddle the knob
left, twiddle the knob right. In New York City, the voice said, the
nighttime low was fifty-seven degrees. I turned the knob some
more. What did I think—that the temperature would drop with
a better voice? No one else was up, probably no one else on the
whole road right up to the Interstate. I'm saving Walter, I
thought, saving him from the Hole. No matter what, I'm saving
Walter. But the weather wasn't on my side. There had been two
tiny frosts in September. Pull up your tomato plants, they had
advised, it's all over. It wasn't, though. The trade winds treach-
erously shifted from north to south. I tuned to a local station and
listened as the falsely middle of the night down-home voice of a
man named Lawrence gave his best regards to the Jingle-Jangle
Club on its tenth anniversary and stated that the local—the
county—nighttime low was forty-eight degrees. "Will winter
come?" Lawrence said. "You bet your bootsies."
"The hell with my bootsies," I said. So much for dreams.
Maybe Walter didn't remember his dreams, but I remembered
mine. I had been dreaming of snow, erotic snow maidens, white
melting mermaids. Everyone indoors. But first it would have to
get cold. The soil must freeze or the snow would waste itself on
the ground. Already I had made three pacts—with whom?—with
the Great Weatherman. If it would get cold, if it would turn freez-
ing cold, then I would cut the snide remarks, the ready-made
food, I would sincerely try to stop complaining about dresses
never being long enough. All that I would do. But what good

were the promises? It was warm. The sun was orange-yellow. The leaves had dried and mostly dropped, swirling across the lawn, the road. Out here, Mrs. Sorley had said pausing in front of my house one afternoon, we use the leaves for mulch, for compost. Last year I had taken down the new copy of the *Better Homes and Gardens Book* and had looked up mulch and compost. If the leaves blew, and I just let them land where they wanted— was that mulch or compost? After a couple of years, Mrs. Sorley had said, you'll get the hang of it.

I thought about my previous experience with land—two pots of everblooming geraniums. Two pots on a terrace overlooking a pile of roofs.

The dog banged her tail against the radiator cover. Country life was hard on her. She liked a leash, her primal memories were of elevators and concrete. I opened the back door. "Listen," I said. "You are a country dog now. Go!" She made the effort, vanishing in the faintest light now appearing, eaten up by the mist like a golden spook. The dog with definite prescience avoided the back of the house, she clung to the side walls until she was able to make those gigantic leaps towards the spruce.

The dog won't go there, I wanted to tell Walter, but I didn't. The dog won't go near the Hole.

I've got this early, early morning routine in which I test the soil. I tested the soil maybe two or three times a week. What I did was to go outside and squat by the rock garden. I dug down and came up with a handful of soil. It's black and sweet-smelling—a little grainy. What had that woman at the local Department of Agriculture office called it? Viable. Yes, the soil was viable. We had a heck of a lot of viable soil, mulching and composting away. But then that representative of the Department of Agriculture had persisted, the government never gives up— What do you want to plant *now* so late in the year? Nothing, I had said, we want to plant nothing. Nothing, thank you. Viable until not viable. How long can you dig in the soil? You can dig in the soil until you can't dig anymore.

. . .

Okawara was a Japanese paper that I liked. It felt permanent to my fingers—it felt substantial, squeezable. What I did was mix some black pigment—some opaque, some transparent. I thought I'd try the look of the soil, the black grains, the bits of bark decomposing. I did several pictures working at my table from morning until four o'clock in the afternoon. A few pictures were black dots, a few were transparent black with opaque shadows. One shadow might have been Chaminade. Yes, it might have been the dog.

When the natural light started to dim, I stopped and cleaned up my table. Having the water from the bathroom up there made it easier. Okawara was a firm paper, so I cut up the sheets in little pieces with my scissors, put them into a plastic bag, and carried them downstairs.

When I was a young girl kids made trouble but the mode of transportation was different. I mean they either rode around in old jalopies or maybe someone's father's station wagon and you couldn't get a scratch on it and that alone stopped a lot. But these kids—on Wednesday night two carloads of them, one Buick convertible and one Lincoln sedan, pulled up in front of the house and when they drove away there were cases of empty beer bottles everywhere, mostly Coors but also a few imports, Dutch and German.

Walter didn't get excited even when they were making a lot of noise. They were yelling, they were calling out, the Hole figured prominently in it. Walter remained calm. "They don't understand," he said. "That's it. They don't have an explanation. I'll go out and talk to them."

"You'll do no such thing," I said. "We'll wait until the beasts go away."

What I wanted to do was to shout back at those kids. "Louts! Stinking sons of bitches!" What I did was sit in the kitchen and hold tight to the dog now shivering and moaning. I put Bruck-ner's Eighth on the phonograph, volume up high.

Conlon was really very nice about the whole business. He was very polite. "Did you get the license plate numbers?" he asked.

"No," I said. "We didn't. We stayed in the back of the house in the kitchen."

It was clear that we were in the public domain.

After Conlon left, and Walter had fallen asleep, I walked into his bedroom that I had abandoned. "I love you, Walter," I whis-pered. One night long ago back in the city Walter sat up in bed, thinking I was asleep, and whispered, "I hate you, and I don't care if you are my wife." Now I never let on that I heard that. In twenty-eight years of marriage you can hear things like that. I don't think that I should have spoken then. But maybe I should speak up more during quarrels.

"The truth of the matter," Walter said to me one morning before he began his work, "is that no one comes to see us any-more."

I thought about that. "Right," I said.

Yesterday, I got into the car and drove down the road to the interchange and then onto the Thruway. It was an impulse. Who could believe that it was late fall. Every day was warm, dry, the temperature pinching seventy. The leaves not wanting to let go rattled in the wind like stop signs. I imagined a hundred pictures of winter. But the windows were rolled down, and I wore sun-glasses to darken that postcard sky. What should I do next? It was an impulse. I'd give a party.

I thought that Jay had liked Walter the best—so I called him. I'd invite Jay and Marilyn and Arthur and Louise.

"Jay," I said on the telephone.

"Sara? Sara baby, well how's life out there? We were going

to ring you up—saw that little article in the *News*—the damndest article. Is that hole as big as they say?"

"Yes."

"Imagine that. Listen, Sara, do you ever get into the city?"

"Yes. Sometimes."

"I'd like to see you, Sara."

"Why?"

"Why do you think? I've always meant to see you."

"Not me," I said.

"Sara," Jay said, "I like you. You're real, Sara. You are definite. I have the use of a place—I can have one with a little notice." He hesitated. "I see us in bed naked. I see me running my hand down your tawny back."

"Tawny?" I said. "For Christ's sake, Jay—tawny!"

"I want to make it with you, Sara."

I hung up.

We had our own little revival meeting behind the house. I saw them, saw the white sheets. I thought, My God, they're going to burn a cross. I ran out there. They were kneeling, two women and two men. The sheets were very clean except for circles of mud where the knees were.

"Private property," I said. "Scram!"

"God sent us," one of the women told me. I looked into her eyes, the expression was veiled. I don't know which one she was—Jane Doe One or Jane Doe Two. I had gone outside because after all it was only four o'clock in the afternoon.

"Go," I said. "Now!"

"We are here to witness," the same woman said. All four of the nuts were kneeling.

When Conlon arrived, three of them had climbed into the Hole. They were digging. For what, I didn't know. The women were using two of Walter's shovels, one man was using his hands. The other man just watched. "A little to the right," he advised the women.

I went back into the house, in my mouth the taste of bile. I washed my face with cold water at the kitchen sink, let the water rush across my neck dripping down to moisten the blouse.

Go away for a while, Conlon advised. Take a trip. Conlon was polite, he was nice. Did Conlon like us?

notes to conlon

I was twenty when I married Walter. He was twenty-three. These were not extraordinary ages. Two years ago at a party I met this man who was married to a sixteen-year-old girl. He was thirty-two. They had to get a letter of permission from her parents. She didn't have to be pregnant. She was beautiful. So he married this baby just before her father was transferred to Duluth, and the mother and father left her behind. The girl was taking correspondence courses to finish high school. The husband doted on her, but I looked at her face. In about three years, I figured, she will give him a hell of a lot of trouble.

I'll tell you what's the problem with simple explanations, Conlon. Nobody believes them. I'm certain that in your line of work you understand the validity of this. Everyone forages and roots for meanings. What do they come up with? More often than not they come up with sexual. Now I'm not talking about certifiable nuts to be explained, like the ones found on my lawn. Like the ones you have in your file, the file about my family. No, I am speaking about perfectly ordinary people seeking to explain Walter's behavior. First of all, no one ever said that Walter was disturbed. At least not to me. Waddington, the doctor whom I consulted, sat me down across from him. When I was a child my family consulted a doctor named Rice who had a small dog named Bubbles. Against all codes of the Department of Health the dog regularly roamed the office. Rice would never I am certain have suggested that Walter and I were not fucking enough. Rice might have referred in some oblique fashion to the brevity of sexual congress. But Waddington sat there smartly dressed from the pages of *GQ* and said, Sara (he does not know me), how often do you and Walter go at intercourse? Screw?

Now this conversation occurred after I had abandoned Walter's bed, but I didn't go far. I only went to the small bedroom at the end of the hall where I am now. The room with walls and door of cardboard. That's how I can hear everything. But to return to Waddington. Before I can answer, before I can say not at all anymore, Waddington is slipping me pamphlets both glossy and not. *Sex and the Middle-Aged. Difficult Years for Men.* What has happened, Waddington says, is that Walter has been forced to sublimate his sexual urges. Walter is digging the Hole to compensate.

I'm thinking bull.

Waddington without a decent pause goes into his thoughts. I might add that Waddington is on the City Council (for the incorporated city limits of Shilton). The Hole, Waddington says, stands for vagina at the narrow end and for womb at the bigger end. Thus, Walter is both fucking and regressing. He is in fact having it both ways. Waddington is saying we have the shovel as penis, the hoist and tackle as birthing devices, the pump as bidet.

Alexander showed up one Saturday at ten a.m. What did Alexander do with that five thousand? Shirley wanted a co-op. They bought into a co-op. Alexander looked out the kitchen window. Mother, he says, is he rational? What do you mean? I say. He's rational at all times. When isn't he rational? I know, Alexander says, but when he's out there—in the back—how is he? You've heard him explain about the Hole, I say. He has explained to you about the Hole—about Lazarre, about the apartment building, about historical significance. Yes, Alexander says, and the explanation—I mean when he explains—it's all right. But then when you stop to think about it—well, it gets strange.

Strange, I know. Strange was when you actually saw the Hole. Strange was when you got a good look.

Conlon, my son went to see our lawyer. I didn't send him. Alexander went on his own. Jack R. V. Haight has been our lawyer for more years than Waddington has been our doctor (ten years versus two visits).

The following conversation I report to you, Conlon, as I remember it from Alexander's account. Maybe verbatim, maybe not.

"As I hear it, you're telling me that your father has a mental aberration, digging a hole, spending his money wildly on motels, et cetera," Jack said.

"There seem to be influences," Alexander said hesitantly. "People from the Historical Society. Look at this." Alexander gave Jack some recent photographs of the Hole.

"He dug that?"

"It's deep," Alexander said. He gave the lawyer the description.

"Dug it by hand?" Jack said and whistled.

"Hardly any equipment."

"What the hell for?"

"He was digging for ruins," Alexander said.

"An archeological dig? Ruins of what?"

"The remains of an apartment building, circa 1910."

"The man is digging up an apartment building?"

"Yes," Alexander said. "Yes, an apartment building. He has old pictures, sketches."

"Let me understand," Jack said. "Walter is digging up an apartment building. Did he find anything?"

"He found some bricks."

"From the apartment building?"

"They look like those in the sketch the Historical Society has."

"Then let me get this straight. He was digging up an apartment building built in 1910, and he found it—part of it."

"Yes."

"Eccentric—but permissible."

"Permissible?"

"Yes."

Jack invited me into the city. We went up to Windows on the World. We had little hors d'oeuvres, we had tiny skish kebabs. We stared down at the city, at the lights. "You ought to paint this," Jack said.

He knows nothing about artists, I realized.

"I don't know how to begin," he said.

This reminded me of all those people who put their cards on the table. The excuse for a hell of a lot of bluntness. "Begin," I said.

"Walter," Jack said, "is in trouble. I mean he seems to be in some kind of trouble."

"What has he said?" I asked.

"Nothing more," Jack said. "Alexander told me to ask him again. I asked him. He just gives that same explanation."

"That explanation is true. I mean I believe it is true."

"You tell me," Jack said. "Say it."

"Walter is digging a hole," I said. "The Hole is in the yard behind the house. It is exactly as Walter says. He is digging up the ruins of Shilton Court, an apartment house circa 1910."

All right, Jack, he is digging up an apartment house.

"Jesus," Jack said. "Tell me, Sara, how often do you and Walter make love?"

"How often do *you* make love?" I ask.

Jack doesn't hesitate, the modernness of it all. "At least four times a week," he said.

Our Jack is married to Donna Rae. Donna Rae was born in Savannah, and her family moved to New Jersey when she was six. She didn't get back her Southern accent until she was eighteen. She weighs one hundred twenty-four and collects first editions of Civil War biographies. I believe that she would sleep with Jack four times a week. Why not?

"If it's true," I said to Jack, "about lack of sexual congress. Why not extracurricular? I mean why is this my fault? I could name a lot of people who are getting it enough, if not at home then elsewhere."

"I don't know," Jack said, "I just think that the root of the problem is at home."

There's that word again, Conlon, *root*.

Back to sex. Jack himself who is getting it by his own admission four times a week at home used to get it with a girl named Nita. Young, maybe twenty-two. And there's Max with Patty, Arthur with Marilyn, Sylvan with Monica, George with Marie, Carl with Babba. So why not Walter with someone? He goes into town. Do I know *exactly* where he goes? So why not Walter with some Madame X?

"Fidelity," Jack said. "Walter has confessed fidelity."

I believed him. Walter loves me. I love Walter.

I love Walter. And yet, I am not thinking about him so much. Maybe hardly at all.

I was sitting in my room on the third floor painting. I was smoking one of those new cigarettes for women. All the new cigarettes are anonymous in brand. I have recently resumed smoking, and I do it on the sly. I burn the butts downstairs in the fireplace with the shreds of my pictures. I took my thumb and with firm intention made a smear of the sky, a blue to grey wet transition.

notes to conlon

Conlon, something so frightening happened to me—that thinking about it, I still tremble. How do things happen? Is it by chance? Who the hell knows. I finished a picture. There was nothing particular about that day, no meteorological phenomena. It was after I moved from Walter's bed. Should I have put one of those advertisements in the newspaper—you know—the ones that begin having left the bed of _____, I am no longer responsible for debts, etc., etc.

It happened this way. I went upstairs. It was early morning. Walter was digging. We owned the motel already. I went upstairs carrying a mug of lukewarm coffee. I sat in my room staring out the window at the Hole. It was a dark day. The Hole looked like a pit. I thought how that pit was going to get us. I took down my first morning sheet of paper. I took a charcoal pencil. I drew the Hole, Conlon. My perspective was good, my balance of mass and space worked. I did the rim of the Hole, quickly—the darkness below just hinted at. The picture was realistic in detail. The trees were there, the ruined patches of grass, the latest mountain of waiting earth. In the distance was the fence of stone. One streak might have been Chaminade running along the side. I was uncertain. The texture of the paper was smooth, the back tone a pale tan. This sheet of paper was twenty by twenty-four. I worked on the picture about two hours. I finished. There were highlights, there were contours. I drank the rest of the coffee, now ice-cold. I waited. What happens at these times, Conlon—I don't analyze. What happens is this—I look at the paper, then after a bit I tear it up. Why?—because I don't like it.

I have tried to learn from the great masters. I have surveyed their lives. The peak can come at any time, Conlon. I mean the age of the artist is not a factor. Was it possible then that I had not reached my peak yet? That I was peaking now? I sat there with this piece of paper, this single sheet. My arms ached from the effort of drawing, the need for control. I did not tear up this paper. I didn't. I took the can of acrylic spray and set the charcoal.

During the following half hour I expected any moment to destroy the paper. I carried it into one of the unused bedrooms, opened the closet door, and put the paper on the shelf. I was shaken. I didn't dare attempt anything else.

It was hard not to tell Walter. Listen, sharing is half of everything. He was out there with his shovels. I wanted to tell him what had happened. But we weren't speaking. I went downstairs. I scrubbed the kitchen floor. I searched my cabinets for ingredients and I made a Linzer torte. I decided to wait twenty-four hours before going back upstairs. Certain in my soul—surely as deep as the Hole—that I must destroy that picture.

How I passed the remainder of that day—I hardly know. Did I eat? Did I read? Did I speak to anyone? I know that the telephone rang. I heard Walter's voice. It was Stopwood. Not too good a week, he was saying. I was listening on the extension. Not to worry, Stopwood was saying. Our season will begin. Walter didn't sound concerned on his end.

The next morning, Conlon, I tried to remain relaxed. What I did was to stretch out full length on the floor. I sit so much, bent into neat squares. So I stretched out full length. My breathing was catarrhal. Afterwards I went upstairs. Never mind where anyone else was. I went into that tiny, that much unused bedroom. I took the paper from the closet shelf and walked to the window. Conlon, I liked the picture. It *pleased* me. That, Conlon, was the first of my series of Hole pictures.

There are at the time of this writing, sixteen Hole drawings and paintings. They are all stacked in the closets of the two third-floor bedrooms. Yes, I had to expand to the other bedroom.

Do I have favorites? Yes.

There is the gouache entitled "Picnic at the Hole." In this painting people are sitting around the Hole, dangling their feet down quite as if the Hole were filled with water, but it isn't. The faces are very distinct, and everyone is dressed up as if it were a social occasion, a Sunday picnic maybe. Then there's the oil of the lovers, a dozen couples in the shallow end of the Hole. I used a layer of white gesso, covered that surface with a glazing mixture and sketched in the figures, outlined them in black.

There are, I admit—depending upon your view—touches of obscenity in poses, shapes, who is doing what to whom. There's a great picture of the fat women at the rim with a strong color combination of orange and red, and several others.

Shirley called me. Shirley is Alexander's wife. In one of Shirley's evening school courses they spent time discussing the benefits and restrictions of the extended family. In an extended family, Shirley said, there would be room for Walter—for eccentric behavior.

What I think listening to her is that someday she will pile me off someplace, if she gets the chance.

I have faith in Alexander. He is certain that Walter is not crazy. But Alexander is not often on the scene. We are communicating by telephone. Still, Alexander believes that he has both sides of the issue: on one side, Walter is explaining calmly—never mind what; on the other side, I sometimes scream my complaints. There is also the car incident.

Swathed in mystery? No, I'll explain what happened, Conlon. I had gone to town for food—it was a clear day. I came home and heard voices, then laughter. A strange cream-colored sedan was parked near our front path. The sounds came from behind the house—mostly laughter. I peeked around the side of the house and saw Walter and a man and woman.

"Drop something down it, Harriet," the man was saying.

"Sure," the woman said and rummaged in her purse. Soon a Kleenex drifted on its own power to the bottom of the Hole.

"Hell," the man said and threw a cigarette butt over the rim.

The woman was tittering, the man's laugh louder. They winked, they nudged each other.

Walter—where was Walter?—he was telling them the story of the Hole.

"Get out," I yelled at the sightseers.

The visitors stared at me. "Beat it," the man said. "The geezer invited us."

I walked back to my car, Conlon, and drove off the driveway onto the grass right towards the Hole—in the general direction of Harriet and friend. I rolled down my window. "Walter," I said, "make them go, or I swear I'll drive the car right into the Hole."

What I planned, you see, was to move the car to the edge of the Hole, release the hand brake, get out, and push. Now I don't think that I would have actually done that, Conlon. But it had the right effect—those people left in a hurry. I backed up my car and reparked it in the driveway.

Today I think they have cut the tranquilizers, Conlon. At any rate I am aware of different possibilities. Like where Walter is. Walter is in a hospital. Which one? I don't know. Conlon, I have just realized that I have not asked about Walter. I mentioned that to Waddington. My impression is that he looked at me funny.

Walter, he said, is in coma.

I keep saying, Conlon, that there is nothing that I won't do for Walter. I suspect that is not true. Suddenly I find that there are limits to my sacrifices. I mean it is possible to sacrifice everything when there is less to sacrifice. But, Conlon, since the creation of my Hole pictures—I am unwilling to give up. These pictures have importance, they have permanence, they are worthy. These pictures, Conlon, are more important than the Hole.

I trust you—that is why I place knowledge of their existence in your safekeeping. I can imagine the pictures on display at an exhibit. Just wait until they come out—the debut of the Hole pictures.

Remember, Conlon, that the entire series of Hole pictures is in the two closets on the third floor. I have told no one. They are good.

seven

I have developed through the creation of my pictures a kind of ecstasy. I am an artist. What happens when things are going good—when you are satisfied with what is painted? What happens is that you pay attention to everything else. I even thought that I might return to Walter's bed. I began speaking to him again. Maybe I'd suggest that we sell the motel and the house and return to the city. I began thinking of practical matters. I went through our mail.

That's when I found a letter from the DeLeuce Foundation. It was addressed to Walter, though. What the hell did they want with him? The man has enough problems. I opened the letter. Walter and Castleberry had applied for a grant for a project entitled "The Restoration of Shilton Court—A Classic Dream." *We regret*, the letter said. The letter was signed by Program Officer Dennys.

I went out in the yard. "Walter," I yelled, "why did you apply to the DeLeuce Foundation for money for this stupid Hole? Are you trying to embarrass me? Are you trying to get me?"

"You did not enter into this. The grant was for historical purposes," Walter said. "Castleberry said that it would be good for the project—give it stability, status, put the Hole in perspective—supply needed money for further explorations."

"Bull," I said.

"I think," Walter said, pausing in his digging, "that you do not want me to succeed."

I went back into the house. I was shaking, though. I was shaking in fury. Needed money? Did you need money to dig a hole in your own yard? Just where were we financially? I had from choice ignored the Marybeth money. Were we broke? I could go back to work, if necessary. I went rummaging. Searching for what? I went through the last envelope of canceled checks from the bank. My God! I read the check twice. It was made out to the Shilton Historical Society—endorsed on the back by Castleberry. A donation. Hadn't I heard that the Society had left the basement of the library, vacated the area, rented a suite of offices? The canceled check was for *twelve thousand dollars*.

I called Alexander. Never mind the time.

"Hello," Shirley said, her voice lacking awareness, coming from sleep.

"It's me," I said.

"Mother?"

"Let me speak to Alexander."

"God," Shirley said. "Alex, take the phone."

"Mother? Mother, what happened?"

"I found a check—from the bank. Walter gave money to the Historical Society," I said. "He gave them twelve thousand. I think he's wiped us out."

"Twelve thousand? Did you ask Dad for an explanation?"

"Alexander," I said, "I just had a fight with your father. Ask him? Would he tell *me*? Call your brother, call Norman—call him now."

I was floundering. But what else could I suggest?

It began to rain. Out in the yard slipping in the grey ooze of mud, Walter turned on his pump. There was a low melodious roar. "Yo ho," he sang above the sound. "Yo ho!" He dived into the hole with a length of rubber tubing. On very wet days he wore a black rubber scuba diving suit.

norman

one

When I woke up the armpits were wet and there was a Mississippi
flow of grease on my nose, pores open and lubricating. If I had
been wearing my glasses the plastic nosepiece would have slid
down to the Giapetto position. Hell, I didn't have to lay there and
suffer. I could have crossed the room and turned on the air conditioner. Never be uncomfortable again, the advertisement had
said. The air conditioner hadn't come with the apartment, I had
bought it. I had made a resolution, though. I was Going Natural.
It wasn't like Going California—organic alfalfa, avocados, suntan
parlors. No, this was to be a matter of health, my own prescrip-
tion. Live naturally in the environment. Wasn't my father's life
strictly additive, as mother would say? How did I feel? I felt like
a genetic time bomb. Did you know when your IQ started to slip?
Baby, is it hot today, the man on the radio said. Oh baby, feel
that wavy heat. I stretched out my arm to reach the knob and
turned off the radio, it was connected to the timer and turned
on when the surf sound machine cut off.

Exercise. It was time to exercise. I let my arm hang down
from the mattress until my hand rested on the floor and then
rolled cautiously from the bed downward. I had a real bed with
innersprings and all. Maybe I should get a futon, maybe try just
sleeping on a mat on the floor.

Push-ups. Wake up and do push-ups. I was face down on the
grey and white tweed acrylic rug. The long fibers pushed into
my nostrils and the filaments of fuzz into my mouth. I raised my
body, resting the weight of it on my hands, back straight or only
slightly sagging. One, two. One—oh God, two. Ten times. Could
I go ten times? What was in the rug that I was breathing and
eating? The carpeting had come with the apartment. Uncleaned,
never cleaned. The color wisely chosen by the Palm Court Real
Estate Management Company to wear forever and show no dirt.
I sniffed the rug. So many people had walked on it, spit into it,
dropped into it—that it smelled of nothing. It was one hell of an
anonymous rug.

I sat up cross-legged on the floor. I wasn't going to do ten. I couldn't physically possibly do ten. Anyway, in place of the exertion I would take a one-a-day, a kelp pill, a zinc tablet, and two thousand milligrams of C. I checked the time on the six-inch red numbers glowing from the digital clock. The clock had been a present from Eileen, given when we were still married. What time is it? I used to ask, waking in the middle of the night, waking her in the middle of the night. And where were my glasses? "Get a look at these numbers," Eileen had said upon presenting me with the clock. "Even you will be able to tell the time from a distance."

It was five o'clock in the morning. Not a bad time for Southern California. I could walk to Cantor's for a coffee and a bagel, I could run to the Farmer's Market. At the kitchen window I poked one finger between the slats, opening the blind a crack at eye level. The slats of the blind were plastic made to look like bamboo. It was an early dawn sky, a kind of brown-blue. The last sky I had seen in New York had been grey-blue.

When I first moved here a year ago I used to joyously fling up that blind to explore the world until a note was shoved under my door. *Exposing yourself,* the note said, *is a sin before the eyes of our God—too late to repent.* Then a cop came. I apologized, I explained. I used to live twelve floors up, old habits were slow to atrophy. The cop understood, the cop didn't think I was another nut. Just don't do it again, he had said. Yes, I agreed, never again. Listen, I had asked, who called you? The cop wouldn't say, maybe didn't know.

There was movement outside. I squinted at the half-darkness, at a shape. It was the dog Margo going to relieve herself on the square of lawn between the sides of the U-shaped building. If Margo was out, then Mrs. Coover was awake. I stepped back from the blinds and reached for a pair of running shorts. I found my glasses on the white table in front of the couch. I had to hurry. She might be on her way back to bed—or just going there. I grabbed my keys and fled.

Outside the air was damp, and surprisingly chilled. Margo

didn't look at me, she was a bull terrier without curiosity. Mrs. Coover stood in her doorway waiting for the dog. She was fully dressed in blue jeans and a tee shirt that said *It's Me*. "Norman," Mrs. Coover said, "what are you doing up this early?"

"Thought I'd take a run," I lied.

"Put on a shirt," she advised; "there's a cold wind, an East Coast wind. Anyway, wait a half hour, let it get real light, let it get past mugging time. Read the papers. What streets are safe?"

"Yeah," I said. I was shivering. "Yeah, maybe I will."

"Coffee?" Mrs. Coover said. "You want to have a cup with me before I turn in."

"Thanks," I said. "Yes, thanks. I'll just get a shirt."

"It's all right," she said, "in my place it's warm. Don't worry— your bare chest won't excite me. Margo," she called. "Get in here."

I followed the dog and Mrs. Coover into her apartment. All the lamps were on.

"Sit at the table," Mrs. Coover ordered. "I made the coffee already."

I pulled one of the solid maple chairs away from the table. Those chairs had a power of gravity that resisted movement. Mrs. Coover had shipped all her furniture from the East Coast. I had met the old woman on the first day I moved into the building when I had stopped to pet Margo. It was an act of charity, she was not an appealing dog. "So," Mrs. Coover had demanded that day, "you like them old and ugly with dangling tits."

She was a widow. Her husband had wanted to go to Florida, she said. She had wanted to go nowhere. But he gave up their New York City rent-controlled apartment to spite her, and then while he was wrapping the china plates in newspaper, he died. "So," Mrs. Coover said, "I moved to California."

She said that she had given advice. Professionally, she said. I was licensed, she said.

She poured coffee into two restaurant size thick-rimmed mugs. We'd shared before, she knew that I drank mine black. From the top of the refrigerator she took a purple and white

Dunkin Donuts box. "I've stopped fooling around," she said, "now I buy just the chocolate-frosted with coconut."

"Sensible," I said and took one. I felt better, better than with the push-ups or the pills.

Mrs. Coover sat down at the table across from me. She stared at me. "You went to that doctor I told you about for a check-up?"

"Yes," I said. "He was really something."

Mrs. Coover smiled and lit a cigarette, no filter. "He shipped his furniture too. Brown Naugahyde."

"A bit of home," I said. Should I take another doughnut? I could buy her a box. The chocolate had pleasantly coated my throat.

"Take one," Mrs. Coover said. "I buy them to be eaten and of the two of us, you're the thinner. He didn't find anything— the doctor?"

"No," I said. "Pronounced that I'm fit."

"You look fit. Why'd you want a doctor anyway?"

The nice thing about Mrs. Coover was that she never apologized for asking questions. "I was curious," I said, "about my health. About certain genetic factors."

Actually, this doctor hadn't really helped. "What are you worrying about?" he had said. "What do you know anyway? Your father is probably just under strain. East Coast strain, business worries, the prostate. I myself don't hold with those theories about inheriting that stuff."

"What?" Mrs. Coover said.

"My father is going berserk," I said.

"What?"

Was it my imagination or had Mrs. Coover pushed her chair slightly away from me? "I don't know for certain," I said. "I have been receiving these letters, these postcards from home. I mean he might be going crazy. And then there's my grandfather—he might have been crazy or at least strange. But he died too young to be certain. My great-grandfather—now I believe from what I have heard that he definitely was nuts. So you understand—I've become worried."

"Jesus," Mrs. Coover said and put out her cigarette in the mug. She stood up. "I'll have to scald the dishes."

"It's not contagious," I said. "For goodness sakes, you can't catch hereditary madness."

"Get out of here, Norman," she said.

Did I argue? I got out of there.

The family had summoned me from Los Angeles—or rather they were trying to summon me. What can I do? I wrote back.

You are the oldest son, my mother said.

I had an answer. Let's be honest—I am not as capable in such matters as Alexander. The order of birth should have been reversed.

"What the hell is the matter with you?" my sister-in-law said on the telephone. "It's Eileen, isn't it? That's why you don't want to leave California. You care more for your ex-wife than you do for your flesh and blood!"

I had an answer—but she slammed down the telephone.

I lived in the Fairfax area of Los Angeles, and if it was true that I was pursuing Eileen as the family implied, then I was certainly doing it the long way. I mean Eileen had moved to an apartment in San Bernardino. She had a job there. She worked in a store that sold only leather. Not that kind of leather, she said to me on the telephone. We used to do leather skirts, boleros. Now we're heavy into Western, early Sears.

Eileen was certainly not subject to daily visits from me. Furthermore, she had moved to California in March. I had moved to California in February. This fact I had triumphantly announced. But you knew that she was going to California—they said that, used that as an argument. I was following my ex-wife. That is the dumbest thing, my mother said. You should be grateful that she has left you. I never once believed that she would ever leave you. Age, my mother said, is important. You can scoff now—but do you know what aging does to a woman?—Norman, just you wait. This referred to the fact that I had been twenty-two when I married Eileen. Eileen had been thirty-four. We had been married for three years, divorced for two. Although I had closely observed her, I could see no signs of deleterious aging in Eileen.

notes to alexander

Alexander, Alex, brother, you dumb asshole. Do you have the slightest idea how you scared me? What the hell do you mean waking me up at four-thirty in the morning?

I jumped right to my feet, naked, shivering, knowing nothing good comes this way.

Alexander, you say to my hello.

Now I know that my Alexander knows about appropriate emotions. If necessary, you'd display them. So right away I figured no deaths.

Time zones, I shrieked. Don't you know about time zones?

I assumed with your life-style, you'd still be up, Alexander says.

That—Alexander—I don't deserve. I mean don't you ever leave it alone?

Come home.

In truth, brother, I don't want to—but before you protest—I will. Yes, I will.

I envision the entire scene.

Don't pretend, Walter says. You haven't come by chance—you were not passing by.

All right, I say. Yes, I received letters, I received calls.

I stare at the old man. I am shocked, I say, at the change in you. I smile. You have never looked better.

I honestly don't remember him looking so good, at least not in memory. There he is tanned, muscled.

Now, how do I seem? he says.

All right, I say.

Talking to myself? Incoherent? Walter asks. He smiles.

Hell no.

· · ·

That's how I see it, Alex.

So I told Eileen. Eileen is nothing if not practical.

My father is going berserk, I said to Eileen.

I've given up smoking, she replied, a plump pigeon on her way to Weight Watchers.

There I was a Jell-O bowl, thinking about Kentucky bluegrass special, about Valium, about amytal, about fifty kinds of dementia—and Miss-Glory-to-the-Republic told me she's given up smoking.

My old man has gone berserk, I tried again.

Jeez, that's too bad, she said. Did they commit him? Better check that out. Is there a second wife? Money involved? Check that out.

Alexander, I am very like Father. This I have always said. Even if I was the only member of the family who thought so. I'm not referring to physical resemblance. Dad's five-ten. I'm five-eight, a great believer in modern athletics. Dad suspects that a ball may be round. Nevertheless, there exists a positive familial bonding, even our disagreements are kindred. For instance one afternoon, one fine fall afternoon, we were sitting in the living room of that apartment in New York. We had Scotch that afternoon. Dad was talking about his often expressed belief in serendipity as a moving factor in life. I was countering with my own belief in definite moments. Sometimes when the discussion was right I called him Walter, he didn't mind, sometimes not. I'll tell you what, Walter said, you make me a list of some of your definite moments, and I'll make a list of my serendipitous events. You'll discover that definite moments are serendipitous. Never, I said. Afterwards, Alexander, you caught me in the hall. What the hell do you find to say to him? We talk, I replied. But I can never talk to him, you said.

Actually, Alexander, you talk to him all the time. I've heard you.

In point of fact I was heading towards a definite moment and never did get around to making up a complete list, but I scribbled down a few definite moments and sent it to Father. Beating you up, an early attempt at fellatio, discovering that my most important definite moments were remembered only by me, and then grey sky.

The grey sky was the newest. One morning I rolled over in bed and stared out the window. From my body angle—flat on my back—all I could see was the sky. It was grey. That was when I decided to go west. I was alone in the room. No one to offer an opposing argument. Being alone is a majority opinion.

Before I left the city, Walter called me up. Beating up Alexander, he said. How? He's huge. Six-two, two twenty-five. Not always, I said. You forget. He was a shrimp, a genuine little kid. Maybe, my father said. I don't remember. A school-teacher loses a lot of his kid's youth. So you beat up Alexander. I would have given him the whole spiel, but he said okay and hung up.

I really would have wanted to see Walter's serendipity list.

But beating you up, Alexander, was a definite moment. My friend Duncan came to see me one Saturday morning. Confidentially, Norman, he said, your brother is ruining you. He is making out of you top ass material. Then he tells me the story. I had to go hunt you up, Alexander. Where were you? Sitting under a tree with a blank pad of paper and a pencil. What kind of crap are you saying? I accused. Our father is a financier? Zurich? A private airplane? I punched you, maybe once, twice. I bloodied your nose. I felt rotten. We went into the basement of our building and I washed your face in the laundry room. You were little and skinny. We were alone down there, Alex, and so I hugged you. Listen, I said, don't let them get at you. If you need help, remember me. I'm your brother.

The first thing I ever did in my life because I wanted to do it was marry Eileen. She had long hair. Blunt cut, she told me. She went every six weeks to Bergdorf's. She was a small girl, slim. I could see the veins beneath her skin pumping blood. Her mother lived out in California. Her mother has lavender-colored hair. No kidding, Alexander, the hair is lavender.

I'll try to get away for a few days. I make no promises, Alex baby. But maybe I'll be able to get back east for a few days and see the old (read that new) homestead.

TWO

I received copies of the newspaper clippings. They were bombarding me with mail every day—along with postcards from the Russian Tea Room, unreal shots of the Verrazano Bridge. The message was the same. Save him, Shirley wrote. His wife—your mother—is out to get him.

I also suspected that Mrs. Coover had taken to peeking in my mailbox if I wasn't home when the mailman came. I was positive that she read the postcards. Our friendship was over. I had found the box from Dunkin Donuts on top of the garbage in the can—the one I had eaten from, the professionally retied string-bow unbroken.

I couldn't stand the mail. The mailman hit my box at nine-fifteen. His name was Petrelli. We'd shared a beer once. Petrelli used to live on 170th and the Grand Concourse. This is the life, he told me.

It was morning, the third week of my pain. I was hungry. I needed to do some shopping. What was left? Slices of pastrami, still in its delicatessen white paper, some bread. I unwrapped the meat, the slices bonded together by the cold glue of fat. I dumped the chilled, moist pile onto a piece of aluminum foil and put it into the toaster oven. By the time I had showered, the whole place smelled of pastrami, a peppery scent reminiscent of grey skies. I'd make a sandwich and some coffee. I liked eating this way sometimes, liked the freedom of having childhood delights whenever I wanted.

I heard the metal flap of the mailbox go down. I was in no hurry. Ever since the session with Petrelli, that man waited to see if I'd come right out and offer another beer.

I filled the coffee pot with water. When I thought it was safe I opened the door, my arm shot out with perfect aim into the brass plated box. One plunge and I had it all.

I just left the mail on the table while I fixed the sandwich. I licked the mustard from my fingers, savoring the sharpness. The sandwich was piled high. Only two slices of bread.

Well, Norm baby. The mail. Maybe two letters, some ads. I wanted least of all any word from home. We weren't a letter writing family. I mean when my father sent that check for five thousand, there wasn't even a note in the envelope.

I had driven right over to Santa Barbara to show that check to Eileen. How do you know? she said. Know? I said. Yeah, how do you know that it's a fair share—that it represents what you're entitled to?

This from a woman who had never told me to go out and make something of myself, who truly believed that we had hidden powers, hidden talents, and that money was unimportant.

Eileen that day was a deep disappointment.

I poured a cup of coffee. I took a bite of the sandwich, rich, juicy, a proper edge of grease. That delicatessen was a Fairfax Avenue find. Brown skies above, I sang softly.

There was an ad for Thom McAn Shoes, a flier from the Quik Market, an invitation from the House of Redemption for ALL FAITHS.

I decided to eat one-half of the sandwich and drink one full cup of coffee before I opened the envelope. It was a quarter to ten. In fifteen minutes I had to leave and drive to the classroom where as Adjunct Assistant Professor I would tell some crisply wide-awake faces about the perils, joys, and social significance of urban life. Last fall I had taught that class at night. Everyone had been older, everyone seemed to be from the East. They had sat there nodding their heads, shuddering. A memory trip, one woman told me. This year the class was in the morning, everyone was from Santa Monica. They paid a lot of attention to facts, there was no remembered pain for them.

Norman, you are a man without soul. Open the letter. So I dropped the sandwich onto the plate, did not wipe my hands on the paper napkin, and the fingerprints of grease on the envelope made it impossible to deny that I had read that letter.

Dear Norman,
    I guess I need to talk to you. Call me when you can.
                                                    Alexander

Now how's that? I shook the envelope too, expecting another paper to fall out. The one that would say—in red ink—*God, Norman, how can I handle what has happened?* Would they stop writing to me? Subject of the postal connections was always my father. Daddy, Pops, Pa, Sir, Walter.

Call me when you can.

The Mystery Man Strikes.

I grabbed my manila folder with its burden of unmarked typing paper. A student had once protested that I came unprepared. Now I always carried a folder, opened it from time to time, angled from public view, turned pages, examined the watermark.

Call me when you can.

I can't.

I started my car. I did not have a radio in my car.

But what do you do when you're trapped in traffic?

I knit, I said.

Today, I would tell the class, we will discuss the problems of mental stability in urban life. For instance, my father is going berserk—the source of his disorder could be the city—or its loss.

I only taught two classes. I was not part of any benefit plan, and I was paid a contact-hour rate not enough to keep pigeons alive nor palm trees in water. So I also sold appliances at a store called Cutter's. I used to have a better job in a music store, but they had let me go. I remembered the names and records and all the groups. I had a series of mnemonics for remembering all that, but the manager said that I didn't look the part. I wasn't even too old, just didn't seem right. I didn't look as if I believed, the manager said.

I spit on the mindless ass, Eileen had said.

Now that was the girl I had loved. The squint at the check had been one minor lapse.

. . .

After class I was always trapped by some students. The substance of my course led them to questions, to conversation. They felt that they could grasp it. "I don't think," the girl was saying, "that mental stability is broken by urban life. I mean by the tight overcrowded urban life that you describe, sir. I mean it can happen out here—by loneliness, for instance."

I nodded. "But I was not talking about loneliness. Loneliness is another ball game. I was talking about urban stress."

I saw Goddard and Angell in the hall. A man cannot exist in Los Angeles without friends. Goddard pointed his finger and motioned.

"Excuse me," I said to the last four students still clustered around the desk. "I have another commitment."

"Wait up," I called and clutched the manila folder to my chest.

"Coffee," Goddard said.

"Doughnuts," Angell said.

"Oh wow," I said and fell into step.

We walked together to the coffee shop two blocks away. I didn't choose it. I didn't like it. It had no pictures of impossibly wonderful food to order.

Angell and Goddard were on the permanent faculty. They had the benefit plan.

"I got my check already," Goddard was saying. "Less the deductible on the dental package, they still paid back one-oh-five."

The coffee shop was crowded. We usually took a booth. But today there was only a table available.

"Can't wait," Goddard said. "I got to pick up my daughter from nursery school today. My wife's got a job interview."

"My blessings," I said.

"Oh, she won't get it," Goddard said. "Interviews for these nice staid-type office jobs and she goes in her black get-'em dress with half her chest hanging out. The interviewer is a woman, see, or when it's a man she gets an invite for a drink. Then she comes home and cries all evening. What's wrong with me? she says."

"Coffee."

"Coffee."

"Coffee and a talcum-covered doughnut."

The waitress didn't smile. We didn't know her name, she didn't know ours. She had a handkerchief with a crocheted edge twisted into a cloth version of petals and held to her shoulder by a chipped black and white plastic name pin. The pin said *Dee*. We did not believe that was her name.

"Norman, baby, how's refrigerators?"

"Cold. Maybe I'll go to New York. Go home."

Angell sipped his coffee. "Permanently?"

"No, for a visit. A trip home."

"Ah NYC! Ah snow, ah sleet, ah exciting throb of real life, nostalgia for the city of my youth," Goddard said.

Angell broke his doughnut, showered the table and my sleeve with the powdery sugar that stuck like crazy glue to whatever it touched. He offered no one a piece but dunked one end into his coffee. "You were born in this sovereign state of California," he said. "It's no use pretending, your accent gave you away."

"It's my father," I said.

"Yeah."

"My father is going berserk."

"You mean really?"

"Yeah. Yeah, I guess so."

"Tough," Goddard said. "I'm not close with my father. Not distant, not close. They live here, my parents, ten miles away. My wife calls them our holiday relatives. You know—like Thanksgiving, Christmas, the rest. They appear at the table scrubbed and in finery. My mother walks around our house and sighs. Children, she swears, would make the difference. Once she whispered in my ear, Don't have them with her."

"I'm hot for someone," Angell said.

"Under twelve or over forty?"

"You know her. The lovely lady Clare."

"Kiss and tell."

"Not actually. I've got an entire scenario planned. I'm going to pick up my kid, take her home, wait for the little woman in her bazoom hanging dress, she'll tell me about the interview, she'll cry, I will insult her dress code, the fight predestined, I leave. I drive to my assignation with the lady Clare. I couldn't have planned it better if I had more time, I mean she put her hand on my leg at precisely eight-oh-two this very a.m. on the pretext of borrowing my fine-line mechanical pencil."

"I think my grandfather was crazy," I said. "I don't know for certain. I just think so."

"So it is in the genes. My mother-in-law may be crazy—or perhaps I too just think so," Angell said.

"He died young," I said. "The grandfather. So I can't be certain. Maybe I ought to consult someone."

"What the hell for? You don't have any kiddies. Listen, your grandfather was probably driven crazy by his children and so on ad infinitum."

"You know what my father said to me once. He said, You have no vanity."

The two men looked at me.

"Did he really?" Angell said.

"Not as a compliment, you know. We were not being buddy-buddy. It was like at breakfast, I think. No, I know it was at breakfast. He put his cup down and said to me, You have no vanity. It's hung with me. I thought of him all that day as a person. All that day I thought about him as someone named Walter."

"When I was ten," Angell said, "my mother was on nights at the hospital for more money, so my father had to make my lunch before he went to work. He hated that and then he was mad at my mother. One day he put prune pits in the sandwich right on top of the cheese. Four prune pits."

"Are you an only child?" Goddard said to me. "Have you got someone to help?"

"A brother. He's back there—where my father is."

"Then it's not so bad. Stick your father in a hospital. That's the way. My wife has a retarded brother. Her parents were sensible. He could have ruined everyone's life if they'd kept him home."

"Listen, bubbalas," Angell said, "I have a commitment. Waitress, puis—je avoir la note, s'il vous plaît?"

We pushed back our chairs. The chairs slid smoothly on the waxed floor. One thing about that restaurant. It was very clean.

"Good luck with Clare."

"Good luck with your father."

"Avoid all children."

I walked back to the parking lot where I'd left my car. On Tuesdays I had five hours after my last class before I was due at the appliance store. There was only a chance that Eileen would be home. I didn't know her schedule anymore. I'd chance it. I never called, but then I only went there during the day.

I tilted the rearview mirror to see my face. I had shaved, hair though curly was neat, shirt and pants clean. Had I no vanity? But that was not what my father had meant. Tell me, Walter, I should have said, just how do you define vanity?

But not as pride. I suspected that my father never confused vanity with pride. Was I a disappointment to him? Or was it possible that my father did not care? After all, I did not think about my father often. Therefore, I must recognize the possibility that my father did not think about me often. It was part of the problem of being an adult, of seeming less needful.

I headed to Eileen. I hadn't seen her since the afternoon when my girl Joan moved out of my apartment. It hadn't been a traumatic event. So long, Joan had said to me, I think I'll move up the coast.

I arrived at her apartment just as Eileen was putting together a pile of clothes to be dry-cleaned. It was mostly blouses dropped in the middle of the floor on the rattan rug. They had fallen like a besieged harem rainbow, reds and blues and yellows, all different, all wildly inviting.

"The trouble with silk," Eileen said, "is that you can't wash it properly, but I love it anyway. It's worth the trouble. I never mind the effort. My skirts though, my skirts I can wash." She hated to be thought extravagant. She had many economies— they kept her even, but not ahead.

"There's lots of food," she said. "Take some."

"No, that's okay. How you been?"

"Fine."

I sat down, stretched out my legs, and pushed off one shoe. My toes waded in the waves of silk. I could imagine Eileen in every single color. I was certain that during our marriage she had only worn natural homespun. I seemed to remember that.

"Did I tell you that I'm working in an insurance company now?" she said.

"No," I said. "No, you didn't."

"Only three days a week. But I'm going to classes too—in business management."

"There's a problem with my father," I said.

Eileen dropped her last blouse and sat down across from me in a beige chair. She had bound her hair into one thick black braid, the braid flipped across one shoulder. She looked as if she had been drawn by a quick hand—slashed mouth, slitted eyes, swell body in something definitely orange—she looked sketched for the Sunday papers.

"I didn't know him very well," she said. "Your father."

"Yes, I know. I'm sorry. That was my fault."

I hadn't notified my parents about the marriage right away. When did the ceremony take place? they asked. Six months ago, I said, remembering too late to lie. Well thanks, my mother said. Thanks a lot. I'll let them cool down, I told Eileen.

"What's wrong with your father," Eileen said.

"My father is going berserk," I said.

"The old do that," Eileen said. "I mean it isn't so uncommon."

"He's not that old," I said. "He's only fifty-eight."

"My father was almost seventy-five when he died," Eileen said. "But that's because I was from the second marriage. His first wife died in Bloomington, Indiana, and then he came out here to L.A. and married my mother. But what I'm saying is that he went strange before he died too. He went strange from the illness."

"My father is not sick," I said. "Not physically."

"My father had six cancers," Eileen said. "Six discrete cancers, the doctors said, not one that grew. My mother couldn't take it at the end, so I went to the hospital alone every day the entire week before he died.

"A bad time. His mind wandered. He spoke freely. He didn't usually talk to me much, you know. I mean not too much. But one afternoon when I was sitting by his bed in Cedars, he started in about what happened to him in 1951. I wasn't even born yet, he wasn't even married to my mother. In Bloomington, he said, when he was a developer, when he was still in construction. He built subdivisions there, he built suburbs. Two-, three-bedroom houses. He lived in a house like the ones he built, only bigger, with his first wife and his three sons. One afternoon coming home on the train from Indianapolis, he got picked up by this girl. Maybe fifteen, twenty years younger, he said. She had long pale hair. She didn't know his real name or anything about him. Twice a week he went up to her place, this large room over a store, the streets deserted at night. My father said that it was a miraculous time, like nothing he'd ever known, the mattress on the floor, great jugs of wine. He said that it could have gone on and on. Then she wanted something more, she seemed to think something more was going to happen. My father decided to divorce his first wife. Then whatever the girl wanted, she could have. What did she want—the girl? She wanted to live in a house, she wanted trees around and a lawn. Forget the candles burning, the mattresses on the floor, the everflowing wine. Adventures don't go on, my father said. Eventually, they end in domestication."

"The story is apocryphal," I said.

"There on his death bed? Why would he do that? His mind was going."

"Doesn't sound like it, it sounds connected. He wanted you

to know before he went that your youth wasn't special. He was delivering a message."

"His mind was wandering."

"Listen, did he go into details—maybe you're skipping them for me. Did he go for instance into their fucking habits, did he free associate about lovemaking? I mean why the hell should he ignore the best stuff."

"My father wouldn't have spoken that way to me." Eileen was annoyed, she was flushing.

"Maybe not," I said. "You are turning red, you know."

"He was of another generation, another time, and his mind was wandering."

"He was delivering a message."

"And your father," Eileen said, "is he delivering a message?"

"How the hell do I know. All I know is that he's going berserk."

"Who says?"

"Everyone, the whole damn family. My mother says, my sister-in-law says, my brother says."

"I'm sorry," Eileen said. "You know that I am really sorry."

"I suppose," I said, "that there is nothing that I can actually do."

"I don't mean to say anything," Eileen said, "but that brother—does he have power of attorney?"

"Jesus! My brother is very nearly perfect."

Eileen stood up. "I have to get dressed," she said. "Go to the cleaners. Meet someone."

"Maybe I'll have some food," I said. "Any chicken?"

"Go help him," Eileen said, her voice suddenly urgent.

"My father?"

"Sure, maybe they're after him."

"No way," I said. "He's after them, if you ask me. Maybe I should pass on the food. I'm due at the store at half-past." I went over and kissed Eileen on the lips. I had the impression that she hadn't aged at all.

notes to alexander

Look, you wanted me to come. I came. I arrived at Kennedy, rented a car, and drove right down here. I arrived around seven in the evening. Get the significance of that, Alex. It was *dark* already. I could see nothing. The country is not lit. They had waited dinner for me. Mother looked great, wearing something green and loose and silver earrings, and Dad seemed to be ten years younger complete with muscles and a deep tan.

We had drinks, we had dinner. They wanted to know what I was doing. They were properly nosy. They asked about Eileen. Nothing seemed strange. What I noticed right away was that neither of them was trying to get me alone. I mean I had been certain that was going to happen. But it didn't.

Then after dinner we were sitting in their living room.

"Don't pretend," Walter said calmly. "You haven't come by chance—you were not passing by."

"All right," I said. "You've received a lot of publicity recently."

"Ah," Walter said. "And you don't approve—well, neither do I. The emphasis has been wrong. It's been Barnum and Bailey. Wrong emphasis, Norman. Everyone speaks of the Hole. The emphasis should be on what I hope to find. Lazarre's buildings. I've acquired some of the man's writings—got them from a dealer in the city. Lazarre had a vision, Norman. How many people have a vision? Life as it might be—gardens of beauty, scenes of peace, plenty of space and tranquility."

"Sounds French," I said. "Sounds Louie the Fourteenth." I was warming to the subject. "Also sounds aristocratic. I mean who was supposed to be able to afford to live out here in when was it—1915?"

"Nineteen-ten," Walter said. "Also, you are wrong about the rich angle. A vision takes money—I'll grant that—but a good idea cannot be limited to those with money. Lazarre wrote about a different kind of life. I don't expect to dig that up, Norman. But what I hope—whatever I could find might stand as a symbol of a search, a search for beauty."

"My field, Dad," I said. "Scratch a beautiful life-style and what do you find? The same old worker bees making it possible."

"Symbols," Walter said, "have value."

I looked across at Mother. She wasn't looking at me—she was staring out the window at the stars, at a myriad of stars.

But Walter was not sounding excessively weird. I'd run across a lot of yearning for the past—the old neighborhood, the torn-down elevated, the wonderful movie house. My father did not sound mad. Why couldn't he do what he wanted? How often could he? Or anyone? So he fell into a pot of luck—the money. Let him use it up. Tomorrow when it was light out I'd look the place over. Already I thought of it as the site of a dig, a real archeological dig.

"Another drink?" Walter asked.

"Hey," I said. "I will have another drink." I felt all right.

"That's my boy," Father said. He poured a strong one. "Long trips wear me out," he said.

"I'm going to bed," Mother said. "Yours is the last room on the right, Norman."

"Fine," I said.

It was amazing, Alexander. There I was in a room in which I had never spent a night and yet it was my room. Not that there was any reason why they shouldn't have kept the furniture. And Mother was never the person to spend time shopping just so something would be new. Anyway, the oak looked good here. Fit. The furniture dates from high school, from the Riverside Drive apartment. You'll use the same bed, Mother had said, but you can get something different for the rest.

I had a budget. I had gone looking at stuff with my friend Duncan. My mother, Duncan had said, would have just bought whatever she wanted. Lucky if it wasn't chintz with apples. Know what I mean? he said.

Shopping hadn't turned out to be fun. I was embarrassed by the salespeople. Here son, they would say. Solid rock maple.

In the end I found what I wanted in one of those outlet places for a storage company—abandoned furniture, orphans of wood. Hell, I didn't believe my luck. But I was young. Did I trust my judgment? I brought Mother to see. Her pleasure made it perfect. You really found it, she said.

The oak desk, I still like. It's here in this room. Line, my God, I had an eye for line. The dresser looks good too, but the desk was the best.

I rubbed circles on the wood. I undressed. In my mother's house I wore pajamas. I had packed some. I would have liked one more drink, but I didn't want to bump into either parent again tonight. But Walter had been all right, like himself, sometimes sarcastic, sometimes easygoing.

I sat on the bed. The mattress was different all right. We could afford quality now. On the wall was the 1953 Maeght poster, the squiggles of grey and brown.

It was almost one o'clock—should I call California? Only ten there. I'd call Eileen. My room, I'd tell her, the same. Can you beat that? I mean the same in a different house. Because this wasn't my house or even someplace where I knew where everything was. I tried one bounce—the innersprings groaned and then settled, the groan wasn't repeated. These springs didn't squeak. Alex had been the great squeaker, through the hollow core walls of Riverside Drive. Good old Alex—squeak, squeak, squeak. Alex with Alex, I had thought. Jesus, the time, that shadowy evening, I saw Alex pull that beige charmer down the hall— right down the hall and knowing that all of us were there. Alex had guts. God, what guts! First Libbie and then the Sachs girl and then two I didn't know.

I fell asleep—one minute sitting up, next not. I was asleep when the yelling began. It was *her* I heard.

"Stop," she was screaming. "Stop!"

Was I oriented? I didn't know where I was. But I jumped up. Ran to the window. It was dark out there—but there was a glow.

This room I was in faced the road. All I saw was a glow. I grabbed my pants, pulling them up over the pajamas. Shoes? I couldn't find my damn shoes. There was more screaming now, louder, much louder. Hell, I'd go barefoot. I ran to the stairs, down the stairs. "Mother," I called. "I'm coming."

What had happened? Special lights, special rigged kleig lights. The backyard looked like Yankee Stadium prepared for a night doubleheader. "Oh Christ," I whispered. There was the Hole, the Pit, the Crater, Dante's Inferno.

If only they had some close neighbors—if only there had been someone around to file a complaint, to stop that mad digger. At the rim of the Hole at the farthest side I saw the hoist attached to the back of an ancient tow truck. Walter had run a rope from it to something deep in the Hole. "Yo ho," Father sang in a loud voice. "Yo ho, ten men in a bottle."

My feet were slipping—as I got close to the Hole, the ground became wetter, dampness spreading between my toes. I saw my father, the Mars man in a black rubber suit, pulling the rope, turning a crank on the pulley.

Was that Mother there? Shouting, flaying the air with her arms. Mother in a long yellow nightgown. "Stop, stop," she screamed. "Not at night! Not at night too!"

"Stand clear," Father yelled. "I'm hoisting it up."

Up? What up?

"Pulling up what, Dad?" I called.

The straining pulley squealed. How could that sound be so loud as to be heard over our combined shrieks? I saw Father standing on the far ridge, his legs spread wide to keep his balance. The final squeal occurred. A concrete lump appeared over the rim of the Hole, but then emerging, its silhouetted shape was unmistakable. It was a stone fountain.

My father was pulling up a fountain.

"Eeeh! Eeeh!" Mother shouted and pulled at her hair.

Tenderly the fountain swayed through the air, swung over solid ground, and was deposited next to the tow truck.

"Eureka!" Father shouted.

I was running towards those apparitions. I felt no pain, like an Indian mystic facing a bed of nails; the tender soles of my feet did not translate the sharp edges of the broken stones. I was sucked by the mud, slid, and went down on my knees.

It was at that moment that Father lost his balance and fell backwards into the Hole. When I got to my feet, Father was flat on his back at the bottom of the Hole and unmoving. And Mother seeing it all had collapsed into a dead faint on solid ground near the rim. Unless of course she had hit him first with a piece of concrete. There were certainly plenty of pieces around.

I have heard that the police sometimes put witnesses under hypnosis in the certainty that they saw what they do not remember. Of course, they have to have your permission. I believe that Father was possessed in the moment of his success with ecstasy. I *know* that I heard that in his voice. The "Eureka!" was a pure, exultant tone—the pulling out of his Excalibur. And Alex, when you consider the circumstances—I mean happiness can dazzle. Think of Hasidim, brother, whirling in joy. So we have Walter floating in spirit. Doesn't that lead to carelessness—to a misstep? Why not? And Mother, Alex, has her side too. I mean the man was out there in the mud in the middle of the night with his roaring, his hoists, his damn baseball lights. What was she to think? To do? She wanted him to stop, to return to the house, to remember that it was the middle of the night. That was certainly reasonable.

I do not consider myself a good candidate for hypnosis, Alex. I cannot imagine giving myself over to that kind of control. And should they ask me—I refuse.

I'm jotting this down, brother, because I want to remember what to tell you and what to ask you. There's a country cop here every twenty minutes or so. His name is Conlon and he has a brown stain on his left incisor. He seems to know his way around the place, but still I try to trot along. The guy is small, thin, and never takes off his green plaid shirt. He has a triangular-shaped face. I am trying to place him—maybe his ancestors came from Poland or perhaps the Ukraine. He arrived prepared all right with some high rubber galoshes, the kind with black metal clips that look like little ladders. He slid around a lot in that mud. He saw, I believe, how easy it is to lose your footing, slip right down to the bottom of that Hole. There wasn't any actual water in the Hole, but Conlon mentioned a rank odor. I didn't smell anything. Maybe he is unusually sensitive. He kept on writing in a little book, some of it I could make out by walking slightly behind him. He was noting the position of the rocks and the small boulders, the pump, the pulley on the back of the tow truck. About a hundred feet back from the Hole the woods begin again—underbrush, a network of thick vines choking some of the trees, plenty of poison ivy. Conlon wants a statement from everybody.

Everybody, Alexander.

Our conversation goes like this, brother. First of all, there are lots of repetitions—he is slow, he is careful. "Norman Simon," he says. "Your name is Norman Simon?"

A schoolboy buying time, I'm thinking.

"Yes," I say. "Norman Simon."

"The time of the occurrence?"

"The accident," I say. "About midnight."

"Where were you?"

"I was in bed," I say.

Colon is neither glum nor impatient. "What were you wearing?"

Now this one I do not understand. "Pajamas," I say.

"What did you hear?" he asks. "What made you get up?"

"Noise," I tell him.

"What did you see?"

. . .

I tell him what I told you, Alex. I tell him nothing else. I give a complete description of the events. I believe that he knows Walter and Sara. At least, I think he knows Mother. He also inquires about her health. He wants to talk to her. I do not see that as possible. She is sedated, I tell him. She is in shock.

He is definitely coming back.

We have not been together much these last years, Alex, but now I see us united on this issue.

Meanwhile, I will do what I can.

To tell the truth, Alexander, things are in a mess. Until I checked the papers in his desk I had no idea Dad had inherited that much money. Don't misunderstand, I am not saying that the five big ones that he gave me was ungenerous. But my God, Alex, they were practically rich. Where is it now, Alex? I'll tell you where. They bought a damn motel, they bought this gentleman's house. I couldn't believe the motel when I saw it. Twenty-four abandoned units. Where were you, Alex, when all this was happening?

Hey, don't misunderstand. I don't blame you. But how long can I hold off that cop. Mother looks better every day—emotionally is another thing—but she looks better.

What I'd like to do, Alex, is order up a couple of trucks of soil and fill in that pit. That's what I'd like to do.

THгee

How organized was I? For instance, if I had a job and was supposed to be someplace at a certain time. All right, I was there. A man must eat. But the rest—hell, if it was Tuesday—so what. I mean I didn't go to the dentist every six months. I paid fines on library books, sometimes I had to buy the books. I went to an accountant who hated me. H & R Block, he'd say, go there, Norman.

In the kitchen of my parents' house where I couldn't find anything—you know, like where were the frying pans—now I wrote things on the blackboard. Originally on that blackboard—a new one, a green one, the chalk yellow—it had said, *Spag, btr, tmc.* I left that for a long time. First, it was untouched like it was evidence. As if Sam Spade would arrive and read that and interpret. So if I erased—I'd throw everything off.

Hell, no crime committed.

Therefore, no evidence needed.

I erased. Then I began on that blackboard my own lists. Organization. I was becoming organized. I adopted a small, an artificially small handwriting. The size of the blackboard imposed its limitations. I developed a tiny, cryptic handwriting. There was a list entitled *Calls to Make* and that list said *lawyer, doctor, banker.*

First I searched my priorities. I found a cast iron frying pan. I placed an order. There were deliveries from Stop & Shop in Shilton. If you didn't eat, you felt worse. Stands to reason, Dr. Waddington said. I bought all sorts of food, heavy on already prepared, but also some of the fresh stuff.

With the cast iron frying pan, I did bacon and eggs. I splashed fat, sent its sizzle across my fingers, and I plunged my fist into my mouth to suck at the pain. Afterwards, I made coffee. I made for two. I went up the stairs whistling loudly. I didn't want to surprise Mother. I wanted her to know that I was coming. "I been working on the railroad," I sang. "Mom," I called out before

I reached the door. Let her know how close I was. "Hey Mom!"
I knocked at the door.

"Norman," she said.

"Me."

"Come in."

In my section on urban family stresses, I gave out ques-
tionnaires at the start of the course. In one class there were
eight from small towns, less than twenty thousand population,
and fourteen from suburbs, and then the remaining core were
from the heart of the city, the tight, crowded part. To test
family stresses, I divided them. I made Team A, Team B, and
Team C. Be truthful, I urged, like in sack races, rallies. It wasn't
who had it worse. It was who had it different. We took apart
the family, we probed, we uncovered. This was not innovative
work, this was a repetition of classical experiments. We did
crowd behavior and clustering. Like for instance it was nine
a.m. on a weekday, and you had spread your towel on a Redon-
do beach, and no one was within five hundred feet. Then
other people arrived carrying umbrellas, vinyl bags. They surveyed the beach and then came and spread their towels within
ten feet of yours. We discussed why. Then we did the essays.
I assigned the one called, "My Mother." I selected some from
the class to read out loud. A representative sampling, I told the
class. Who was telling the truth? There were the dypsomaniac
mothers concealing behind Sen-Sen, the seducers of small
children, the grim bearers of beatings and other bad tidings, the
kindly old orifice cleaners, the kleptomaniac-hypochondriac-
arsonists.

I read these essays anonymously. So I read mine. I wrote
about my mother, the urban mother. A transient childhood, I
wrote, yields stresses. I wrote about how my mother yelled, how
she cooked, the pressures of mothers on the eldest, about her
hobby of painting. The class discussed, but they were actually
more interested in some of the other mothers. The juicier ones.

.   .   .

What was I afraid of each time I opened her bedroom door? What did I expect—the Madwoman of Chaillot? I mean it came at you fast, all that stimulus, you didn't have time. I didn't have time to think of Walter.

But Mother was always lying quietly in that bed, two pillows behind her head. She had combed her hair, though. She looked neat. She wore a blue bathrobe, old, tightly belted. There were paint stains on it here and there. She had a lot of clothes like that. Red, blue, green stains.

"Hey Mom," I was saying. "Come on down, Mom. I've made bacon. I've made eggs. Also, coffee."

"I don't know," she replied. She stared at the wallpaper, the ceiling, the floor.

"Listen," I began again, "it's lonely down there, just me. This is one big house."

"Turn on the radio," she said.

Do not at this time, Dr. Waddington said, mention Walter, if she does not.

She did not.

She sat up slowly, as if movement made her dizzy. "All right," she said. "What the hell."

"Good girl," I replied. "You want help?"

I was certain that she would refuse, would not take my arm. But she did. I was frightened. Overwhelmed. I could see a lawn, a long expanse of sloping grass, trimmed. I was walking down that lawn and with me, hand on my arm, was this woman, my mother, in a bathrobe. Moving past us were other ladies similarly garbed, each one with a visitor. It was visiting hours. Thus, was I influenced by the media. This was a media-induced vision.

Mother took hold of the banister when we reached the stairs and let go of my arm. "It's the damn pills," she said. "I feel like a sailboat in a strong wind. And if that half-ass doctor says relax to me one more time, Norman. Anyway, what kind of a doctor makes house calls?"

I started to say relax, but I sucked in my breath for an isometric exercise instead.

"I'll tell you why he comes," she said, carefully putting one foot in front of another as she went down the stairs. "He comes for gossip. He would hate to miss anything. After all, he has a foot in the Hole."

I listened closely. It was terrible when your parents were wise.

In the kitchen I removed the inverted soup bowl that I had used to cover the bacon and eggs. They were still warm on the platter.

"I should help," Mother said.

A good sign. Guilt.

I poured the coffee, and she went to the refrigerator for the butter.

"Listen, Norman," she said after we were seated. "I think that you should marry again. One mistake means nothing. What does it mean?"

"Certainly," I replied. I didn't want to upset her. In the kitchen she looked pale, fluorescent light was heartless. She looked pale and sick.

"Are you writing that study you used to mention?" she asked. "Urban life?"

"Yes," I said. "But I'm still gathering data. Need plenty of data."

Across the room on top of the radio—which I had forgotten to turn on—were envelopes. Every day I put the mail there. My parents received a lot of mail, more than I remembered.

"Mother," I began, "are there things I should do?"

"Like what?"

"Affairs. Your mail—your bills. Aren't there matters to be taken care of?"

Mother was chewing her food. "Possibly," she said.

Funding had been her business. Where did I come off asking her fiscal questions.

"You should have power of attorney," she said.

"What?"

"Call what's-his-face. Have him write up something. Pay the bills, Norman. I trust you to take care of our affairs."

I nodded. "Sure," I said, "but this is only temporary."

We drank our coffee, ate our eggs, cracked the too-crisp bacon.

Jack R. V. Haight drew up the papers. Power of attorney. Did Alexander want it? No, he said, you take it, you're the oldest. I sent Eileen a postcard right after the signing. There were plenty of postcards on the desk in the living room. This one had a picture on it of Fifth Avenue at twilight, blue-grey sky. One of the buildings on the left had been torn down since that postcard was printed. Not a new postcard. *My brother,* I wrote to Eileen, *is the salt of the earth.* I scratched that out. *My brother is all a brother should be. You would understand, if you knew him. Love, Norman.* I put a stamp on the card and gave it to the Stop & Shop boy. He probably mailed it, I tipped well.

I wasn't putting calls through to Mother. In truth, I didn't actually ask her. I just didn't put calls through. I pretended to be a friend just answering the phone. Did it work?

"Norman?" the voice would say. "Norman, that's you. This is Louise."

"Yes," I would reply, no use disguising my consonants.

"For goodness sakes, why didn't you just say so? This is Louise, Norman."

"Yes."

"How is Sara? How is your mother? Should I come out? Should Arthur and I drive out?"

"No."

"We had no idea—until the newspapers. We tried to get through to Walter. We're old friends, Norman. We want to help. After all, Walter and Arthur were one-time partners."

"Beg pardon?"

"Partners," she repeated. "Walter and Arthur were going into business together."

"I didn't know," I said. It came to me what the power of attorney meant. I would have to go through their papers. I would have to go through the desk drawers. The family voyeur, the envelope peeker. Maybe when I was a kid that would have given me a thrill. I didn't want to know what was there anymore.

"Yes, they were planning a business venture," Louise said. "I have to tell you, Norman, you have my sympathies. We would really love to help."

"Thank you," I said. "Not necessary."

"You will call, though, for anything? Do you have a pencil? I'll give you my number."

"Yes."

She gave me the numbers slowly, and I dutifully repeated them. I had no idea where a pencil might be.

"No," Jack said. "Don't fill the Hole."

"Why the hell not? He's not going out there again. You know that. Even when Walter wakes up, gets well. He's not going out there again. The Hole is there, it's big. I want to have it filled."

"Norman, calm down. It can't be done right now, Norman."

"Why not?"

"I think, Norman, if you tried to do that—maybe the county sheriff's office would stop it."

"How the hell could they? My parents' land, my parents' goddamn Hole."

"Norman, I have a particular lawyer in mind."

"You are a lawyer."

"A different kind of lawyer, Norman, is what I have in mind—should anything come up."

"What could come up?"

"I am only being cautious, Norman. Thinking of the family's welfare—thinking about Sara."

"Mother is all right. Mother is recovering daily." Sara, I meant to say, leave Sara out of this.

"Has your Mr. Conlon questioned her yet?"

"No."

"Precautions," Jack said soothingly. "Precautions never hurt."

. . .

I used the downstairs bathroom to vomit. I vomited convulsively. I had done that twice before, both times I had been drunk. I had been exceptionally drunk. I have been told that you can tear your gut vomiting that way. The second time was after a divorce. I don't actually remember the circumstances of the first time.

That was the start of it. Organization had begun. Lists, telephone calls, the bank. You know how I felt? I felt as if I had broken into someone's house, going through the drawers, searching for treasure.

Walter had an account at the local bank. Mr. Orckin at the local bank did not like me. Maybe it was the way I kept whistling through my teeth. Everything had been done through this bank, you see. The house, the motel, the accounts. Did I suspect something? I suspected everything. I mean, originally, I figured Dad had got maybe thirty or forty thousand.

Are you crazy? Alexander said to me. How could they get the house with thirty?

House—I hadn't seen it. I was in California. I had been thinking cottage.

I described it, Alexander said to me. I told you.

I hadn't listened.

All right then. Up the ante. No thirty or forty.

Then the motel. The Lost Continent of Atlantis, the Missing Tribes of Israel, the Hanging Gardens of Babylon. Then came Walter's Hoax—The Great Hole!

Mother said that Walter had a loan outstanding. Maybe we could make the motel a roadside attraction. The haunted motel. Bedsprings leaping out at you, ghostly chambermaids.

Pass on that.

Mr. Orckin, I said. I do have power of attorney.

I got my hands on records.

I couldn't believe the actual sum. I couldn't believe it.

I didn't know what to do.

I called Eileen in L.A.

Hello, I said.

Do you know what time it is?

Two a.m. your time, I said. You were up—weren't you up?

Yes, she said, but I might not have been.

I figured you were, I said. I could see her suddenly, I could see her in colors.

You're alone.

Yes, she said, as if it were a question.

Eileen, I whispered, they were rich. Christ, they had so much money. I never dreamed.

What? she said.

Money, I said.

Where is it? She was whispering too.

I'm not exactly certain. Spent, I believe.

The house, she said. Full of new furniture? Minks? Jewels?

No, I said. Old stuff. From their NYC apartment. No furs.

Check that brother.

What?

He's got it, Norman. I feel that in my bones, sibling rivalry, old Greek myths, birthrights. He's got your birthright, Norman.

Bull, Eileen, I said.

You, she said, spacing the words, have been warned.

The doorbell had a good sound. I like to think they put it in. It's the sort of change Walter would make. *Water Music*, the bell played.

"That must be the lady!" I yelled my words up the stairs. I knew Mother heard me, but she didn't answer. Maybe I shouldn't go. Maybe I should stay.

I opened the door. The woman standing there was about sixty and all dressed in white. She shone in the sunlight.

"Hell," I said—thought I whispered.

"I beg your pardon?"

"Uniform," I said. "I specified no uniform."

"I'm not contaminating my own clothes for nobody," the woman said. "I'm entitled to a uniform. I'm a practical."

This wasn't the city. I couldn't ship her back and try another agency. There wasn't another agency.

"All right," I said.

"I'm Mrs. Sorbitol," she said. "I'm licensed."

"Sure," I said. "Come in."

She marched past me. She was an authoritative waddler, five-feet-two, a squat lady. Her grey hair was wound into coils. I imagined her standing next to Mother. It was not a good image—up to Mother's shoulder. No, not quite.

Mrs. Sorbitol looked around the living room. "Ought to cover the upholstery," she advised. "Too much light. Want me to drape with sheets?"

"No," I said. "Listen, my mother is upstairs. First door on the left. She expects you, knows you're coming. I don't think she needs anything, though. Probably nothing to do for her. Probably nothing to do at all."

"All right with me. The one thing I need is coffee. I drink a lot of coffee."

"Sure," I said. "Yeah. Come, I'll show you the kitchen."

Maybe I shouldn't go and leave the pygmy here with Mother. But I hadn't been to the hospital. All right, I was bothered. I didn't want to go. It was Alex who had been going. You have to, he had told me. I think, he said, that Conlon checks to see who went.

Mrs. Sorbitol inspected the kitchen. "This is very old-fashioned," she said. "I'm surprised it wasn't torn out. You should see what I've got. Formica, stainless. I could give you the name of the dealer. Terrific price, mention my name. His sister and my brother-in-law are cousins."

"Not my house," I said.

"Well, when your mother gets on her feet, tell her, it'll give her a lift. Every woman loves new."

Mrs. Sorbitol was at the window. She pressed her nose to the glass. "That is something," she said. "The pictures don't do it justice. Fuzzy, the pictures, except for that colored one in the Sunday Magazine. What a Hole! Imagine."

"Yes," I said. Now I wanted to go.

"You got a television?" Mrs. Sorbitol asked.

"Certainly," I said. "Here in the kitchen over on that counter."

She looked at it "Twelve inches," she said. "You're kidding? That's something for besides a pool or maybe in the john. Nothing bigger? Nothing with color?"

"No," I lied. Bigger and with color was upstairs in the back bedroom. I envisioned Mrs. Sorbitol up there, gleaming white in the room, right down the hall from Mother. Loud laughter, voices from the screen.

"To each his own," Mrs. Sorbitol said. "This will have to do. I don't watch morning junk though. And no soaps. Enough tragedy in my life as it is. I watch public television. I watch 'Good Morning America.' That's what I like."

"Yes," I said. "I'm going upstairs now to tell my mother goodbye. I'll be back home in three or four hours."

Mrs. Sorbitol stared at me. "Full day," she said.

"I beg your pardon."

"The agency makes that clear. I get a full day."

"Yes," I said. "A full day. I don't care about that. I'll pay a full day, but I'll still be back in three or four hours."

"Just so we understand each other. I like to put my cards on the table."

You bet.

Mrs. Sorbitol was already at the sink. She was making coffee, spilling out what was already there. "Fresh," she said. "My middle name is fresh."

I realized that I should pay her for a full day and send her off. But I couldn't leave Mother alone. Could I leave Mother alone?

I sang out as I climbed the stairs. "I'm on the way. I'm on the way."

I knocked. "Mother?"

"Yes."

I saw her lying on the bed. Why did I think she looked worse? I thought that shadows had appeared across her face. No, I couldn't leave her alone. Even grin-and-bear-it downstairs was better than no one.

"Mother," I said. "I have to go out for a while." Do not, Dr. Waddington had said, mention Walter. "I'll be back soon. Downstairs in the kitchen is a Mrs. Sorbitol. If you want anything—anything—need anything, just ask her. Right?"

Mother looked at me. "Right," she repeated.

I remembered a thousand inquisitions. This had never been a distant mother. Where are you going? she had asked. She meant it.

Now she didn't ask. I was an adult. I could go where I liked.

Suppose I told her I was going to the hospital. Suppose I said I was going to see Walter. Would she cry out? Would she come with me? Tell me what happened in that moment when the brown mud rose up in front of my eyes. No, of course not. She had fainted.

"Be back, Mother," I said. I bent over and kissed her cheek.

I heard Mrs. Sorbitol calling me. "Hurry!" She was really yelling. "Hey, Mister! Hey, Mr. Simon!"

I ran down the stairs, ran down the hall to the kitchen.

The little woman crackling with stiffness was bounding pogo-stick fashion in the kitchen and pointing to the television. "Look!" she said. "Hurry—one more min, and they'll be on to something else."

There was a man on the screen. Thin, grey-toned, his hair looked freshly combed. He was bare to the waist, all they were showing of him. I had never seen this man before. He was being interviewed by someone off-camera.

"What was the purpose of the dance, Mr. Meinhard?"

"Not an exorcism," the bare-chested man said. "That was

positively canard. And not for publicity. Although it is true that I am presently an unemployed dancer. My reasons were symbolic. The Simons have dug up my ancestral land. What I was performing was an ancient dance to appease, to soothe the disturbed spirits of my ancestors, an expression of my regrets. I am an Indian on my mother's side. The Simon Hole disturbed me greatly."

"The Simon Hole," I whispered.

Mrs. Sorbitol was pulling at my arm. "Geez," she said, "and we are here. We are here at the Simon Hole. Right out there in that yard." Mrs. Sorbitol's crepe-soled feet squeaked generously. "This," she said, "is some day."

"Some full day," I corrected.

notes to alexander

Alex, I have a set of memories just like anyone else. Take for instance out in L.A. last spring. My friend Frederick was giving a party, a birthday party for his mother. Her seventieth. Fred was her last child. Unlikely for me to be invited. I mean what the hell was I doing at someone else's mother's birthday party? Do it for me, Fred said. I got to have someone to talk to there, Norman. I mean I cannot just be there with all those people by myself. So I said what the hell. I went. I didn't know anyone. Fred turned out to be all right. Actually, Fred was having a good time. His cheeks were flushed, he was downing toasts.

There I was trapped in someone else's family. I found myself a plate of food. No place to sit. I was wandering around the house. I went into the sunroom just as a kid went out. I snatched his seat. There were maybe eight, ten people there, all eating. Someone was talking, a woman maybe fifty, fifty-five. Anne, she says, is having a bad time. Her husband ran off with that woman from the hotel. How such an ugly man could find someone—never mind two someones.

The conversation shifted. There were operations, miseries, mergers. I knew the conversation, I listened, I nodded my head. The names I didn't know, but the tones, the accounts. I could have adopted those relatives, could have fit right in. So I dropped my plate on the windowsill behind a creeping Swedish ivy. I fled.

Alex, brother, you called me on the telephone. You screamed, you yelled—how the hell was I supposed to answer? Mother was sitting in the room. Could I say excuse me, I'll pick this up elsewhere? No, I stood there, Alexander, jackass. I stood there and permitted that calumny to be shouted. I admit that what happened at the hospital was unfortunate.

All right, I was wrong.

But I don't know exactly how you heard it, what you heard,

what motives you ascribed to me. Shirley may be your wife, but she is not an unbiased observer. That nurse—what's-her-name—didn't understand. Furthermore, she didn't want to hear an explanation. Nothing, not one word. And before I forget, fuck face—you too have been remiss—you sure as hell should have told me the entire matter. I thought he had a concussion, I thought pain pills were keeping Walter unconscious. In short, I misunderstood the circumstances. And you—you did not tell me. For that, you are responsible. For what I did, I am responsible.

Face facts, brother mine, only *I* know what happened. All right, Walter knows too.

I had your directions to the hospital. I was driving Walter's car. That hospital was big, a stone and brick castle spreading deep shadows and that was comforting. Because basically I'm thinking Hicksville. I did like you said, Alex—followed the procedures outlined.

To the woman at Reception I said, "Walter Simon."

"No visitors."

"There's a list," I said. "I'm on the list."

She looked at me. I would have preferred indifference.

"I'm the son, one of the sons. Norman Simon."

She looked at a paper a long time. Hell, I could see the list, there were only three names on that list. You, Shirley, and me.

"All right," she said. "Fourth floor, four-oh-one, but stop at the Nursing Station first."

"Yeah," I said. "Sure."

Now to alert you to what I was thinking, where my grasp of Walter's condition was, for the first time I wondered whether I should have come empty-handed. I was ashamed to have arrived without something for Dad—like flowers, candy, maybe a book.

First of all, when I got off the elevator I did not stop at the Nursing Station. After all, I was on the list. I trotted down the hall, checking the numbers first to the left then to the right.

Four-oh-one was a private room, a single. There was a little white card in a slot. *W. Simon* was printed on it. Another sign says NO SMOKING and beneath that NO VISITORS.

Walter is in the single bed, the sides up, a miniature crib.

In one of those absurd shifts of life, even though he is there, and I am standing, I am a little kid and he is Daddy. I am approaching the bed and risking wrath if I wake him up, because if he doesn't have to get up—if he doesn't have to go to school—then he wants to sleep late.

Christ, I think. I go up to the bed. He is lying on his back—they have shaved his head, but no bandages, no bandages anywhere. And he's not all that pale, I mean Mother is paler these days. There are tubes, tubes into his arms, and bottles dripping. Saline solutions, food solutions, unknown solutions.

"Dad," I whisper. "Dad? Walter?"

He didn't reply.

"Father." I have now reached a conversational tone.

Never once did I stop looking at him, so I see him move his arm (right arm) and bring that hand up to his face and then the arm goes back down.

"An itch, Dad? Should I scratch for you?"

I see the legs move, the corner of the mouth jerk, and maybe the eyelids raise.

"Dad," I try again. This time my voice has acquired a stronger pitch, not however—no matter what you have been told—a shout. I did not shout at him or in fact at anybody. Although it is perfectly true that I may have cursed once or twice at Shirley. Have I ever denied a temper?

Think about it, Alexander. I'm looking at this man on his back in bed, I see him stretch—definitely stretch—I see him yawn. I'm thinking he's been anesthetized or calmed or fully doped. I am hoping to bring him up.

I reached over and took his hand. It was warm, felt familiar, and I was certain that the fingers tightened over mine.

"Pop," I said, "it's good to see you. Everything is all right. Everything is all right in your house. And Mother," I said. No

one had told me not to mention *her* to *him.* "Mother is fine. She'll
be here to visit you soon."

Walter lies there. He was my father, and at no time did I feel
that he was not in command of the situation.

"I'm taking care of everything," I lied. Should I mention the
Hole? "If it rains," I tell him, "I'll turn on the pumps to drain the
water out of the Hole. So don't worry about it."

"What are you doing?"

It was a nurse. Probably the same one who caused the uproar.

"Visiting," I say.

"You were supposed to stop at the Nursing Station. Didn't
they tell you that downstairs?"

"No," I lie.

She does not believe me.

"Mr. Simon is not having visitors."

"I'm on the list," I say. "I'm a son."

She looks at me. I figure she knows the visitors.

"I'm the other son," I say. "How is my father?"

"Unchanged."

"What does that mean? Unchanged? What kind of description
is unchanged? Who else can I ask?"

"You can ask Dr. Heller—he may *still* be at the Nursing Station."

"Yes," I say. "Sure."

"And," she says, "try not to disturb the patient."

I dropped my father's hand.

Who ever told me on the telephone that I should have spoken
to Dr. Herschl? Who the hell is Dr. Herschl? I spoke to Dr. Heller.
When I ask him, Do you think my father will awaken? he stares
at me. Your father, he says, is in coma. Yeah, I say, that I can
see. But how long? The medical paragon shrugs. Mr. Simon, he
says, these events are hard to predict. The prognosis, he says, is
clouded. Now what the hell is that, Alex? Clouded. The nurse,
that sweetheart, says, Please lower your voice, Mr. Simon. So Mr.

Simon lowers his voice. Doctor, I say, while I was in the room, my father moved. My father rubbed his face, he yawned, he made distinct grimaces.

You bet, the doctor says. I understand, he says. You understand? You understand what? These are spontaneous movements, Mr. Simon, he says. Adventitious movements. I beg your pardon, I say. He doesn't look strange, my father does not look strange. He looks as if he's asleep. Yes, Mr. Simon, *coma* in Greek means sleep. I don't give a shit what it means in Greek, Doc— I want to know when will he wake up—and what the hell is he getting in those bottles? Mr. Simon, I believe that it is best if you discuss this further with Dr. Waddington, Heller says. I understand your agitation, he says.

The truth is, Alex, I do not want to be understood by that doctor. For the first time, I am really worried. I mean how hard did Walter fall?

I am trying to put myself in Walter's place. Not in coma. In his thoughts. Look, Walter was not peculiar. Our father was— is—a hearty lover of life. An intelligent man. I said to myself suppose I got involved in some half-brained scheme. Like for instance I decided to dig up an apartment building. And I got started on a lark maybe. I am digging a hole. And one day I am digging a bigger hole and so forth. Then suddenly there I am with a hole that in all honesty is too big. What do I do? There is publicity—none of it good. I am making a spectacle of myself with this hole. I have done this thing. What now?

Thus, Alex, it followed logically that I would try to get out of it. I would consider alternatives—one of them would be to get sick. Why not? You get sick, very sick, and the heat is off—then your family, if they have any sense, fills up the damn hole. After a short interval you get unsick—no semantics, please—unsick will do just fine.

So I left the doctor and went back to Walter's room.

"Dad," I say, "it's me again. It's Norman. I'm ordering some trucks, Dad. I am going to fill in the Hole. It's the right thing to do. Anyway, when you recover, you certainly can't dig anymore back there. But the fountain—the stone fountain I will leave in the backyard. Maybe for a bird bath." I hesitate for a meaningful pause.

"Think about what I'm saying, Dad. The problem is over, solved, gone."

He lies there, Alex. No adventitious movements. Not one damn one.

I go over to the bed, lift the covers a bit. He's got a jungle gym of tubes down there, he pisses into a damn bag.

"Dad," I say. "Wake-up time, Dad. Cut the act. There is nothing to worry about. The Hole is gonna vanish. Dad, wake up."

To tell you the truth, Alex, I would have thought that people knowing that I was there with my father would have knocked.

I reached down, touched Dad's side.

I pinched him.

He groaned.

"Are you crazy?" Shirley said. She was behind me. She was all dressed in yellow. I hardly recognized her. "Are you a sadist? Get away from that man!"

That man is my father.

But behind Shirley is Sweetheart Nurse. "Don't," she hissed, "touch the patient."

That's the gist of it, Alexander. There was a slight uproar. But I never took my eyes off Walter, never once. They summoned someone. A uniform. I do not recall saying that I planned to wheel Walter's bed down the corridor and into the elevator and out the door. But maybe I did.

I was ejected. I believe that I am off the list.

Walter never opened his eyes, Alex. Not once.

Four

I went out and brought Chaminade back from the kennel. She was happy to see me, her tail slapped against the upholstery of the back seat all the way home. Then I was sorry, which was stupid. What happened was not the dog's fault. How could I know what went through a dog's mind? Chaminade wouldn't go into the backyard. I didn't know that. She wouldn't go anywhere near that Hole. Then too, she would not go into Mother's room. She stood in the doorway and moaned and then ran away. Mother didn't actually seem to pay any attention.

Chaminade liked Mrs. Sorbitol, though.

"Good dog," she said and fed her crusts of toast.

"Mother," I said, still standing in the doorway even after Chaminade ran away, "I believe that I will have to go through the papers in the desk downstairs."

"Yes," she said. "Go right ahead."

"Unless," I began, "you would rather I didn't. I mean I don't want to—if you don't want me to."

"Why wouldn't I want you to do that?" she said.

"Mother," I said, "listen, would you like to go through those papers with me?"

"Not at all," she said. "I never liked the dollars and cents part of funding. Anyway, I'm busy."

Now that bothered me. "Busy?"

"I'm trying to remember what I knew about galleries."

"Galleries?"

"Yes—like on Madison Avenue—art galleries."

That sounded all right. She was always interested in art. "You want to go to a gallery?" We could do that. If she wanted to go, I'd take her.

"Not right now, Norman. Don't be foolish. I'm in no condition to go anywhere."

I stared at her, smiled. I thought that she did look worse than Walter.

"Time for the desk," I said out loud as I walked down the stairs. She could hear that.

The desk was walnut veneer. There were three drawers down each side and a center drawer. The same desk used to be in their bedroom in the apartment, crowded into a corner—it looked smaller there. When I was ten maybe eleven the desk was kept locked. Alex and I tried to jimmy it open with a nail file following closely observations made at the movies. A little more to the left, Alex had said. We had been in the middle of the act of crime when Mother caught us. Her hand came down hard across our corduroy pants. I'll teach you, she said. Alex yelled that it was my fault. She paid no attention. I think it was no movies for two weeks, maybe one.

The desk was no longer locked. The top was littered with papers. By nature and training we were not neat with our papers, none of us. Walter had two wire baskets that fitted together one on top of the other. These too were filled with papers, envelopes.

As part of my new organization routine, before picking up Chaminade I had stopped at a store that favored miscellany and purchased several brown paper accordion files, the kind labelled *Important Documents*. Also, manila folders and felt-tipped pens in three colors.

I touched every envelope on that desk, every piece of paper with a sense of violation. Who violated? *Me*. Yes, me. Involvement violated me.

There were bills, plenty of bills. If they didn't say second no-tice, I ignored them. Walter seemed to be fairly up-to-date. Bills from the motel chilled me. Laundry, sundries. Miscellaneous at one hundred and four dollars. What the hell was that for? Made a note to ask the Stopwood man. Made a note to make a prolonged visit to the motel.

The hardware bills were something. There was a lot more to making and maintaining a Hole than I ever imagined. All Walter's hardware purchases were made at the Shilton Do It Store. Average monthly bill at three hundred eighty-five dollars. Except March, June, and August—average bill, eight hundred fifty-five. We were good customers. I read out loud some of the purchases. "Chop saw, square wave transistorized inverter, torque cordless drill, orbital sander, speed reversing drill, and assorted hammers."

The folder labelled *Bills to Be Paid* grew larger. Also, I made another one labelled *Lazarre's Folly*. Into that one went the remnants of papers found everywhere—Xeroxes, photostats, clippings, four booklets. I thought I might read through them, but I was uncertain.

Mrs. Sorbitol was still in the kitchen. I came back early from the kennel. You can go, I told her. A full day, she said, is a full day. She sat in the kitchen watching public television with a few lapses, drinking coffee. Sometimes she laughed out loud at what she heard.

I went into the kitchen for some coffee. It was not during a lapse. A debate at the UN was going on.

"Get 'em," Mrs. Sorbitol was saying to the man on the screen. She shook her fist at the tiny head. "Get 'em."

Now why I asked the following question shows how the unconscious carries the message, no matter what.

"You lived around here long?" I said as I filled a brown ceramic mug with coffee. She made good coffee.

"Born, bred, and raised here," Mrs. Sorbitol answered.

"Who owns the Shilton Do It Store?" I asked.

"Used to be the Lancings. Hilga and J.D. He leaped off a bridge into the Pasonic two years ago, deliberate. She, the Widow Lancings, sold to Castleberry. He got a buy, let me tell you." Mrs. Sorbitol touched her head and nodded significantly. "Hilga wasn't a brain, if you get my meaning."

. . .

I went back into the living room and plugged in Walter's calculator. I reached into the accordion file for the pocket labelled *Shilton Do It* and pulled out a handful of bills. I added them up, maybe I hit the wrong buttons a few times for the cents—anger did that. Also dread. Totalled, the bills came to six thousand four-oh-eight and fourteen cents. And that was just for ten months.

I went outside. I suspected that Mrs. Sorbitol was watching from the window. Maybe I shouldn't have gone outside. I pretended to be whistling for the dog. I bent over, picked up a stone, cradled it in my hand before tossing it into the Hole. I waited for the sound that meant it had hit bottom. Then I put my hands in my pockets and walked around the rim of the Hole. It hadn't rained recently. The ground was dry, crumbly. The mud was still caked on the stone fountain. The fountain was in the exact spot where the hoist had dropped it. I could see a rubber hose coiled in the grass. I had seen it before. I knew that it was there. All right, I was going to wash down that piece of stone. I thought about pretending that wasn't what I intended. But that didn't seem likely. Still, I practiced idle movements for a bit—with my foot I traced the length of the hose from coil to hook-up. Hell, it was already connected. I swooped down on that hose, untwisted the green edge, turned the faucet on. Was it too cold? Would the water have frozen? No, the stream was swift, good pressure. I aimed at the stone shape. The mud slid away. The fountain was grey under the mud, just grey. It was an ordinary fountain, no architectural seventh wonder. Some curlicues around the edge, slight chipping. Small letters on the inner lip. I focussed water right at that spot, removing any dirt trapped in those blurred indentations. The letters were distinct, easy to read.

Lazarre, 1910.

"Son of a gun," I said. "The apartment building. He really found it."

I looked back at the house expecting Mrs. Sorbitol's entranced gaze. But she was not standing at the kitchen window, nose flattened. Mrs. Sorbitol was not in sight.

What I thought, although I was not certain, was that Mother was watching me. Was that Mother at the bedroom window?

I gathered a small bouquet. Yes, there were still things growing, not at the center of the property but at the periphery. I brought the flowers into the house. Mother always had vases, easily found. I should have been satisfied with the flowers, even shedding as they did a tiny snowfall of green bits. I checked it out, though. There was a sheaf of multigraphed papers, fading purple letters and lines. The papers were thumbtacked to the back of a cupboard door. It was a list of native flora, descriptions, pictures. Every plant I admired, every wild essence, turned out to be a weed. The strong yellows, lavenders, whites—all weeds. I kept them anyway, plunged them in water. Put the vase in the middle of the table. The flowers did not live long.

For supper that night we had hamburgers, canned corn. Mother hardly ate anything. I offered her many choices—I would have cooked anything. But no, she said. I'm not hungry, Norman, she repeated.

After I cleaned up the kitchen I went back to the desk and the papers. Words from our history came back—*consolidation, bankruptcy, intent.* With power of attorney, could I sell the motel? Should I make an appointment to see that Stopwood character at the motel or just walk in? Walk in, I decided. I set up an appointment with Mrs. Sorbitol, though.

I made a pile of motel bills. We'd discuss the motel bills. Stopwood and I. That's what we'd do. I went into the kitchen. *Motel,* I wrote on the blackboard. Under it, I listed possibilities. *A) Sell for land, B) Sell to factory, C) Close up—for tax loss.*

Would anyone buy the motel? I felt suddenly like my parents' protector. Like Walter's White Knight. I was normally not aggressive.

I left the papers and went and made myself a Scotch and soda.

. . .

The Stopwood man had a crewcut. Odd thing about that style of haircut—it looked ominous, tough, made one think of gangs. But there he was with a crewcut and he couldn't have weighed in at more than one-forty. He didn't have mean eyes either, not small, shifty eyes. He looked rather like a picture of a share-cropper in a book, eyes both shrewd and haunted. He wore a faded bleach-splattered flannel shirt, never mind the warmth of the day.

I turned down his offer of coffee. I had come in with my clutch of papers.

"You manage this place, don't you?"

"Yes," he said. "Mr. Simon asked me to stay on, until he took over."

"You have managing qualifications?"

Stopwood rubbed that crewcut. "M.B.A.," he said. "Branch of the State University."

"These bills," I said and waved my hand to rattle the papers but the sound was hardly strong enough, more of a flutter. "You send these bills?"

"Yes."

"I cannot understand these bills," I said, my voice growing louder, growing contemptuous. "Take laundry for instance. Our costs must rival the Waldorf's. Do you take the clean sheets off the beds and launder them for effect? No one stays here—who the hell uses the sheets?"

"Look, mister," Stopwood said. "I don't have to take this."

"It's not mister—it's Mr. Simon. I am paying you. Understand?"

"Like shit you are. I am employed by Walter Simon."

"As of yesterday—today it's me. I don't know what went on here before, Stopwood, but I am protecting my father's interests."

Stopwood stood up. He was about five-four standing, a tired-looking man, but young, I thought.

"I never cheated your father," he said. "Your father was decent. I used to talk to him about my plans. I was going west as soon as he learned this business."

I was choking. "Learned this business? What business! No one registers here. No one uses this place. Who the hell uses this place?"

"Who uses this place!" Stopwood was now shouting back. "This is one profitable business, mister. And I never cheated your father. Not one dime's worth. Your daddy got my receipts less my share—have you checked? Have you checked my receipts? Every last dollar was deposited to the Stopwood Motel savings account at the bank."

Had I checked the Stopwood Motel savings account? I didn't even know there was one. Mr. Orckin at the bank was not helpful.

I left the motel, the shabby, thrift-store-rejected motel, and drove to the bank.

The Stopwood Motel savings account. Bucks, real bucks, big bucks. Cash deposits. Why not credit cards—why not American Express, why not MasterCard, why not Visa?

Why?

It's a brothel. Set up by young Stopwood in gratitude to my daddy.

The place is a fucking brothel.

Empty by night—full night that is.

Deserted—cars park around back.

We have our own chicken ranch.

I had a headache that went around my head in an endless spiral motion, pressing tighter as it zeroed in like a spring-action toy—snap, zing, whack. I did a time calculation—eight o'clock in New York, five o'clock in L.A.

I dialled the number.

"Eileen, it's me."

"Wait a minute, let me turn down the hi-fi."

I was good with sounds. I heard the click. She had not turned down the hi-fi, she had closed a door. Someone was out there with the hi-fi.

"Eileen, I am getting progressively less and less happy," I said.

"What is it?" she whispered. "Is he worse?"

"No," I said. "He isn't."

"Then it's just depression—East Coast depression."

"Guess what?"

"What?"

"The motel—the motel my father bought. I thought it was a horror, an empty twenty-four-unit by the side of the road—the back road."

"Yes?"

"It's a brothel."

"You're kidding."

"No—my dad owns a brothel."

I could hear her breath draw inward. I clarified.

"Actually, he doesn't know about it," I said. "But he runs one anyway—it is owned by him, operates in his name."

Eileen was hesitating. "That I imagine," she said, "is profitable. Isn't it?"

"Yes," I said. "They are raking it in."

How did I meet Eileen?—my bouncing, irresistible Eileen. I met her in the New York University library. I followed her across Washington Square Park in the earliest darkness of evening. It was August, a season of short dresses that year. I had spotted her before, was grateful she wasn't one of my students. I rarely dated one of my own students.

But I specialized in night school students—they fit into my schedule. Thus, I followed Eileen into the library, followed the gentle curve of her body.

This girl, I decided, was worthy of a little time. Together we went straight through English Literature to Poetic Thought.

We took our selections—substantial books—and went to sit down, she on one side of a table, I on the other. Was I obvious? I was trying.

"A soul," I said—I had a good library voice, a hollowed bass— "that knowes not to presume is Heaven's and its own perfume."

"Andrew Marvell," she said.

For the first time, I thought that this might not be easy.

"Yes," I said.

I decided that I was partial to everything about her. "My name is Norman."

"Eileen."

"Coffee?"

"Bourbon."

"My pleasure."

We did not however go to either her place or mine, we went to a bar. "Being picked up is an art," Eileen said as we walked together down the street. She was quite short. "Some girls think that if the place is all right then the guy is all right—that's ridiculous. I have my own criteria—sincerity, unbitten nails, no careful dressers."

"I fit the picture," I said. I was visualizing Eileen as an overnight guest.

While we had our drinks, Eileen went through the preliminaries. She was an English major, she said. An evening student. By day she worked in a boutique that specialized in Italian shoes. "I can get them dirt cheap for myself," she said, "and at first I did, of course. But they hurt—God, do they pinch. It's in the last—lousy last."

"Right," I said. I ordered myself to pay attention, speed was not everything.

"I've switched advisors," Eileen said. "I believe that my spirit was too strong for the last man. I'm doing a senior thesis on literal sexual allusions."

"Beg pardon?"

"Sexual allusions—in literature, and of course how they enter the language."

"Really?"

"Yes, for instance, I have indexed at least five hundred and seventy-three references to piece of tail. You wouldn't believe how long that's been around."

"No," I said and pulled my chair closer to the tiny table.

"If we become friends," Eileen said, "I would appreciate it if you would keep your eye out for choice phrases—for instance real terms, medical terms have not been in literature all that long. Take cunnilingus for example."

"Yes."

Eileen sighed. "I'll be at it forever, though. I have to discipline myself to set limits."

We went back to my place. I have learned through experience the importance of leaving your rooms neat enough for the unexpected rewards of life. I offered to remove Eileen's clothes, but she shook her head and took them off herself. She was very slow about it.

First we tried out some ordinary words, and then we moved on from there.

"I want you to know," Eileen said, "that I am never physically jealous."

"What?"

"I don't believe in possessiveness towards the body. Do you know why I am telling you this right now—right up front?"

"No," I said, "I guess I don't. No, I definitely do not."

"I believe that we will see each other again—so I want you to know that seeing me is freedom."

"Gotcha," I said.

Three weeks later I learned Eileen's age. When you were four, she said, I was sixteen.

notes to alexander

Yesterday when you called, Alexander, I was abrupt. I was grilling two steaks. Red meat, I thought. I'll give her red meat. Mother wouldn't eat. She said that hunger has left her. She said that the meat had a sour smell. Think of her frame, Alex. She's a big woman. I see her becoming cadaverous. Think of those photographs of Isak Dinesen.

Also we had a chocolate cake. An extraordinary cake—really home-baked. Mrs. Sorbitol brought it with her. Made with one hundred percent real bittersweet chocolate, Swiss. I bake, she told me. I believe that it is a dying art. So I bake—but for whom? My husband can't touch the stuff. Eat, she said. Give your mother some. Mother however refused. Give what's-her-name my apologies, she said.

The thing is, brother, your call disturbed me. Set me on edge, killed the appetite. Alex, what are you getting at? Mother was downstairs so I could say little. Why do you ask the same retelling? I mean do you realize that you do it? Relate what happened, you say. You were running, you say, and then you slipped. The wet ground was slippery. The mud smooth, the mud glass, a Hans Brinker setting. You fell, you say. Norman, did you fall? What the hell kind of a question is that? I fell.

Walter fell.

She fainted.

As you fell, you say, what did you see?

You mean like did my life flash before me? Alex, I saw mud. More correctly I saw a kind of brown darkness.

Did they have a fight?

I heard no fight. I heard her yell to him. Stop, she yelled.

That's all, Alex. Honest. Nothing else. She was maybe twenty feet away from him. It was slippery, dark. All right not dark—bright. But around the lit area, it was dark. In some places the mud was soft, a rennet custard of mud. There was a slapping sound from my feet in and out of the mud. I couldn't find my shoes—I hurried—the shoes were somewhere in the room. Why hurried? Had I heard something terrible?

Never.

I was startled, awakened that way. Pulled upward through dreams, REM sleep disrupted. Hell, I was surprised.

I thought something was wrong.

Why wrong?

It was night, I was asleep, I had a bit to drink, I had too much to drink.

Is Mother amnesiac?

There are no signs of her being amnesiac. Listen to me—I sound like all the others. Signs of amnesia. Christ! She just doesn't want to think about it.

I understand.

Something you don't want to think about.

As I wander through these rooms, Alexander, that are full of furniture, the detritus of that apartment we knew, the pictures, the books, I become certain that I grew up here. I believe that it was here that everything happened. Now I know that is not so. But still the memories persist. All my memories, Alex, are attached to objects. I mean I thought I was beyond that. But hell, it is not so.

By the way Alex, how well did you know Dad's father? Now it is none of my business, but is there any reason why you and Shirley have not had a child? Forgive me, brother. I mean do you know anything I have not been told? Genetic problems? That old man (Grandfather) was strange. I remember the summer he first arrived and gave me some firecrackers as a present. First, Mother was going to throw them down the incinerator. Are you nuts? Father said. Then she held them under the faucet. Alex, I think he (Grandfather) showed up one night—drunk or something. I set fire to the hardware store, he said, I think. With a piece of celluloid. Personally though, I am uncertain about this last—I don't remember the man too well. Did this happen? Think about it, Alex, and let me know.

About eleven o'clock three cars arrived drag racing to a stop in front of the house, the noise began almost at once. I ran up the stairs and turned on the television in the back room and left the door open. I wanted to block those outside noises, but I don't know if I did. I don't know if Mother heard.

I waited. If the action was going to be brief, I'd wait it out. First, there were the yells, the catcalls, the insults. They were not very inventive. I watched from the darkened front windows. Maybe five men in each car—early twenties. You know what I was looking for—I was looking for crewcuts. But from that distance, they all looked like dark shapes. I waited ten minutes, I waited fifteen minutes. They were settling in, they were tossing beer bottles. But the fact of the matter is that I did not call Conlon. It was someone else who called. Actually, I don't blame whoever called. Those voices carried.

Conlon came with a red light flashing on top of his car. Very impressive. Two of the parked cars started their motors fast enough and got away. One, he stopped. Kids in that car. In the circles of the headlights they looked like kids. He must have known them. They were afraid to run away. Then Conlon rang the doorbell.

Would you mind turning on that light on the lawn? he asked.

I turned on the light.

The kids walked on the grass. They were picking up beer bottles, they were picking up garbage.

I gave Conlon a black plastic bag. He gave it to the kids, and after it was filled, one of the boys put it into the trunk of his car.

There is about Conlon a persistence, a fierceness, a tenacity.

Jack R. V. Haight counsels patience. Wait him out, he says. This man, says Jack, is a country cop with limited duties—in short, he's not busy enough. Give him time. He'll go on to something else.

Alex, I have considered approaching our local constable. Conlon, I'll say, my father fell into a Hole. Now what the hell else is there?

What else can he say, Alex? Be reasonable.

I *mean* what else is there?

But Jack advises me—say nothing.

Why?

Money, Jack says. There seems to be a considerable amount of money to be inherited.

Telephones. I wrote this on the kitchen blackboard. I want to tell you, brother, that I am considering an unlisted number. No, we have not received more than a few nuisance calls. But people can get through. Take for instance the call from Dad's friend Jay. Who the hell is Jay? I mean I believe he is for real, because he knows a lot about me, about Mother, about Dad. Not information from newspapers—other information.

What does he want?

He spoke about investments. He spoke about how he and Dad were planning—had planned—had executed joint ventures. All right, that I can handle. Then there's Hole curiosity. Tell me the truth, he begged. Norman, he said, I love your father like a brother. Ever since our joint days at the Bronx High School of Science. Like a brother. What is the true story of the Hole? What has Walter found?

He's talking mineral rights, Alex. The bastard is talking mineral rights. Geological layers, assays, corporate buyouts.

Then I got a call from L.A. From the Chairman of my department, Alex. A man, who I would have assured you, did not comprehend my existence. I am an Adjunct in his department— I am a cheapie, an employee without benefits. He must have sent the secretary for my file. I can see his hands with manicured nails picking up the dirt from my file. That's how he got my telephone number. Where you have to write next of kin in case of a sociological disaster—I wrote the names of my parents and their telephone number.

He called me all the way from the Coast. Norman, he said, you are in the news. I am not in the news, I tell him. Your family, he amended. Exactness is important. What I think, Norman, he says, is that we may be on to something here. Beg pardon? I say. The Hole, Norm. The Simon Hole. The L.A. *Times* only described the Hole. But I see it as more, Norm. I see it as a subject for a dissertation, a book, a study. It reminds me of a similar project I began in collaboration in '67—a freak quarry accident—but we were too late. Others got there first—mined it for all it was worth. But this, Norm—this is a Hole that we could have exclusively. We could limit access to the data. It would be our collaborative study of sociological significance—meaning, societal response.

The new telephone number, Alex, will be one about which I believe we should be most circumspect. Give it out to no one.

Alex, did I tell you about the inscription? On the fountain. Lazarre was here, brother. Here, just like Dad predicted.

Yesterday afternoon, brother, for two minutes—I swear for only two minutes—I slipped on a pair of Dad's rubber boots—they fit. I climbed down into the Hole. That is some drop, let me tell you. All right, I took a shovel. The soil was dry, light, powdery. I dug at the site of the fountain—where he had found the fountain. Two minutes, Alex, I swear. Bricks. I found ten bricks and a piece of tile. A piece of cracked tile about two feet by a foot and a half. A grey-blue glaze. The bricks I tossed up in the air to the surface, the tile I carried under my arm. It was hard getting out of the Hole, especially with the tile.

The reason I am mentioning this, Alex, is that as I was reaching the surface two things happened. One, Conlon was walking towards me from around the side of the house. The second is that Mother was definitely watching me from the upstairs window.

Five

Jack R. V. Haight came out to the house from the city. Just meet the train, he said. He didn't enjoy highway driving. The trouble was that Jack had dressed for a day in the country. Tweed jacket, leather buttons, dark grey slacks. He looked so damned formal, so out of place.

"Get him!" Mrs. Sorbitol whispered. "La-de-da."

"This is a private meeting," I whispered back.

"Excuse me," she said, and went into the kitchen where she turned on public television too loud.

Jack didn't seem disturbed. We went out around the side of the house, but he was careful not to step off the stone path. He was wearing brown loafers with tassels, good ones.

We both stared down at the Hole.

"I've seen it before," Jack said. "Once."

"When?"

"Walter had me out—two months ago, I think it was. Astonishing. Astonishing, you know, that Walter made that Hole. The number of ordinances broken—amazing."

We went back inside, and I fixed Jack a drink. I fixed both of us drinks. Jack was catching the six-fifty back.

"The way it stands," he said, "based only on what you have sent me, is that the degree of solvency is greater than we originally thought."

"I want to sell the motel," I said.

Jack pursed his lips. "Don't be hasty."

"Stopwood's family will buy it back."

"We'll take that under advisement," Jack said. "Now as for the Historical Society—how much do we know about the exact extent of Walter's involvement?"

"I mentioned the Society to Mother," I said. "I mean just once I mentioned it. She got very disturbed. She got agitated. Don't speak of that, she begged. So I've been afraid to ask her more— Waddington said not to upset her."

"Right," Jack said. "That is unfortunate, though. I calculated that they got twenty-five thousand dollars from Walter. But there could be more."

"Yes," I said. "All of that. And today Castleberry sent a message by way of Mrs. Sorbitol, Mother's companion. He wants to meet me. He wants to come here."

"What about?"

"He wouldn't say."

"Norman, don't sign anything."

"Sign anything! I want to go after him with a whip. I hold him responsible for this, you know. He put Walter onto Lazarre's Folly."

"We'll get to all that," Jack said. "Never you fear, Norman. I'll have the Historical Society's accounts examined."

"You think I should see Castleberry?"

"Why not? Maybe he thinks he can get more money from you. He can't—can he, Norman?"

"You bet he can't."

I wondered if Castleberry had a crewcut.

I left a message with his wife Faith. Tomorrow, I told her.

Castleberry was supposed to arrive at the house at noon. Mrs. Sorbitol offered to make lunch. "I don't do housework," she said. "But listen, I wouldn't be against making a touch of lunch for us. Beef stroganoff with noodles, maybe, and a watercress salad."

"Lunch? This is a business meeting. That man does not eat in this house."

"Suit yourself," she said. "But this is a man with connections. I'll have the fixings, if you change your mind."

At noon he was scheduled to appear, but at eleven Castleberry came. I was outside, I was picking up branches, twigs, making a pyre. I was wearing jeans, Dad's boots.

I turned around and there he was.

I understood the whole scene. He was at an advantage. In truth, he looked like me. Jeans, work shoes, old shirt. A country working man. Not a social call.

"Mr. Simon," Castleberry said. His voice was hearty. He came towards me extending his hand. "I didn't even try the house," he said. "Saw you out here when I was driving by. Stop now, I told myself, kill two birds. No need to drive back this way then at noon. You're our Walter's boy, aren't you? All the way from Cal-i-for-ni-a."

"Yes," I said. I felt obligated to shake his hand.

"My heart," Castleberry said, "oh yes, my heart has been breaking for your mother and father. You don't know how I feel about Walter."

"I imagine I do," I said. Walter as the well of plenty, I was thinking.

"No," Castleberry said and shook his head, "you can't. Love. Respect. Admiration. Your father and I were partners."

"Partners? Partners in what?"

Castleberry smiled at me. "Partners," he said, "in admiration for this country, for the very ground on which we stand, for the environs of Shilton. We both felt the same way about preserving memories."

"How could my father have any memories of this place?" I said. "My father didn't live here long enough to have any memories of this place."

"History," Castleberry said, "is a universal burden. Your father—our Walter—became in a short time—a beloved member of the Shilton Historical Society. And with your permission, our next collection and exhibit will be called *The Walter Simon Collection.*"

"Touching," I said. "Was that it, Mr. Castleberry? Was that what you wanted? To tell me about *The Walter Simon Collection.*"

"No," Castleberry said. He reached into his pocket. "Now that our Walter is ill—and we are all praying for him—and awaiting his return—but still fair is fair and I called a meeting of myself as Secretary-Treasurer with the President of the Shilton Historical Society."

"Who is the President?"

"Mrs. Stopwood," Castleberry said. "She and I agreed that under the cloud of illness, the Society must come second. We polled the membership and have unanimously decided to return Walter Simon's last generous donation to the Society."

"Beg pardon?"

"Here's a check."

I reached for the piece of pale green paper, taken neatly folded from Castleberry's pocket.

What was written on it? I read out loud. "Twelve thousand dollars."

"Walter," Castleberry said, "perhaps needs this now in the time of illness."

Do you thank someone for returning your very own money?

"Thank you," I said.

Castleberry bobbed his head modestly. "Also," he said, "I have taken the liberty of leaving at your front door a cauldron of soup."

"Soup?"

"Yes, I set it down before I came on back here. I am very proud of my soup and do regret not leaving some sustenance sooner."

Castleberry nodded, half-bowed, and went away.

I was left out there in the yard next to the Hole holding a check for twelve thousand dollars. "Damn!" I said and went back to the house.

"Mrs. Sorbitol," I called out, because I could definitely smell food cooking, "he's come and gone."

She stuck her head out of the kitchen, her cheeks flushed. "Then I'll take it home," she said. "My husband will probably eat it."

I went straight to the telephone and called Jack.

"I met with Castleberry," I said.

"How did it go?"

"He gave me a check."

"What?"

"Yeah," I said. "I'm surprised—no astounded. He returned Dad's last donation as he called it. A check for twelve thousand dollars."

"Really? Norman, you have the check there?"

"Of course."

"Look at it."

"Yes?"

"On what account drawn?"

I read what was printed on top of the check. "Prentice Castleberry, Faith Castleberry."

"Personal check? Say Historical Society anywhere? Say signed for Historical Society anywhere?"

"No," I said.

"Make some copies of that check, Norman—both sides."

Suspicions led to more suspicions. That's the way affairs function. I started a Castleberry file. But besides the ten copies of the check, I hadn't anything else to put into the file. There wasn't any Castleberry correspondence. No Castleberry notes. Historical Society letters were signed by Mrs. Stopwood. No, there was little Castleberry paperwork.

Except then I found a copy of a grant application in a black three-hole binder. That evoked a whistle, a catcall whistle. I didn't find that grant in the desk. I found it in Dad's room on the closet shelf. What was I doing looking on the closet shelf? I was searching for boots in that closet, more boots.

I kept staring at that binder. A grant application had been sent to the DeLeuce Foundation by Castleberry and Dad. On the cover of the binder was an official label, *The Restoration of Shilton Court—A Classic Dream*. Submitted to the DeLeuce Foundation. There was also a letter of turndown inside the binder. The letter had been written by Program Officer Dennys for the DeLeuce Foundation. Did Mother know? Maybe not. That would explain why the stuff was on the closet shelf instead of in the desk.

I pulled a chair from the corner of the room to the closet doorway and stood on it to get a better look at the shelf. That's when I found another letter. Also from the DeLeuce Foundation.

I read it, the envelope was already opened—then too I had power of attorney.

> *Dear Walter,*
>
> *Re your grant. I can overrule, Walt. If I choose to do that— I can give you the grant. You like it in the country? You want to dig for something? I can help you, Walt.*
>
> *I, Eric DeLeuce, have the authority to make it possible. Hell, I can give you a five-year grant. Hear that—a five-year grant guaranteed. What do I want in return? Not a grant report, Walt. Not that. I want Sara, Walt. I want to be honorable. I am willing to marry her. Fair exchange. Reply to above address in Florence by 15th or if by 20th send to Geneva address.*
>
> *Best regards,*
> *Eric DeLeuce*

I put the binder back on the shelf. I tried to replace it at the exact same angle—a slight slant to the right. I spent some time repositioning the letters.

I felt lousy. I clumped my way down the stairs—never mind if Mother heard. That wasn't important. What was important? Did she know? How could Dad have permitted Castleberry to talk him into applying to the DeLeuce Foundation! Was he trying to get her? Wrong—wrong—I'm wrong. Not Dad—he wasn't going to hand Mother over to Eric DeLeuce. Who would do that?

I remembered Eric DeLeuce. I remembered him from when Alex and I were little kids. Sometimes, something would happen—no one to stay with us, no school, troubles. Mother would bring us into the Foundation then. Be quiet, we were ordered. Behave. This, kids, she would say, is part of our bread and butter. We understood. Alex and I would stay close together as we were escorted down the hall. It wasn't bad, it was fun.

We were taken to the supply room. They kept a little table there for sorting papers. Sit, mother ordered. The smells were rich—paper, glue, erasers. Maddy the secretary would come in after a while. She was kind, she brought containers of chocolate milk, packaged sweets. She also gave us construction paper, colored pencils, file folders. We stared, we were little kids—we were scraped, scratched. What should we do? I asked. Make grants, she said. Put together grants. Words and pictures. We understood—there was a lot of talk about this at home. We assembled our presentations.

Promote your interests, Maddy advised. More funding for libraries was Alex's theme. I did baseball cards—money for printing more cards. Eric DeLeuce came in once in a while. Quiet, he said. Good.

He was old. All right, we were children. To children, everyone is old. But even then he was a grandfather's age—any grandfather—he had white hair, had canes, smelled of endless years. The man was ancient.

Not for one second was I going to call L.A. and tell Eileen.

Tell Eileen what?

That a rich man wanted to marry Mother.

Change that—a rich *old* man wanted to marry Mother.

Waddington was not happy. "I have to tell you, Norman," he said. "I am disturbed."

He spoke as if he had always known me—had in fact delivered me into the world—not possible. Waddington was a young man.

"What about?" I said.

We were in the upstairs hall. He had just left Mother. "Disturbed," he repeated.

I tried to maneuver him down the stairs. The man had a low center of gravity.

"Come," I said finally. "Downstairs."

"What?"

"Walls." I pointed. "Like paper." Who knew what he would say?

"Certainly," he said.

We went downstairs together, our footsteps echoing—we sounded like the changing of the guard.

"How much does she eat?" Waddington said when we had reached the downstairs hall.

"Enough," I said. At that moment without preliminaries, I vowed not to confide.

"Norman, your mother is steadily growing thinner. I predict anorexia ahead. That's what I predict."

"Vitamins," I said. "I'll get vitamins. How about chocolate malteds?"

"Norman, we must face facts. She is becoming depressed. In fact, she is already depressed."

"Maybe," I conceded. I rubbed my head. "Maybe I should take her to the hospital."

"Yes," Waddington said and moved two steps closer until our shoulders touched. "Perhaps admission is the ticket."

"What? I meant take her to the hospital to see Walter. To see my father."

"Absolutely not." Waddington went pale, we broke contact.

"You think not?"

"Absolutely. Her system, Norman, cannot bear any more shocks. I'll prescribe a food supplement, high caloric. We'll try that."

"Certainly," I said, trying to be cooperative.

"Stimulation," Waddington said. "Also, add stimulation."

"I'll consider it," I said.

Stimulation. Now that was probably a good idea. I thought about various forms of stimulation all day. Maybe I should push the upstairs television set down the hall into Mother's room? It was big and with color. What did she like to do? How much did I actually know about her? I would have to be selective. It probably wasn't wise to throw television, books, and newspapers at her. Anyway, which books? Did she want to read Jane Austen?

There were hobbies, of course. Painting was a hobby. She had even planned to paint here in this house. I had seen her art materials in the attic. She had a whole setup there.

Chaminade accompanied me up to the third floor. "An easel, dog," I said. "Lookeehere—an easel with folding legs. Now that's the ticket." I folded up the easel. Mother kept the room neat. Perhaps she hadn't started to paint yet. The room did not look used. I put together some paper, a set of watercolors. I carried it all downstairs. Managing the easel was difficult, the ends were sharp. "Get away, dog," I ordered. But Chaminade went as far as Mother's door.

"Mother," I called out. "It's me, again."

"Yes."

"Can I come in?"

"Yes."

I opened the door and stood there trying to pull the easel into the room without dropping either paints or paper.

She raised her head from the pillows. "What the hell are you doing, Norman?"

"I thought," I said, "that you should have something to do up here. Can't lie in bed all day, Mother."

"What?"

"I know that you like to paint, Mother. And it won't tire you— you can even do it sitting down. I brought you the implements— a few."

"Get that stuff out of here, Norman," she said. "Get it out of here."

I stood there. She was sitting up in bed, her voice growing rapidly louder. The paper dropped. Suddenly there was a puddle of paper on the floor.

"How dare you!" she said.

I didn't understand that. The dog started barking in the hall. Mother was shaking her fist at me. I pulled the easel out of the room, scratching the doorframe. I would go back for the paper later.

notes to alexander

I am no health freak, Alex. Nor do I believe that I will live to be one hundred if I take advice. Read the newspapers—half the advice-givers fall down dead in their prime bodies, loaded with vitamins, drowning in kelp and seaweed. This is not to imply that I do not take care, especially now. Brother, I've started to take walks. Plain walks—not jogging. After all, since I arrived here my regimen of health activities has just gone to the dogs so to speak. I've been heavy on processed food, heavy on alcohol, low on rest and relaxation. So I've begun to take these walks, strolls, saunters. I walk on Simon property.

When do I do this? At twilight when the light is cold. The damp air seems to aim right for me after a day spent in hot, dry rooms. I put on a sweater—I borrow one of Dad's. You can't avoid the Hole if you walk. How can you avoid the Hole? Sometimes I walk around the Hole, circling the entire rim from north to south. In the distance I see that some people have started their furnaces. The further away the smoke, the stronger its shape. Often the smoke assumes a corporeal form as if passing through an unseen funnel. Frosts are rolling in, the tools turning silver—silver-edged anyway. I even do a little K.P. duty. I pick up stray twigs, branches, put them in a pile. I haven't actually moved anything, disturbed anything. The tow truck is still in place. But by and large I believe that I have improved the general appearance.

The bricks I've piled up in a wall formation. What do you know about bricks, Alex? Bricks take on the coloration of the soil used to make them—i.e., clay available. That's significant, Alexander. These bricks found in the Hole were not made locally. Even if you take into account aging—still, these were buried—no fading from light. Examine the bricks, Alex—next time you're out here—the pink tones are representative of the amount of calcium and iron in the soil. Do we have that around here? We do not. Out here the local bricks are more orangey, definitely more orangey in tone. Therefore, these bricks are imported.

Even considering the prices in the first decade of the twentieth century—those bricks must have cost. We are talking money. To date, there are fifty-three bricks. The ten I found the first time, and the others I found later. There may be more down there.

You think digging is picking up a shovel? There's a lot more to digging, Alex. Knowledge is needed. Take Schliemann. I mean a lot of people think Schliemann and then think Troy. But Schliemann, Alex, dug up a hell of a lot more than Troy. I mean Schliemann also dug up Mycenae and Orchomenus. I can see him and his Sophie digging away, heaving up the earth. There were scoffers, brother. Surely there were laughers. But Schliemann kept at it—walls, fortifications, limestone blocks—the whole works. He could have just stopped at finding civilization. What more did he need to find than civilization? But also there was gold. A real cache of gold. Sophie, he must have said. Look, Soph!

I have been thinking about that and also about Knossos of Crete, the poetry of time, and the labyrinths of society.

What surprises me, Alex, on these walks, these saunters around Simon Land is the lack of silence. City people do not know. I mean whenever I thought of the country—not often I grant you—I thought of silence. I said blue skies and green grass and no noise.

I was wrong. There is noise. There are cracklings from bushes, animal mutterings, a wind tunnel effect created by the Hole itself. Not a frightening sound—this isn't an account of a haunting.

The wind does not howl down and around that Hole. No, rather it is a whoosh sound. Whoosh! Whoosh! Therefore on these walks I am assaulted by stimulus. For reverie I go indoors.

Yesterday, brother, I was sitting in the living room with my drink. I unrolled Lazarre's plans for the site. There was nothing on television, no talk shows on the radio—I was alone. I read the plans. A lot of weird-shaped rooms. It would have taken some getting used to, I guess. But imaginative, Alex, and even today, I don't think these plans have their equal. All right, environment versus life-style is not unknown—but this man was unique. Not equalitarian, though. The aristocratic approach is necessary at the beginning, he wrote. A question of costs and the willingness to experiment. But just at the start, he wrote, at least according to his pamphlet *Life and Society*. Later it will be for all—this in *Digressions*.

By the way, the bricks that I've found so far—no signs of fire damage. It wasn't one day a building and the next day none. Don't think that I am comparing these bricks found at the Hole to Crete or anything. But still, in essence, I could see Schliemann walking around his find—if, for instance, it had been here with these bricks. The urge to recreate, to embellish, to make again a civilization, is not my cup, of course. Mine is modern society— alive and unwell. I wonder, though, you had this building—Lazarre's building—and then poof off the earth like that. A societal response to what it didn't want.

I have always been particularly interested in the family unit, Alex. In family stresses, the ticking of the family, its mores, the private language. The comings and goings of the larger view— the Mysteries—that's the part I don't bother about.

All my assembled data are about families, both close and distant. Listen, I even interviewed Eileen. Eileen had a previous husband. I was married a short time, she told me. It felt like one and one-half days. But really it was eighteen months. That other husband was a bone doctor—the real thing, not chiropractic. He had some kind of government service to do, like doing time. They sent us to South Dakota, she said. We had a second-floor apartment out there. That husband was a man from the city. Break-ins, he said, are a definite possibility. So he grated the windows to keep out burglars. People drove by the building just to see the metal grilles at all the windows. The entire apartment—it was a floor-through. Our neighbors thought he must be a doctor who treated crazy people. I begged that husband to take the bars down. It was the idea of them that I hated.

"Did you leave the bars on the windows when you moved?"

"Yes," she said. "They're probably still there."

. . .

I received a postcard yesterday—actually Mother did—from someone named Malka R. *An apartment building down there,* she wrote. *Who are you kidding, Sara baby. I cannot wait until I return for the true scoop, the real poop, the actual findings.* The postcard was mailed from Lyons.

I have tried to give Mother her mail three times. That is, I brought letters and postcards upstairs on a tray with her breakfast coffee.

Thanks, she says, but no thanks.

Alex, for breakfast she drinks coffee. For lunch she drinks coffee. For supper again coffee. Sometimes a taste of meat or vegetables.

I want to report a conversation, Alexander.

Yesterday at about nine p.m. I had just returned to the house from my walk, and I was hanging up the sweater on the hook behind the kitchen door when she appeared. I was startled. To tell the truth, I haven't seen her leave her room by herself. Mother just did not walk down the stairs alone.

God, I said. What's wrong?

Norman, she said, what the hell are you doing out there?

Out where?

Cut the crap, she said. In the yard near the Hole, near the abomination, near the end of the world.

I've just been walking, I said.

I'm warning you, she said.

Wednesday, I went to town to buy the newspaper and some rope. It was just ten o'clock in the morning, and I went into Paul & Marie's Diner for a cup of coffee. I was sitting in a booth—it's an old-fashioned diner, Alex—dark, heavily varnished wood—the food mediocre but the coffee excellent. I was sitting there stirring my cup of coffee. The diner is directly across from Orckin's bank. I saw them come out together. I saw Castleberry and Stopwood—the Stopwood who is my employee, the motel Stopwood. For a long time they stood on the sidewalk and spoke to each other. I am certain that this was not a conversation about casual matters. Why? Their stance, the slight curving inward of the bodies—it was a conversation of secrets. I'll tell you what I thought of doing. I thought of running outside and yelling at Stopwood. Hey, I would say, what are you doing wandering around town on my time?

When the two men finally parted, their hands brushed together in some conspiratorial fashion. Remember, Alex, there is some link between Castleberry and this Stopwood.

I almost forgot. Along with that postcard from Malka, a letter arrived by Federal Express to me here at Bayley Farm House. My no-holds-barred Chairman in L.A. has offered me a permanent position on the faculty—permanent tenure-track position.

Kindly reply by return mail, he says.

What did I do?

I accepted it.

Send contract, I replied.

notes to alexander

Alex, you inquired about the uproar. It wasn't actually an uproar. It was just that several things occurred simultaneously. If these incidents had occurred singly, they would have gone practically unnoticed.

What's true? It is true that I told Waddington to haul his ass away before I inverted his body.

How did he get our new telephone number, Alex?

Waddington showed up at Bayley Farm House with someone else—the doctor of his choice. Your mother, he salivated, needs a rest. Come on now, Alex, I've heard better lines in second features on Saturday afternoons when I was nine. Rest—what the hell does he think she's doing upstairs? Am I taking in washing for her?

An examination, he says. Mental status. Sara is going to get another examination.

However, Alex, I did not push him.

It was during this conversation that the doorbell rang—the second movement where the water gurgles forth.

I shouted for Mrs. Sorbitol.

She shouted back. I don't do housework! I don't do doors!

I opened the door.

Standing at our door was one Mary Ellen, age thirty plus. In, heaven help us, a pinafore with ribbons. In her right hand she had a candle. Not a *yahrzeit* light. A genuine Jack-Be-Nimble candle.

Behind her on the path—at least not on the porch—was a cluster of six or seven others. Adults wearing a style of clothing called Plain Folks.

Yes? I said to the spectre at the door.

When I light this candle, she replied, Our Heavenly Father will send forth a spring from the Heavenly Hole. And the curative waters shall flow. I am his messenger.

What did I do? What could I do?

I broke the candle, Alex.

Chaminade barked but did not bite. True, she growled, but at Waddington not at the people assembled.

Directly in front of the house at least five cars were parked.

The people on the path started wailing. The pinafore tore her hair.

Conlon arrived.

He must have us under surveillance, Alex, else how could he have shown up so quickly.

SIX

I have developed a craving for Walter. Something that I cannot understand. At night I wait expectantly for Walter to return. From where? Dad, I call out. There is, of course, no one. There is only the melancholy cackle of the radiator. I keep the house very warm at night to bring on languor. The heat makes me drowsy, I yield easily to sleep, my eyelids closing. Yet I crave Walter. I wear his sweater, his boots. I have borrowed his socks. If it snows, I will build a man from the fresh-fallen snow and wrap Walter's scarf around his neck and put one of Walter's old caps on his head. But that snowman, I suspect, will smell more of the world than of Walter.

Bayley Farm House has a very large country mailbox, askew on its pole. You would think such a large box could never be filled. On the contrary, it overflows with messages, catalogs, forwarded mail for everyone. One envelope was addressed to "Simons"—as if we were a breed or a generic designation—and the envelope was thick with clippings. Our correspondent was someone who subscribes, I concluded, to some science magazines. The parts of the brain are (I quote): cerebrum, diencephalon, cerebellum, medulla oblongata. All are related. Walter's brain is in trouble. Some of the words in the clippings were underlined with a yellow marker.

The wind, I have observed, has a pattern. I stood outside and watched it go first to the top branches of the spruce, these branches were green in the daylight and skeletal at dawn. Another fact I learned from a clipping was that the prognosis after age forty was not good.

Every day now grew colder. I thought of the Hole filled with snow. How would it feel to drop into such a depth of snow? Would it be safe? In the mornings the dew on the grass was already a winter dew, a grey-toned lacquer. From a distance, from perspective, it looked blue like a sea. There were coarse strands of grass not so much taking over as making a padding for the more attractive fragile blades that poked among them, a motley grass. Around the rim of the Hole hung a beard of icicles. They were always gone by noon, trimmed by the sunlight in this endless autumn. In truth, I didn't know what to do—how did one prepare for winter in this house? Even the Hole was different in winter light—an optical illusion of greater depth—a haze at the bottom. Overhead the blackbirds were nonchalantly in flight. But I didn't have a sense of oasis, it was rather a feeling of being cut-off. By four o'clock these winter afternoons the Hole builds its shadows, and for the first time I have noticed that the left side is terraced for half its distance and then has a straight drop. The frosts, the coldness, have hardened footprints and handholds. The Hole looks like a reflection of some ancient time. I have found traces of schist and zigzagged veins of greyish-white limestone. The Carboniferous age? Some of the stones were crumbling at the top. I have not figured out what anchors the rim of the Hole— what keeps it intact.

"You have got to get organized, Norman," Jack R. V. Haight was saying on the telephone.

"I thought I was organized," I said. "I'm halfway through that desk. Everything in folders."

"Listen," Jack said, "there's a lot more to be done, Norman. You have to consolidate. When you are dealing with large sums of money, you have to be certain. Everything is everywhere. I would advise you to search the house, Norman."

"I beg your pardon?"

"Norman, it's your parents' house. That's the way to look at it."

How was I going to search the house? This was a very large house. I called up Alexander. No way, he said. I'm not helping. I have enough to do right now.

The truth was, he didn't want to—and I didn't want to either. Jack had been definite. Start with Walter's bedroom, he had said. I always advise that. There's a lot less in sugar bowls than people imagine.

I woke up the morning of the search with a pain in my neck, a distinct muscular tightening. Breakfast was going to be easy. I didn't want anything but coffee. I would psych myself into this.

I began by looking into the mirror as I shaved. Walter is sick, I said. Father is sick. I was only helping him. I didn't give a damn about what was in his room. Whatever he had in his room was none of my business. That was the proper approach. I didn't want to find anything—and I wouldn't find anything.

There were two ways I could do the search. I could just go upstairs as if I were packing for Dad. For instance if Walter had called me from the hospital. Son, he'd have said, I want to abandon this hospital gown—these damn things are open down the back. It's filthy anyway. Bring me some pajamas, also a robe, and clothes to wear when I go home. I could accept that conversation. Yes, that way I could have a matter-of-fact searching operation, opening drawers, closing drawers, selecting clothes.

The other way was different. I went to see Mother—I decided not to make a big thing out of it—I'd mention the search when I brought up her morning coffee.

"Mother," I said, "I thought perhaps I might look around Dad's room, It has to do with the power of attorney—Jack told me to do it. But if my looking disturbs you, then I won't. Let Jack—well anyway I won't."

"Look," she said. "Search, open, close." She drank her coffee. "Make it stronger next time," she said.

"I don't expect to find anything," I said.

"Why should you?"

"Jack is trying to put things in order," I said. I stared at her. Didn't she look better today? Stronger? "Mother," I said, "can we talk about the Historical Society?"

"Get out of here," she said.

I went back downstairs. I drank my coffee. I put both cups into the dishwasher. I went up the stairs singing, "From the Halls of Montezuma . . ." I sang all the way down the hall right to the door of Dad's room.

Mother and Dad used to share this room. I remembered that double bed from the apartment in the city. Why Mother moved out was her business—it certainly wasn't mine. I had been in the room before. It was where I had found boots, a sweater, a grant application.

There were suitcases in the attic. I was tempted to pack a suitcase—but then I would have to explain what I was doing with a suitcase packed with Dad's clothes. For a man in coma? they would say. Come on!

The two chests of drawers in that room were familiar. One was tall, five drawers high. I used to borrow Dad's socks from that one. I had already taken a pair. Hey Dad, I would call out, can I have another pair of socks? The socks already in hand. For Christ's sake, he would say. Now I opened the third drawer down, pulled it out cautiously. There were two piles of underwear in that drawer. So I did the other drawers. First, I did an isometric breathing exercise, but it was all right. It was easy. Dad's clothes were not frightening. Neatly folded, and in all the right drawers, as I remembered. His clothes were intact, and he was coming back to wear all of them.

What did I find? I found nothing. I suppose that seemed a bit strange to me. What should I have found? More of the leavings of life, I thought. How cleansing was country living? In the pockets of one sweater I located a key labelled *Garage*.

There was more furniture to examine—two chests. I had only finished with one. The other chest was long and low. There was a mirror on the wall above this one. Both chests were covered with walnut veneer, both had scratches from their long existence. Six drawers in the low one. I opened them—empty—mostly empty. Mother had placed her clothes elsewhere. Not completely, though. In the bottom left-hand drawer were folded scarves, handkerchiefs, a green wooden doorstop with a painted flower. Spare evening purses—black satin, beaded, pearl-covered. Discarded costume jewelry, unopened boxes of bath powder.

Look carefully, Jack had advised. Don't be squeamish, Norman.

I looked carefully.

I found the bankbook between the folds of a blue and white striped silk scarf. Could I say that it was hidden? No, it was just there. All right, not in the desk—but why did a bankbook have to be in a desk?

"Mother has an account," I told Jack on the telephone. "A savings account at the local bank, the bank managed by Mr. Orckin."

"Not unusual," Jack said, "in today's world women often have their own savings accounts. When opened?"

"Two months ago."

"The deposits," he said. "Frequent?"

"Yes."

"How frequent, Norman?"

I held my breath, sucked in my stomach according to the *U.S. Air Forces Isometric Guide.* "Sometimes biweekly, sometimes more."

Jack whistled. "How much per deposit?"

"Usually two thousand."

"Most recently?"

"Three thousand dollars per."

"Norman," Jack said, "this is what I want you to do. Go through your father's cancelled checks."

I don't believe that I have a low pain threshold. Therefore, the extreme trembling spasms accompanied by sticking jabs in my gut were probably the result of hunger. Going all day on a cup of coffee. A man must eat. I went into the kitchen. I had been neglecting Stop & Shop. There wasn't too much available. I made myself a peanut butter and jelly sandwich, I drank ginger ale, I had a chocolate ice cream sandwich.

Eating has become an acute sensation. This I have noticed— eating has changed. I was never an interested consumer of food.

I mean I enjoyed good food, but I didn't dwell upon it. But now I felt food—sharp, tart, soft, sour—it coated my tongue.

The cancelled checks were in the bottom drawer on the left side of the desk, the side I hadn't gotten to yet. Walter had the checks together in their monthly envelopes, the whole bunch held intact by a red rubberband wound around the envelopes twice.

Were Walter or Mother interested in money? I didn't think so. Money was seldom mentioned when I was growing up. My parents were not concerned with that, I believed. Now Mother was always employable. There are many ways that she could earn money. Take consulting jobs, for instance. She had the background. And then part-time employment was a possibility. Therefore, two things I was not thinking were cancelled checks or Eric DeLeuce. Money was always on Jack's mind, though. He had his code words—*inheritance, power of attorney, accidents, Mother.*

The food did not work. Mrs. Sorbitol kept a drugstore remedy for heartburn on the kitchen windowsill. I took two teaspoonsful. It helped.

In my own cancelled checks mailed to me monthly by a bank in the Greater City of Los Angeles were always names and words I did not recognize. I wasn't denying the checks, my handwriting was recognizable. But who was J. Henty for fifty-six dollars? And why C & D for ten eighty-six? In one short month a life that I had definitely led had left my consciousness. Maybe I'd assign an essay about that next year. Remembering the month.

I went through Walter's checks starting from the period when they moved into the Bayley Farm House. I did not start from the month in which the first deposit was made into the bankbook listed for Sara Simon. But eventually I got to that month. It was inevitable that I would.

In those checks surrounded by the anonymity of someone
else's life was a check made out to Cash and signed by one Sara
Simon. It was, of course, coincidence. But I compared the dates.
Date of check to date of first deposit. It went faster then. I just
had to skim through the checks each month, pick out the ones
made out to Cash and signed Sara Simon, cross-referenced to
the bankbook. Mother was withdrawing from the checking account of Walter and Sara Simon and depositing to the savings
account of Sara Simon.

Didn't sound duplicitous—why shouldn't Mother do that?
Her money too. Wasn't it her money also? A transaction between
husband and wife. Anyway, she deposited the money in a local
bank—not a different one. I did not believe that if you were going
to hide deposits that you would put them in the same bank.

"Shrewd," Jack said.

I hung up.

The woman at Reception was adamant. If you don't leave, Mr.
Simon, she said, we will summon Security. I said that I was sorry.
But no one seemed about to reconsider. I was off the list.

All I wanted to do was to talk to Father. Dad, I wanted to say,
there are matters that I must discuss with you. I wanted him
(Dad) to say, Hell Norm, my door is always open to you.

But in truth, the door both literal and figurative was closed.
I left before Security arrived. I took the long way home and drove
through Shilton. No one stared at me, maybe I didn't look like a
stranger anymore. It also occurred to me as I drove down the
Main Street of Shilton that Castleberry might own one out of
every two stores.

That possibility did exist.

There's nothing you can do about that.

The trip to and from the hospital had taken three hours. What
could happen in such a short time? There was a red Chevette in

the driveway of Bayley Farm House, not parked on the road in front of the house but right in the driveway. Balls, I thought. Someone was inside. I pulled in behind the red car, blocking their escape. "Hey you!" I shouted and walked towards the car.

"Norman," she called, already opening the car door.

I watched her get out of the car. She was wearing beige, some kind of homespun skirt and matching blouse.

"Eileen?"

"Me," she said. She put her hands on my shoulders, pinching them. Standing on tiptoe she kissed me, aiming directly for the lips not the cheek.

"What the hell," I said. "Why?"

"Honey," Eileen said. "I've been worried every day. I never heard you so muddled on the telephone, so in need of help. And there I am taking at this very time a business management course. I am here to assist you. Flew into Kennedy, train to here, and rented this cute jalopy in town. Not much of a town, Norman."

I noticed that there were two suitcases on the back seat. I stared at Eileen. She looked beautiful, fresh, pearly.

"You should have gone into the house," I said.

"The house," she said. "First, you have to call off your watchdog."

"Dog? Chaminade wouldn't hurt you."

"Chaminade, hell. The little witch lady is what I mean."

"Mrs. Sorbitol?"

"All I know is that I rang the bell, identified myself, and that walking broomstick told me to get my carcass off the porch before she squashed it. That's a direct quote, Norman."

"Come," I said, pulling the suitcases from the car and leading the way.

Mrs. Sorbitol had been watching. She flung open the front door. Chaminade was beside her, she bared her teeth.

"It's all right, Mrs. Sorbitol," I said. "This is Eileen. We used to be married. She flew all the way from Los Angeles."

Eileen smiled triumphantly. "See," she said. "See."

I carried the suitcases into the hall. They were heavy.

"All I know," Mrs. Sorbitol said, "is that I never laid eyes on her before, and I wasn't about to let her in."

"I understand," I said. "Mistake. Simple error. Anyway, I'm back now, Mrs. Sorbitol, you can leave."

Mrs. Sorbitol nodded. I could see that she was prepared, her black purse was on the hall table.

"Good," Eileen said.

I tried to nudge her in time, but it didn't work.

Mrs. Sorbitol stood at the foot of the stairs. "Mrs. Simon," she yelled. "I'm going now. You've got company, Mrs. Simon. Your ex-daughter-in-law from L.A."

I believe that this was the first time that Mrs. Sorbitol ever addressed Mother.

I made some drinks, never mind the hour. Eileen liked bourbon. She was walking around the downstairs rooms. "Big," she said. "Where's the Hole?"

"Out back," I said, "but you can see it from the kitchen."

Eileen found the kitchen by herself. She stared out the window. "The pits," she said. "The pits."

"Yeah," I said. I was standing behind her, I put my arms around her, put my hands beneath her blouse.

"Should I go up and speak to your mama?"

"No," I said. "No visitors."

"This place," Eileen said, tilting her glass, "is a mess. Honestly, Norman, you should have picked up a little."

"I did," I said, "what I could."

She sighed. "Everything needs tidying. Find me the vacuum, some old pieces of cloth, and a bucket."

"Eileen," I said. "Later, Eileen."

"Hell no. I hate a pigsty, Norman. Just show me some closet where I can hang up my clothes. I didn't bring any old slacks or anything like that so I'm just going to have to work around in my bra and panties."

I did what I could to help her. She scrubbed the kitchen, the dining room, the sunroom. I carried out old newspapers. Eileen was a quick mover, her body firm and sleek, her breasts carried high. I wondered if there had been some intended cruelty, a plot to deprive her of any little lines on her face, any indentations of passage. Baby-smooth, she was.

"Work around the piles of paper on the living room floor," I said. "Those in the corner."

"What's there?"

"Accounts, letters, miscellaneous."

"We'll pick them up," she said.

"No," I said.

"I can help you, Norman. That's what I'm here for."

She was leaning forward. The light made her hair transparent.

She was standing very still, but I suspected that I was quivering, throbbing.

"Come on," she said. "What's the use of having me if I can't help."

I thought her voice was cheerful, basic, matter-of-fact. My fingers tingled, it was the way I had been holding them—very still. I thought of Eileen seated cross-legged on the floor across from me, the papers between us. She would sit casually, no modesty panel, the muscular curves of her legs defined, knees up. And as we leaned forward—wouldn't the wooden floor creak a warning? I was suddenly a sad man, moderately intoxicated.

"I am forbidden by the lawyer of my parents from showing these papers to anyone," I said.

"That's for strangers," Eileen said. "Anyway, I never heard of such a thing. I didn't know my help would be taken this way."

She picked up a broom.

"What way?" I said quickly. "What way?"

"I want to shower," Eileen said. I took her upstairs.

Now I was having no déjà vu or hallucinations of other kinds, but as I came down the stairs I could distinctly smell a breakfast. I could smell coffee, also frying bacon. Now I had gone from bed to bath to stairs. There were no back stairs, and Eileen was still in that bed I had vacated, a small, bare-bodied hump beneath the blankets. And I could see a light from the kitchen, a pointed arrow of a glow. I fumbled in the closet near the stairs. There was a broom there. The only weapon that I could immediately locate. "Here I come," I called and approached the kitchen.

Mother stood at the stove. She was wearing black slacks and a black sweater. She had tied a scarf around her waist to hold up the slacks. I wondered if she had taken the scarf from the scarf drawer, if she had noticed the missing bankbook. It's in the accordion file, Mother, I would say.

"Sit down, Norman," Mother said. "I hate cold food."

"Yes," I said. I stared at her.

Mother filled two plates with scrambled eggs, bacon. She poured two cups of coffee. We sat down together.

"Mother," I said finally, "I'm glad you're feeling better."

"I'm feeling lousy, Norman. I wonder how long it takes for all that junk to flush out of your bloodstream. Cut out the pills, Norman. I'm practically numb from them."

"They were prescribed," I explained.

"Not by me," she said.

"Yeah," I said. "Sure—no more pills. You know that Eileen is here? Eileen—she's upstairs."

"Really? Doing what?"

"Sleeping."

"Doesn't she live in California?"

"She came here on a visit—a short visit."

"It's rather tasteless to plump yourself down in the house of the sick."

"I believe she only wanted to help."

"Before you help someone—you ought to wait to be asked. Norman, how is your father? How's Walter?"

I felt suddenly a new pain, this one sharp and keen and inexplicable, with no source, no focal point. An all-over endless ache.

"He's still in the hospital, Mother."

"Conscious? Is he awake?"

"No," I said. I volunteered no more.

"After breakfast, Norman. After I clean up the dishes. I want you to drive me to the hospital."

"I don't know," I said. "I don't know if that's a good idea. Maybe I ought to ask your doctor."

"Fuck the doctor, Norman. Get the car."

Mother went upstairs to change her clothes, but then she came back wearing the same things. The other stuff looks worse, she said. Nothing fits. In the other stuff, I'd scare the dead. But before she had returned I had tried the telephone in the kitchen, but it was no use. Everyone was in transit—Alexander, Dr. Waddington, Drs. Heller and Herschl.

I left a note for Eileen on the kitchen table. *Be back soon,* I wrote. *Gone to hospital with Mother—wait for me.*

I didn't know about Reception. "Maybe," I ventured, "they might not let you in." They probably wouldn't if they saw her with me.

"What room is Walter in?" Mother said.

"Four-oh-one—fourth floor."

I drove around to a back entrance to the hospital.

"Go home," Mother said. "Pick me up at three."

I raised myself on one elbow. I was nostalgic as I ran my fingers down Eileen's belly, nostalgic for our scatological days when we explored the meanings of her collection of dirty words. We were damp there, damp and warm and delightful. I thought about the journey Eileen had made to be here. I thought about anger and separations. I could see Eileen dragging her heavy suitcases, Eileen coming to me.

"Do you have a madam?" Eileen asked.

"Beg pardon?"

"A madam at the motel."

"Christ—it's not like that. I think Stopwood runs the place as a kind of clearing house."

"Oh"—she was disappointed—"he just rents then."

"Not exactly," I said. "I think the house gets a cut and everyone pays a share of the expenses."

"I want to see it."

"What?—the books, the accounts?"

"Don't be silly—the brothel. The motel."

"There is nothing to see. A shabby building, secondhand stuff."

"Come on, Norman." She leaned over, pressing against me. "I don't know when I'm going to get a chance like this again."

"I swear," I said, "there is nothing to see there—no red velvet curtains, no gilt. There's more to see here in the yard—look down the Hole for instance. I've uncovered a gigantic piece of grey-green tile, maybe a section of flooring. Can't figure out how to get it to the surface intact."

"For flooring," she said, "I go to Armstrong."

I have been expecting Conlon to hide and wait for us, Mother and me, when we leave the hospital. I have decided to continue my present policy. If he approaches, I will say *No Visitors* and get Mother into the car as quickly as possible. I heard that one of the doctors told Mother to talk to Walter. I was told that she does, now she pulls her chair up close to the bed and talks to him all day. What does she say to him? I have no idea of the depth of their relationship.

notes to alexander

Alexander, remember our construction paper days—reds, blues, greens—all primary shades. You with your library presentations and me with my damn baseball cards. Guess what, brother, old chap? I made a miniature paper model of the apartment building yesterday. And it looks real good. Like one of those pop-up kids' books. I based it on Lazarre's sketches, those that still exist. I built it from stiff beige construction paper—Mother had some in the attic—and to scale. If the building had been completed, Alex—how the hell did it just vanish? And were there any renters? I have found no personal artifacts to date.

After one of our rains, a gully appeared within the Hole, a natural occurrence. I climbed down for a closer look, but the mud was too clinging. I was panting by the time I came back up to the surface. Next rain, the gully vanished. There are weeds trying to colonize the rim—hardy, winter weeds. Stumps of bushes are sending up shoots, no leaves, just awkward-looking sticks, wallflower twigs.

You said that Mother didn't seem quite well. That is true. Waddington, reappearing, says that this going to the hospital to see Walter is not such a giant step forward. I thought it was. But Waddington explained that now instead of lying in her bed all day, she just sits in Walter's room all day. Actually, she talks to him and also she has begun reading articles in the newspapers about art, paintings, and so forth. Gallery announcements too.

The last twenty-four hours have been busy, kiddo. Distinctly busy. I thought for a while that Mother might need something. I had two capsules ready, but she didn't take them.

First, let's go back to yesterday. Yesterday, I went to the motel. Eileen was excited. She had put on grey slacks tight across the ass, and a white silk blouse.

"Do I look all right?" she said.

She twirled in front of me, the sleeves of her blouse flapping like wings.

"There will be nothing to see, Eileen," I said. But I had promised to take her, ill-chosen words when we were together.

We used Walter's station wagon. Eileen wanted the rented car. Jazzier, she said.

We rode side by side.

"Your mother," Eileen said, "has not been all that hospitable, Norman. We have not even spoken to each other. I knocked on her door twice. Mother Simon, I called. But she wouldn't answer. I knew damn well she was in there. And I am just trying to help. I straighten up every day. The work wouldn't be so bad, but all that dust from the digging. When it doesn't rain, all that stuff just flies up and settles."

"Yes," I said. I didn't want to go to the motel. I wasn't having anything to do with Stopwood. I was leaving that to Jack R. V. Haight.

I knew what the motel looked like. A painted sign that had faded to a watery brown. Additional neon words that were tiny, but easy to see on the road at night, a deserted road at night.

"My goodness," Eileen said and bounced on the seat. "A dump. Does anyone stay here for real?"

"No," I said.

If Stopwood was watching us from his window, I knew what he would think. That I had brought her there. That I was coming for a room, owner's privileges or something.

"*Mister* Simon," Stopwood said and stood in the office doorway supporting the screen door with one hand.

I'll say this for Stopwood, he seemed to come to work every day.

"This is Mrs. Simon," I lied.

"Eileen," she said and wasted on him her smile.

What was I going to tell the man?

"We've come on a tour," I said.

"Sure," Stopwood said.

I looked at Eileen. "What do you want to see?" I whispered. "The bedrooms?"

"Later," she said. "Could we—would you by the tiniest of chances have some coffee, Mr. Stopwood?"

She was set to charm Stopwood. That was Eileen's specialty and she worked it well. Stopwood's eyes followed her rump into the office.

Stopwood nodded at her, but slowly.

What I'm thinking, brother, is that you better drag your bones out here. I want to eliminate this property. Never mind what Jack says. Jack is not family. Furthermore, I have power of attorney, don't forget. This motel goes!

"Who are the women?" Eileen asked. "I mean who do you get out here?"

Stopwood's cheeks were flushed. He was staring at Eileen, and she was angled at her most flattering three-quarter profile.

"All kinds," he said.

"But from where—from where around here?"

"Well," he said, "this isn't that far from everywhere, you know. There are some regulars. I mean if someone calls and just asks, I have a few numbers. Then there's girl friends of people and women from surrounding towns."

"Ages?"

"A good range. Except if I know they're too young, I won't let them in."

"Norman," Eileen said, "you could collect a lot of data here."

On the corner of the registration counter was a note, half-folded. I couldn't read it—it was signed with an initial—a large visible C.

I have by trial and error attached a rope to the winch on the back of the tow truck, that way I can let myself down into the Hole easily. Also, I can tie together any implements and lower them at the same time. I had been damaging the tools by just throwing them down. It's a matter of organization. For raising bricks to the surface I use an old hammock that I found in the garage. I fill the hammock sling with bricks and heave ho. Nothing but bricks so far except for that large hunk of tile which is leaning against one wall outside the garage. There are by count two hundred and forty-seven bricks.

Alex, what the hell do you think I am? Do you think I would have left the two of them alone in the house? Where was I when the trouble started? I was outside in the Hole. Earlier I had left for a few minutes to place an order at the Shilton Do It Store, but I was back before the trouble started. I am certain that it hadn't begun yet. I was there, I was outside—you can hear plenty from the Hole.

Who was at fault? Both of them, Alex. But what I heard at first was noise. To be exact, I heard Chaminade barking from inside the house. It wasn't a pleasant day, brother, rain falling like a veil, making sharp lines waver. I thought someone was at the door, maybe trying to force their way into the house. Eileen could never hold them off. I climbed up from the bottom of the Hole and ran to the house. As soon as I opened the kitchen door, I heard their voices—the pitch was at a level above a shout. Eileen had met Mother.

They were yelling, but I couldn't make out any words. I went to the stairs. "I'm on the way," I called. No one was on the second floor. The door that led to the stairs to the attic was open. That was where they were. But at that moment I heard a scuffling, they were descending the stairs. I was in the hallway of the second floor when they appeared. Eileen first—and behind her, Mother. Actually, Mother was holding Eileen's arm. She was propelling her forward. Their faces were red, their cries spluttered with words.

"Shut up!" I shouted. Christ! I felt rotten.

"Get this biddy off me," Eileen was saying.

And Mother. Mother looked terribly thin. It was five o'clock, no visiting hours at the hospital. Normally Mother would have been in her room. What had dragged her out?

"I heard footsteps," Mother said. "I heard that she-wolf's footsteps overhead. I followed her."

"I was cleaning," Eileen said.

"Cleaning? Who the hell told you to do cleaning?" Mother said.

"Then she"—Eileen pointed at Mother—"crept up the stairs. Did I know she was there? I was only looking at some pictures."

"You are a sneaking person," Mother said. "You are not a member of this family. You are a middle-aged child in bra and panties."

"Norman," Eileen said. But dignity was difficult, her clothes were basically see-through. "I don't have to take this."

The doors slammed, Alex.

Eileen's.

Mother's.

I arranged for Eileen's airplane reservations back to L.A., arranged for the disposal of the rented car by hiring one of the Stopwood children to return it. Also, I used my power of attorney to write a check for two hundred fifty dollars for Eileen. If this does not meet with your approval, I'll repay the account, Alex. But after all, Eileen did a perfectly acceptable job of cleaning downstairs.

About what I found in the Hole, Alex, Federal Express will be at your door tomorrow with a package. Do with it whatever you want. The truth is that I read the first two pages, closed the thing, and shipped it pronto to you.

What is it? It appears to be a journal, Alex. Mother's journal, very recent, wrapped and taped inside a black rubber poncho. I found it in the Hole.

I have at this moment all the responsibility that I can bear. The only thing that I ask of you is that you try to get me back on the list. I mean they let me into the room to pick up Mother— but Alex, I really need to speak to Walter alone.

walter's notes

This is not another psychoanalysis. He couldn't afford one years ago—now he hasn't the time. He has never been particularly fond of turtles—not that he dislikes them. But for him a tortoise walks from beach to the rocks, a slow pronounced amble. Under no circumstances can this stroll be described as a waddle. Do you have any idea how old tortoises can be? Tortoises can be absolutely ancient. This is a very old turtle—maybe his age can be told by rings on the shell. The shell itself is heavy, scarred, someone once carved initials on the side—P.C. 1937. The tortoise is carrying around his house, his mobile world. He makes his way through the shallow water to rocks that are half-buried in mud and green with primitive moss. There by the rocks he draws in his legs, until he is the shell, a granite outcropping. Then along comes a group of workmen with hammers and mallets to bang on his shell. Tortoise hunters. The men are laughing and joking. One of them puts out his cigarette on the tortoise's hard back. Does the turtle feel that? Any pain? Do the vibrating blows hurt? Anybody there? Is he afraid, quivering, mucus seeping outward? The men cannot move the turtle. Maybe they can scare him ashore. Their truck is parked there. Does that particular turtle just let the men bang on his shell?—what the hell, let them make their noise. In the shell he is invincible and too heavy and too old—either he no longer cares or is unaware of what is happening. And thus unaware, he goes on with his ruminations of all that has happened to him, of hundreds of happenings. The men are still banging on the shell. But it doesn't hurt the turtle.

This concludes the first scene except for the interpretation. Now suppose you are inside the shell and you can't feel a damn thing. But you are not dead. Walter is not a tortoise, is not inside a shell, nor is he dead. If the men banging on the shell do not frighten the reptile, if the men can't scare the turtle—therefore it is possible to be inside a shell, not frightened, and not dead. The cause of not being frightened must of course be like protective coloration. Nature then or natural ways or something—what the hell, he doesn't know.

For a few moments Walter considers the possibility that he is catatonic, but he dismisses the possibility. He concludes that he is not dead. He cannot wiggle, though. But he doesn't feel amputated, no phantom limbs floating by. As a matter of fact, he sees himself in his navy blue Brooks Brothers suit leaning against a wall. Standing across the room if there were any points of reference. He is in the suit leaning against the wall across the room, his hair is properly combed, he is relaxed. No matter that he does not know where the hell he is. It will come to him. He could, of course, move the turtle. The turtle is his to command and if he wants the turtle to stick his legs out—then the turtle will damn well stick his legs out.

The remarkable thing is that Walter is not in a state of panic, saliva is not flowing, adrenaline pushing, heartbeat irregular. None of these. And that is as surprising as the fact that he is also certain that he is not blind. It's not that the darkness is not heavy or the blackness incomplete or that there are any reassuring pinpoints of light. This is one complete set of blackness. Yet it seems not so much upon him as raised up over him like a tent. Suppose he wanted to spit? No, he does not want to spit. But if he did—would he spit up, down, sideways? If he were leaning against the wall in his navy blue Brooks Brothers suit, he would either spit out or down. In truth, he neither wants to spit nor eat nor scratch nor piss. No—*wants* is not the word. *Needs* is the word, *needs* or *has to* or *be able*.

It ought not to be bearable.

But it is.

What were the senses? But all that came to mind were those three monkeys covering up certain vital functions. You can buy replicas of those monkeys in tourist traps everywhere.

Never a patient man, Walter has acquired this wonderful willingness to wait. Not that he has another choice. Anyway, he has

always been optimistic. That was part of his nature. A glorious
optimism. The cornerstone of the New World. How do tortoises
fuck? Imagine the tortoise seeking female companionship. And
the continuation of his race. Can the tortoise supply information
about this?

Walter was certainly interested in female companionship.
Sexuality then has not vanished. He could still recall that. Ever
since age eleven he could remember, he was interested in female
companionship. And probably before that. At what age for the
tortoise? But at age eleven, Walter remembered that he had great
passions regarding movie stars, regarding some other child, regarding some child with long brown hair. Remembered the
sticky feeling of pajama pants with their striped line stuck against
his leg. What memories of passion could the tortoise recount?—
hell, it was hardly fair—the tortoise had lived at least four of
Walter's lifetimes.

Could he be wearing pajamas? If you know what you're wearing, you know where you are. Hey, think about pajamas. He could
be encased in pajamas. Pale blue pajamas with a piping of white
and an absurd initialled pocket sent by his aunt from Chicago—
another non-returnable. Yet it was hard to believe that he was
in those pajamas circa Christmas present, 1938. A) They
wouldn't fit, and B) Nothing lasts that long. No, better to stick
to the suit theory—man against the wall, arms crossed.

The scene shifts to background emphasis. Walter is standing on
a small, stone balcony on the third floor looking out not at the
woods but rather upon a neat, fenced backyard, squares of prime
shade, nurtured grass intersecting smaller rectangles of flower
beds. Right off the bat, he knows that something is wrong.

What's that? Walter says and leans farther out, although not
at any dangerous angle. He rests both hands palms down against
the pebbly surfaced railing of stone, bits of mica glittering even
in the pale light. His socks feel damp, he might have come
straight out onto the balcony from a walk through the grass. But

if he stood on the balcony looking out to the west there should be woods, thick grass, no houses.

Hallo, he yells. He doesn't believe for one second that he is on the balcony. First of all, his house does not have a balcony. Second, it is set in a wooded area—a weedy area. They know what they can do with their balcony. What's he supposed to do— play Romeo?

How do tortoises fuck?

All right, he is not on a balcony. Chop off the balcony.

And he is not having a good time in someone's bed either. That's it. First, he does not know for certain that he is upon a bed. He surmises. He'd better be careful. He has no intention of passing into dreams.

All right, he is on the bed. That eliminates the suit and wall theory. Anyway, he rarely wore that blue suit. The body—his body—performed certain functions. How? Who knows? Even if he didn't know how he did them before—they must still be there. For instance, he must be eating, urinating, defecating. Saliva must be forming, ditto for tears in the eyes. Other things not happening—erections for fucking, night dreams, movement. Does he itch? Does he itch—if he does not scratch? Does he moan and make some gesture like scratching and someone does that for him? Is he communicating?

Back to the balcony and house. No, not the balcony. Listen, everyone lives somewhere. People do not have convenient shells. It could be a house in the city. He rode the subway, he ate in restaurants. He was in bed in the city.

It was absolutely amazing to him that he could have selective memory, consciousness, and not panic. From the bed Walter goes directly to a car and is driving up to the Bronx. He is going to Boston Post Road. It's midday on Saturday. He goes to a restaurant that he knows, actually more of a Danish and coffee place. He knows the owner, they nod at each other. There is no one else in the room whom Walter knows. He orders coffee and a piece of cherry pie that is stiff with gelatinous juice of a dangerous red. Then in comes Jack with his wife. They walk right past Walter, busily talking. He pretends to drop his napkin and gets up to go to the counter to get another one. What he wants is a long good look. He sees Jack's wife. She's maybe a little heavier, she was always a rather loud brunette with well-powdered skin. She sees him and makes a signal.

What he ought to do is run through his life in some kind of order. Wasn't that the right approach? What did tortoises do? Maybe if you had a couple of hundred years of memories you found them hard to organize.

He was probably in a bed.

With Jack's wife?

Chop off Jack's wife.

Where I can, someone says to him, I've told the story exactly as it is. Some conversations are then accurate. But where I can't do that, I have invented them based on my knowledge of the people. Many things happen around me based on my appearance which they take to be some sign of idiocy even though they know better. I am considered to have better than average intelligence, am palsied from birth, need special shoes, certain adapted implements, but I go to school, take care of my body's functions, but my face is blanker than it ought to be, less varied, and so sometimes they act as if I weren't present. No one says, Hush, the child is here. No one. And I do not speak.

When the time comes, you'll speak. The right question will trigger a response. Meanwhile, tuck your legs in and ruminate.

one

See if you can get through to him.

Your name is Walter. Walter, speak to me. Speak to me, Walter!

Your wife's name is Sara. Your sons are here, Walt. You want to see your boys, don't you, fellow? Walter, open your eyes—I know you can. Get up—time to get up!

The poor bastard Walter is in coma.

Whoopee!

Walter was in coma.

Thank God they'd said that. Knowledge does not hurt. Suppose they hadn't? Suppose no one ever said that. How would I know what this was? I should be grateful. I am grateful. One man had spoken to another. I understand the darkness. Amazing how reassuring an explanation was. I'm not afraid of the darkness. Was this the first time I thought about the darkness? I think that was the first time. What the hell. There you are Walter, old fellow, teacher extraordinaire. You are in darkness. In bloody darkness and in coma. A double dip of pleasures.

Was I completely in coma if I heard those voices, disembodied though they were? I had heard voices. One man to another. Walter is in coma, one said. No, not both. One man to another. Was it like a lesson. Or had I come in at the end of a conversation? What did I know about coma? Hell, I knew nothing.

Should I list the facts of coma? What facts? Didn't I already say I didn't have any facts? I could describe my coma—complete darkness, yet a sense of myself there. I could, I supposed, equate these sensations to that summer when I was fifteen and broke my leg. The result of an incident with a girl and her brother—but never mind. I awoke in a hospital to find one leg in a cast from thigh to ankle. It had stopped being—the leg. It did not itch, not even exist, no part of my body. That was me now—the total me.

I couldn't move anything. I didn't care that I couldn't move anything. No twitching muscles, no staccato beat in the veins. I was just there. Where in hell was the there? Probably in a hospital. Most certainly in a hospital. Eventually the right words would be spoken. I have faith in the right words. Someone will say exactly where I was. Or I would come up from coma. Assuming of course that I was down. I probably wasn't down—up, down, alongside—I was just there.

This was the first time I was aware that something had happened to me. I thought I remembered that this was the first time. I had walked that labyrinth at Hampton Court—classy topiary—round and round I had gone. I was rescued. This could be like that. I'd rather it wasn't. I'll make a statement. I, Walter, knew for the first time that I was in coma. Knew? Drop the knew. Make it know. Suppose I didn't come in at the same spot again? I didn't want to appear in and out of the world this way, always at the point of someone saying "Walter is in coma." Suppose that happened? Did you sleep in coma? What did the body need?

I hadn't thought about that before. The body. I was in my body—that familiar, much misused Walter body. Yet I was calm, I was relaxed. Was I intact? Had I forgotten how to signal the parts of the body? Hey body! Yoohoo!

I was a mathematician. I wasn't a mathematician for nothing—I'd develop a fucking numbering system.

Walter in coma. Time period One.

That was the way to do it. Should I fall asleep or go down or whatever—should that occur and then when I came back or up—why then I must first say the last number. One.

One is how I got here.

Already I had a system. You can't beat a system.

That was the best way. Later I could invade memory storage and bring back my One and say that was how I got here. No, I would do this in a straightforward manner. How it happened. It happened on a Monday.

I can see it now—at home on a Monday in January. I enjoyed being home, I really liked it, especially in the closed world of winter. The past weekend had been good, had been long. I had awakened restless on that storming Monday, not in need of an extra day of rest. Outside the roads had glistened, every gravelly crack iced. I would go out and get some papers and do some work. I was certain of the correctness of my decision.

Being on the streets felt right too. Hardly anyone wandering about. That was marvelous about the city, any city. How the weather could make people do what it wanted—or give them the excuse anyway.

I stood on Lexington Avenue and Forty-second and waved at an approaching taxi.

Glad to see you, the man said. You're only my second today.

I smiled. Fifty-eighth and Third, I said.

Right, the man said. He was a black man, middle-aged. He wore a grey wool cap pulled down over his ears. It was cold in the taxi, vapor-producing cold. I leaned back against the black vinyl upholstery. I could feel the chilling plastic right through my overcoat. I linked my fingers through the arm rest on the door. The car skidded several times, once through a stop light. The driver was cursing softly. Still, I felt that he was a good driver. I braced myself for the sliding stops that caused a slight tightening in my back. The car spun on a stretch of grey shine at an intersection, no cross-traffic. Fortunate, I said, perhaps out loud. But the car slid farther, spun, the driver not taking his foot from the gas pedal—or did he? Don't hit the brakes, I ordered. The car made a larger circle. We will have to crash, I realized. The car was swinging towards a streetlight. We will hit, I knew, neatly, cruelly smashing into the back half of the car, into the passenger half. There was, of course, nothing that I could do.

What I have here is a reasonable, a mathematically possible explanation. But was there a car? There was no car. I mean for a short moment I was some mysterious fish in dark waters. Better a white fish, better a pale albino fish, thirty, forty, fifty fathoms below. I was not in that car—all right I might have been in that car—probably was in that car and it skidded. Or was I just finishing a scene? At some time I was A) In a taxi that skidded, and B) Afraid that it would crash.

You'll never awaken, will you, Walter? You'll be there forever and more.
Who the hell was that?
New voice appeared. That was the nurse. I decided that had to be a nurse. *It is Wednesday, Walter,* she said. *Squeeze back, Walter. Squeeze back.*
Something was being squeezed—hey, that's what I call a lucky guess.
I cannot be touched. No touch, no smell, imperfect hearing. At any rate I hadn't even heard her come into the room. Unless her soles were rubber. Had she come in on little cat's feet?
They could touch me, any of them. I wouldn't know. I, Walter, am by nature independent. Still, I didn't care. Let them touch away. Kitchee, kitchee. There was probably a series of tubes. Stands to reason that there would have to be. The excreta tubes, the eating tubes. I didn't actually eat, did I? And I had liked my food. I ought to make a list of my favorite foods. Had they put a tube in my nose too? After the operation—the operation that marked my one stay in a hospital, except for this—I had awakened from surgery with a tube in my nose. Clearing the passages, they had said. Get the damn thing out, I told them. They had, they did. Keep quiet, they said.
Let them put their tubes in. I didn't know. Humiliation required knowing. They could tube me to their heart's content.

I'd rather be dead, a voice said. This was a much younger voice, this was a young man's voice.
Not me, I replied.
As good as dead.
Hardly.

Open your eyes. Hey buddy, open up. Your wife's a swell looker. Don't you want to see her? Fuck her? Screw her?

Of course, I replied.

That voice went away. It hadn't been long then. No, from the way they spoke. It hadn't been long. There was nothing that differentiated the days. Days? Why not nights? There was nothing that differentiated the nights. There were no meal times, no pissing times—there must just be needles dripping into me. What did I look like? Was I recognizable?

I must remember to number each period. Sleep would be the dividing state. No matter how long. I would call each period of being, the period of time. I could count them. That was the best. The trick was to remember the last number. For instance, suppose I awoke and thought that the next period was Fifteen when indeed it was Twelve. Let it be Fifteen then. That was reassuring—getting a system in order.

Open your eyes, Walter.

What an uncompelling voice.

Open your eyes, Walter. Today is Tuesday, Walter.

Give me the damn month, lady. What the hell good is the day?

Theoretically, I should be climbing the walls. Assuming of course, that I could climb—which I cannot. I am determined however not to regress. I am not going to go through my life re-arguing all those events. I could do that. The quick rundown from conception to intubation.

But I won't.

I am determined to stay *au courant*.

One.

TWO

Two.

I am somewhat exhilarated. This is certainly my Two—but more important I can remember One. Since we are in period Two, I feel that progress is being made. I am keeping my mathematically inclined wits around me.

I will concentrate during this period upon externals. Actually, I should define that better. External what? External to my present state of being which is not all that uncomfortable.

Back to exhilaration. I am rich. I don't believe I ever stated it that way before. I must have been ashamed to admit that I was rich—maybe I didn't know. All right, I am rich—maybe not Fortune 500 rich—but a damn sight above comfortable. I probably should have been more outspoken about my circumstances. But actually I wasn't really asked. This, of course, was due to the source of the money. Referred to in the past as the Marybeth money—henceforth to be called the Walter money. Or perhaps the Simon Estate. I made a will—I made a new will two weeks ago. Cancel the two weeks ago. Two weeks ago from when? A will is not at the moment called for anyway—I am very much with everyone.

I have learned for myself firsthand that money is freedom, if properly used. I believe that I have properly used it.

Also, I am acquiring an interior visualization of Sara—in short, I can see her face. Sara is a good sport. We have our separate interests, though.

Sara is coming into a room. I should like to know, she says, where you think we're going? My smile, I believe, is disarming. My tone reflects simplicity and directness. Baby, I say, I have this wonderful opportunity, and I want you with me. Sara is shaking her head. I go to work on her. Gently, I assist her from chair to floor where the rug is thick and make love to her. The moments are tender but calculated. They tell me I should stay here, Sara says. I don't even ask who they are. I should paint, Sara whispers. You can paint anywhere, I say.

That's it—Sara paints. She is some kind of an artist.

I hope my being rich has helped her.

What does she paint? I must have seen something—because I am positive that she is talented.

Sara wants a framer.

Probably planning an exhibit.

In some of my scenes Sara is yelling, she is upset, she is annoying me. The artistic temperament maybe.

Is the source of exhilaration the money? Sara's painting? I don't think so. I mean this is a personal exhilaration.

How do I feel?

Damned good inside.

The Hole.

How come I didn't think of this right away?

The Hole. I can see it all right. That's what I've done. Jesus, what a sweet Hole! Big, bigger, biggest—and I did it! Why? For this, I have to concentrate—because periodically I am in Cleveland. And I do not think that the Hole is there.

Walter, someone is saying, the Hole in and of itself is not important. It is what we will find there—that's the key, Walt.

We will find there. So I wasn't in this alone.

Castleberry.

I was in the Hole business with Castleberry.

I was digging up an apartment building.

Two.

walter's notes

Walter has been resistant ever since a thought came to him. He has insisted upon focusing on square roots, the states of the Union in alphabetical order, and the succession of the British Royal Family. That's because he feels cheated. Maybe he is not in such stable condition. Perhaps the bastards are feeding him drugs. Did he lack anxiety because of drugs? Why hasn't that occurred to him before?—perhaps that is also drugs. Are they slipping into his elixir of life a calming potion? He can see some pink-tinted solution slowly moving downward, a thin brew with easily read meniscus—his personal fuel tank.

On the other hand, wouldn't the body adjust to steady doses of pacification—requiring an upping of the pacifier? Maybe he was jumping the gun. Why the hell would they bother? Why calm the already inert—wouldn't that just be a waste of dough? No, just keep it clean for visitors like one of those boxed pictures. What are they called? This is a view of life intact.

Jesus, he hopes his mouth doesn't hang open, those sleepers on the subway, the looks of consciousness gone, sunken cheeks, hawklike noses. But no one has ever mentioned that to him. Not one solitary speaker.

He thinks that he has pared it down to the most basic emotions. He's got it down at least for him. It's curiosity, that's what, just simple curiosity. He must know.

He sets himself a series of questions. What do I miss most? Desire? Food? Touch? Colors? Speech? Awareness? The answer is none. The answer is zero, the answer is zilch.

It's about time someone showed up.

Where the hell have you been, Sara?

You'd think at a time like this, you wouldn't paint. You should have been by my bedside, Walter thinks. Or leaning against the wall next to me. For God's sake, Sara, I stopped alphabetizing the states after Ohio—I lost count—and I got stuck after William of Orange.

The walls of this room are blue, Sara says, *a pale, washed-out shade. Not what I would have picked, let me tell you. Your bed is standard hospital issue. In the corner, they stuck in a table and one comfortable chair covered in blue and green striped vinyl upholstery—the height of hospital fashion. Out the window, Walter, are trees, a lawn. Not bad—the view. The parking lot is around back.*

That's where he is.

Sara's voice is too soft. It sounds thin. Poor girl must be nervous. He was surprised, though, about what she had said. He thought the entire place was done in sterile white, a shining white. He took it for granted that he was not lied to—it rather seemed that they wouldn't bother. The room was blue. But now the surroundings were in order. Nothing can be accomplished without a system.

Could he get her to tell him about his Hole?

How's the Hole, Sara?

What the hell was she doing? Rattling something? Rattling a newspaper. Whatever was happening out there?

He could recall the principle of atrophy, but he can't really absorb that. He tries to imagine his muscles in a slow dissolve, he concentrates. What do I weigh now? I think I weigh the same. I envision myself as the same.

In the next scene Walter is in a state of contemplation.

In Korea I was in the artillery. Nan was my girl. I had a girl at that time named Nan. Sad, young Nan died in an automobile accident at the corner of Lexington and Fifty-third. I have never forgotten that street corner. Nan was perfect. I remember that girl as absolutely perfect. You probably don't remember her at all, my friend Jay said to me.

During period Two I tried to think about what if Nan had lived. I intended to create the days of our lives together. But I stopped before I started—found I didn't want to do that. What if Nan lived? Anyway, Nan is not a person. Can I hear her voice?

How did she sound? Did she push back her hair? Was she given to colds? Obviously, I don't remember her at all.

Now he knew what he wanted to have recorded. How in the middle of periods of coherence—definite coherence and attending to what is going on—suddenly something occurs. He goes someplace.

In the words of Mr. Mowfatt they were "reaching up" when they moved to Shilton Court. It was for them a dangerous move, the move took all the money they had put into their savings. This gesture, Mr. Mowfatt said, is an expression of the faith I have in myself and the results of hard work. It didn't matter to him that his wife went down on her knees. "Oh Lord," she prayed, "save us from this disastrous act." The anxiety was conveyed to their daughters, only ten and eight. The two girls clung to their mother and wept. In truth, they wept less for the financial uncertainties than for the upheaval of their home. Nothing interfered however—no mighty blow to shatter Mr. Mowfatt's convictions. He was not moved by the sudden fevers that put his children in bed, their tossing, uneasy bodies. Mr. Mowfatt signed the papers. Shilton Court was to be theirs.

This is an example of what happens, he thinks. *The Mowfatts?* I mean—come on! If Norman and Alexander weren't always darting in and out of here like nervous frogs I'd try to convey the essence of this experience to them.

Do you know what he'd love? He would love to get his hands on his complete medical records. He'd enjoy reading them. Patient pissed on schedule, patient ingested some yummy glucose.
    They pinched him, the nurse said.

Jesus, the doctor said. *Relatives! Isn't it enough that he's like that—like a vegetable.*

Up yours, buddy.

If he concentrated very hard—could he make Sara talk about the Hole? He tried. It didn't work.

But how was the Hole? If it was allowed to fill up with water too often, the damn thing could collapse. That would be tragic. What if the Hole fell apart before he found what it held?

Found what?

Shilton Court.

That was it—found Shilton Court.

And a life made perfect, a life made idyllic.

Lived in rooms with more than four sides.

THree

He might get up if they wouldn't talk about the Hole. It was Three. It was Three. One, two, three. Why wouldn't they talk about the Hole? He wasn't anxious, but he was annoyed.

His Hole was important to him. You'd think they would be more considerate. It was upsetting him—not knowing.

He should calm down. Could his emotional state make the tubes gurgle? Patient is having a fit. Damn right—patient is having a fit!

How did he get here?

One thing was certain—he didn't walk.

Didn't he have any friends? How come no one was visiting him? Just the wife and the kids. He had friends. There were his old high school chums—what's-his-name and what's-his-name. There were the Stopwoods en masse. There was Castleberry.

Castleberry would have told him about the Hole. He was absolutely positive that Castleberry would have been of assistance.

But he couldn't conjure up a visitor.

How had he gotten here?

It wasn't an automobile accident. Nix the automobile accident. Not a mugging either. It must have been something serious—beyond the aftermath of the common cold.

He hit his head.

Whoopee—on target!

That's what happened. He hit his head.

How?

Sara was sitting in the living room. She looked terrific. What was with her these days? He couldn't remember her looking that great in a long time. He felt horny—he might have taken her right there in the living room—but they weren't alone. Who was there? Norman was there. Norman in from California. Was Norman planning to move back east? A man needed roots.

Tell me, Norman was asking, about the Hole.

Wait until you see it, Walter said. It's the actual site of the most wonderful building imaginable. And I'll find it, Norman. I am convinced that I'll find it.

Why not, Norman said. Here's to you, Dad. Norman raised his glass.

Walter looked over at Sara, but she was looking past him. She was staring at the windows. Outside it was all darkness. Nothing to see.

He and Norman were talking.

I mean who was supposed to have enough dough to live out here in when was it—1915? Norman said.

Nineteen-ten, Walter said. Also, you are wrong about the rich angle. A vision takes money—I'll grant that—but a good idea cannot be limited to those with money. Lazarre wrote about a different kind of life. I don't expect to dig that up, Norman. But what I hope—whatever I could find might stand as a symbol of a search, a search for beauty.

My field, Dad, Norman said. Scratch a beautiful life-style and what do you find? The same old worker bees making it possible.

Symbols, Walter said, have value.

Norman and Walter smiled at each other.

Another drink? Walter asked.

Hey, Norman said, I will have another drink.

That's my boy, Walter said. Long trips wear me out.

I'm going to bed, Sara said. Yours is the last room on the right, Norman.

Walter sat in his room waiting. It certainly took the kid long enough to turn in. He felt foolish sitting there waiting—like he was trying to screw the landlord's wife after all the guests went to sleep. But nevertheless he waited until the house grew silent. Dum de dum, he hummed. He smacked his face with lotion. The hall floorboards creaked under his weight—but with the liquor in him perhaps Norman was snoring away. Anyway, can't stop the floorboards.

He knocked on the door.

Yes? Sara said.

Me, he said.

Come in, she said.

She was sitting up in bed wearing some long-sleeved night-gown. When had she bought that? He had thought that she might have sensed seduction—might have felt the circumstances ripe for seduction.

Sweetheart, Walter said and crossed the room to sit on the edge of the bed. He decided not to say that he had missed her.

He leaned over and kissed her firmly on the lips. He touched the nightgown—full-length and made of flannel. There was no way to get it off without cooperation. She helped. They were experienced in making love to each other.

He awoke later, his naked body half-curled around Sara's. He felt good but not sleepy or lethargic. He was amazed at how awake he was and energetic. Then too, he had been dreaming, and he thought that he didn't dream anymore. But he had been dreaming. In his dream he had made a definitive find—made it in the night. Yesterday afternoon deep in the Hole—hadn't he experienced the same presentiment of success. His shovel had moved up and down setting its own rhythm.

He couldn't just stay there in bed. He had work to do. He slid carefully from bed, he didn't want to wake Sara, and he went back down the hall to his room to get dressed. Yes, he felt it. This was to be the time. Never mind that it was dark out—he had arranged for that contingency.

He had done a good job with the lights and the connections. The Hole looked brilliant. *It* was down there all right. It was waiting for him. Never mind the dampness. He turned on the pump, lowered the rope that he had attached to the tow truck and hand-over-hand climbed down into the Hole.

He felt the metal tip of the shovel hit something large, something resisting. He worked slower now, not wanting to destroy anything. This was it! This was his night!

My God, he had found it—The Fountain! God-all-mighty, that was the fountain. He scrambled back up to the top. He would raise the beast. Tomorrow, he would have Castleberry and the entire Society membership over to view it and to toast his success.

Heave ho, he sang.

The lights went on in the house. He could see that.

There were shouts, screams—hard to hear over the sound of the machinery.

Sara was running towards him. Norman was following. Walter waved at them. It was right that they should share this moment.

The blow of the concrete sent him straight down in the direction of Shilton Court.

Four

Four, Five, Six, One hundred and five.

What difference did it make to him. What were they doing out there—practicing self-control? The one who sits the longest without making a sound gets to stay. Say something! Speak!

A couple of times he thought about waving at them or sitting up suddenly and doing a Frankenstein act. On the other hand just suppose his numbering system has gone awry—could be he was not the Einstein of coma.

All right, he'd face the possibility that they did speak to him. Maybe he just didn't listen. He'll give them the benefit of that. Because in truth he has lost count of some periods. Was this the fucking fourth period or the lousy sixth?

At any rate he thought someone was with him on the inside. Yes here—with him inside this coma, if you will. Not me and my shadow—but he was not here alone. Since he was not delusional, he naturally assumed that this was an induced reaction. New drugs? Who knew what dripped into him by now?

All right. Something—call that someone—was inside. He felt a presence. Like someone with authority. He did not respond well to orders. He had a bad time in the army. Ask him to do something and he'll probably say—What the hell. But order him—and see what happens.

He found himself in his coma with this presence. A feeling but not a cold chill. So right away he nicknamed this figure the Dictator. Nice, huh? He thought of a Hitler. You know, he saw some little guy in polished boots and wearing a Charlie Chaplin mustache marching into his coma. At the very least a Mussolini with a plate of pasta.

He was not about to be ordered around either in coma or out of coma. And certainly not by some unwelcome presence with illusions of conquering his minute kingdom.

For a while this was kind of a stand-off. Walter versus drug-induced reaction. The Dictator was parading back and forth. No

kidding—the Dictator had shouts, he had bands, he had an uproar. Spiffy uniforms, heavy with gold braid. Walter held back.
Parades have never been his thing. In the middle of this—when
he most needed his wits about him—what happened?

In walked his favorite vegetarian doctor.

Walter, I want you to tell me your name, he says.

I do wish Sara would do something about keeping these idiots
away from me.

Open your eyes, the doctor says.

I do.

The doctor got excited. I do believe he pushed a button.

He opened his eyes on command, the doctor told the two
nurses who appeared.

Trained seal—one and only appearance.

Open your eyes, Walter, the doctor said.

Open your eyes, Walter, the nurses said, two sopranos in uni-
son.

Was the Hole everything? That was the Dictator speaking—
wasn't it? By God, it was time everyone stopped saying that. Not
the Hole, damn it. What he would have found there. Listen,
buddy, he said and shook his fist at the speaker. The Dictator
disappeared. They must have switched drugs. The man was
gone. The problem with that was that suddenly Walter was
lonely.

In this period—who knows what number—he found himself
building Shilton Court. One of the workmen. He had calluses on
his hands, a backache, and a splitting headache. The foreman—
or whatever—walked around with his plans and couldn't tell his
head from his ass. Excuse me, Walter said to him. Mind your
own business, the foreman said.

Walter threw his shovel down.

Let them do their own work.

notes to walter

Walter, I am doing all the things that I read in a book. I trust books. You can find out anything you want to know from books. Coma is hard, though. There's coma in acute alcoholism, coma in carbon monoxide poisoning, coma in rabies, coma in typhus fever, coma in primary subarachnoid hemorrhage. Those are just a few conditions, Walter. Coma runs rampant. Instructions and advice are limited, however. What did I find? Rousing the deep sleeper, how to capture someone's attention (this from a booklet). Also, I found a chapter on perception and attending. The sudden surprise—I clap my hands in front of your face, Dad. The sound is sharp, a hollow thwang that would redden your cheek. The hospital doors have some kind of special hinges—I can't slam your door, Walter. One book suggests appealing to the basic emotions. I feel like an idiot, but I pretend to have a scared little kid voice. Daddy! Daddy! I cry in a moronic, high-pitched tone. Also I order you to get up. Rise and shine, Walt! I call your name at unexpected intervals. I lie about imminent tragedies—a tornado has hit your house, I myself am seriously and incurably ill, the car was stolen. I don't know how to tell you this, I begin. In short I do what I can and all the time I look at your body gone smooth and pink.

I brought in a portable radio—a big job with fancy speakers—I played loud music. Ra-ta-ta-boom! The nurse came. Can it, she said.

My choice of music was deliberate, groups with strange unworldly names. I picked what you didn't like. I expected that you would say to me, Turn the junk off, Alex. You did not. It is amazing that I can stand in your room staring at you.

Periodically I give you news bulletins. The world is changing, I tell you—they are subtle but real differences. The election is almost upon us. Have you registered to vote? Will you know who wins? Believe me, Pop, if you keep your eyes closed much longer, you will not recognize the world. You'll be like one of those soldiers who show up from time to time—you know, the ones who hid in the jungle for forty years not knowing the war was over. Dad, the war is over. Open your peepers. New products arrive daily in the marketplace, brands vanish, roads are altered. Prices, Dad, you wouldn't believe prices.

What has always seemed strange to me—no, not strange but hard to accept—are these little shifts in life. Am I so insecure that I cling to accepted views? Like for instance I had decided, Walter, that you were a wisecracking intellectual, a man of spirit. Now having established this in my mind, I am forced to reverse, to slow down. No man of spirit would remain flat on his back.

There is also the Hole. There is you and the Hole, the damned chasm, the vulture crater. Listen Pop, why the hell? Tell me— why the hell? However, I am not completely rigid. Can I adapt? I can adapt. I want you to know now and for all time that I do not care about your Hole. What is it to me? Shove the Hole, Walter.

How did we end up here? The two of us in this room with me staring at you in bright, unshadowed glare. The plight of the youngest son, a biblical plight. Walter, I would like to give you a list of wishes—you know like some kid's Gift List. I wish this wasn't your room. I wish you'd wake up. I wish I was smarter. I wish I had ended up different.

All right as to the last. I know what you'd say. You're a young man, Alex. The world is in front of you. Shit, Dad. That is pure shit. Do you know my rock and cat story, Walter?

Walter, I was at various periods in my childhood a number-one ass. It was in junior high school, Walter—the very age of the children you taught—when I hung around with the Moffitt twins, with Petey, with Salvo, with three unnamed girls. We took a bus one day—maybe on a Tuesday—we took a bus to the country. Who knows why? We went to the country and we horsed around and we climbed hills and we threw rocks. We saw this cat on a ledge near the top of a hill and we threw rocks at it. And it scrambled out farther and farther from ledge to ledge until it got itself caught, too high for our rocks but stuck. The dumb thing was scared. It was out there trembling. Time to go back,

Petey said. We were going to the bus then, bad kids and me. Tough kids, kids of divorced parents and without the wherewithal for warm food. Hell, I said. The fucking cat can't get down. Don't be an ass, my friends said, a cat can always get down. But I knew it couldn't. I went back, I climbed those rocks, tore my hands, reached the animal. The cat looked bad from up close—patchy fur, red eyes, diseased. As I grabbed the beast around the belly, it clawed my arm. I dropped the cat onto a lower ledge. They looked up at me, all those kids. I knew what they thought.

Walter, we are waiting for you to return. Mother is waiting, Norman is waiting, and me too. We do not care about your Hole, Walter. What is it to us? Keep it, Walter!

One thing I wonder about—was there really an apartment building down there, Dad? Shirley thinks about buried gold. She wouldn't admit that, but at night when she is feverish and tossing, she whispers gold. Gold, she whispers over and over again. She reaches over and squeezes my hand, but she doesn't wake up.

Did I mention that Shirley also thinks that you should not have married Mother? They were ill-suited to each other, she says. What do you mean? I ask. He was an adventurous man, she says. He was a curious man. Hell, I say, Mother deserves to die then because she lacks curiosity?

Dad, let me tell you what happened the other day. The medical staff came in. They pinched him, the nurse said. Jesus, the resident said, examining a large purple swelling. Relatives! Isn't it enough that he's like that—like a vegetable.

I'm sorry about that, Dad.

He's faking, Norman said to me. I feel certain that he's faking.

There are tests for that, I told him. I explained about eye deviation, about the drug test.

He's faking, Norman said.

I spoke to you for a while, Walter. But then Mother came into the room, and I can only say words like how are you and offer further glimpses of the world. For instance, I read to you from the newspaper. You always enjoyed the newspaper. But what parts? I read to you first what I want you to know—is that right? Do I read to you from *my* newspaper when I ought to read to you from yours? But that is the streak of pure selfishness in me. When I am reading the newspaper, Mother sits there by your side and does not speak. When I leave the room, she speaks. I have stood at the door and heard the low murmur of her voice, I can't make out the words, I do not know what she says. For a time, I read to you news from the front page, news about catastrophes and disasters. The nurse came in. What are you doing? she said. Giving Walter the world, I replied. Are you mad? she said. Read him the better parts. So then I did the columns of advice, the gardening news, the marriage announcements. But I couldn't continue that, that was false. I read it to you as I saw it.

Walter, yesterday, when I left this charmed establishment I saw that creep outside. I saw him. In his plaid never-washed outer garment.

I put Mother in the car and locked the door and then I went right over to him. "Mr. Conlon," I said, "visiting someone at the hospital?"

"Inquiring about your father," he said.

"He's sick," I said.

"Yes," Conlon said, "that's what they say." He looked over at the car. "How's your Mother?"

"Her doctor says that she's sick."

"When do you think I could talk to her?"

"When she gets well," I said.

Conlon smiled, inclined his head in the direction of the car, but did not stare at Mother. "See you," he said.

Walter, what can I do about Conlon? Is there something he knows, something I should be told? Truth is, Dad, he scares me.

one

Shirley had a new pile of college catalogues. Different sizes, different shapes, they arrived in clusters, stuffed into the mailbox, the excess nearby. Too many. Basically, we had the largest collection of up-to-date college catalogues that I have ever seen. From colleges everywhere, no geographic limitations. Did she really plan to go to Idaho? Utah? The wilds of Delaware? The bound wish books flowed from couch to floor, an annual encyclopedia of education.

"I'm not certain what I want to take," Shirley was saying, flipping through one book with orange covers. "I need direction. I need counseling."

Shirley has red hair, dyed red hair, but she has fair skin and the combination looks good. On the other hand she was always saying things like redheads have difficulty with colors. Gloria made her happy, though. I wasn't present at the time, but Gloria's birth was a pleasure. Gloria has red hair, she was born with red hair. Shirley had been married to Paul, and Paul's family came by their red hair naturally. I knew a lot about Paul. There was a picture of Paul in Gloria's bedroom. I knew that Paul was the only uncircumcised male Shirley had ever slept with. I knew that Paul saw Gloria when she was two hours old and again when she was three and once last year. I called Paul up when I was going into labor, Shirley told me. I said, come and take me to the hospital. The shit says, Considering the legal separation, it is probably not a good idea.

Shirley later forgave him. She said that after she calmed down she understood that Paul felt that he had lost everything—wife, family, the Church. Shirley's mother didn't like Paul. She hadn't welcomed me either. From the fire to you know where, she said. Librarians, she said, make peanuts.

"Why don't you write an essay," I told Shirley. "What I'm going to be when I grow up."

"Don't be sarcastic," Shirley said, pushing her hair away from her forehead. "It's easy to be sarcastic. I just can't settle, that's all."

In truth, she is smart. She and Norman are smart. It's difficult having two smart people in your life. The odd thing was that she really finished these courses that she took. There are already two degrees.

"I have to have something for the fall," she said.

I looked at her. Her voice had a good throaty beat, the best since June Allyson.

"What you are looking for," I said, "is an intellectual dildo."

"Alex," she said and nodded her head significantly in the direction of the child sitting across the room reading.

I knew that book. *The Yellow Book of Fairy Tales.* It is far more frightening than modern parents remember—a book full of treachery, poisonings, thwarted loves.

"You mean," I said, "that she knows the meaning of dildo at seven?"

"The tone conveys," Shirley said.

But Gloria did not look up.

"You'd think," Shirley said to me, "that the first thing upon entering the apartment that you'd do is ask me how he is. You know that today is Tuesday, you know that I go up to the hospital on Tuesday. Wouldn't you think you'd ask me?"

"How is he, Shirley?"

"God, Alex, he's your father, that's how he is. Your father. Lying there in a state of not-being. Every time I come back to the city, I feel as if we have abandoned him."

"How abandoned? He is in the hospital. Every day my Mother sits with him. Norman is only a short ride away."

"You know what I think, Alex?"

"Don't tell me."

"Don't be nasty. He has no one. That man has no one."

"Walter is not a stray dog. He has all of us. God knows, he has you."

"Should he be moved? I would like to go up to Columbia-Presbyterian and speak to someone."

"I told you Norman had consultants. City consultants."

"The right ones?"

I didn't answer. I went from the living room into the kitchen, a tiny walk away. I took a can of beer from the refrigerator. I rubbed the can against my forehead, it cooled me. Shirley was a beautiful woman. A beautiful woman can get away with a lot.

"I'm sorry," I said when I came back carrying my beer.

She nodded, her expression solemn. "It's all right. I shouldn't meddle. It's your family. But I think that someone really ought to take a complete inventory of what's there."

"Where?"

"In the house—Bayley Farm House."

"Go ahead."

"I beg your pardon?"

"You want an inventory, take an inventory."

"Alex, it's not for me. Don't you care about your interests?"

I thought about my interests. For months now I had been thinking about my interests. Also about my material possessions. Mostly books. Things come and go, Shirley said.

"I made a will," I said.

"You made a will? You didn't mention that before."

"It was Jack's idea," I said. "I signed it today. You want to know who inherits?"

Shirley glared at me. "No," she said.

"I left everything to you—and to Gloria. In the will I said to my wife Shirley and in the event of her death to my daughter Gloria."

"I hate wills," Shirley said.

"Shirley, I want to adopt the child."

"What?" She put down her catalogue. She frowned. She was examining my face for seriousness. "Gloria, go read in your room, I want to talk privately to Alex," she said.

"I won't listen," the child said.

"Go."

We waited.

"I want to adopt the child."

"There is a father," Shirley said.

"He is not a father—he is a biological occurrence."

"Do you want her to take your name?"

"Yes."

"Then she wouldn't have a name of her own."

"My name would be her own."

"Does this have something to do with your *own* father? I mean why now with Walter sick? Wills make people morbid."

"My will did not make me morbid. And why the hell should this have anything to do with my father?"

"You never mentioned it before," Shirley said. "We should ask Gloria. I feel she should share in the decision."

"She reads fairy tales."

"I don't see how that applies."

Shirley has an IQ of one seventy-five. God knows what the kid has. I love the child. I didn't feel that at first—not that she was particularly nasty or anything. No, she was all right. But I didn't love her. My love for her has grown. I wasn't stupid—I knew that she wasn't my child in the classical sense, but I loved her, I wanted to be her father.

"Would I have to call you something instead of Alex?" Gloria asked.

"Like what?"

"Like Daddy."

I looked at her. "Yes," I said.

"All right," she said. "Could I use Father or Pop sometimes? Angela says Pa sometimes. Says it makes her father mad."

"All of these are suitable substitutes. The name of your choice."

Shirley was balancing from foot to foot, also, she was nibbling at her thumbnail. "You understand," she said to Gloria, "that if we do this—and I'm not saying that we will—that this changes your relationship with Paul."

"Oh him," Gloria said.

"A serious matter," Shirley said.

Gloria paid no further attention.

"Guess what?" Shirley said.

"What?"

"Martha Kessel called up. She was looking up old friends, traced us through the newspapers."

"Through the newspapers?"

"I didn't like it, either. But she remembered your father's first name, also your mother's. You know how I feel. I feel grateful that Simon is not an unusual name—otherwise most people would think it was us—us and the Hole."

"Why would you care? You don't use the name. You use Paul's last name."

"I'm used to that name," Shirley said. "The thing is—she invited us to dinner—a spaghetti dinner. I'm afraid that I said yes. Gloria can go downstairs to the Plomers."

"All right," I said. "It's all right." I went into the bedroom to change my shirt. I looked out the window, down at the street. I lived in an apartment building. Many floors, many people. All the rooms were probably square, and the outer façade was smooth. Would I dig this building up?

Shirley had put on a high-necked peasant blouse, a khaki skirt, and her new boots and covered it all with a thrift shop outsized coat.

"Martha is working now in an advertising agency," she said. "And she's living with what's-his-name—remember—Karl."

Yes, Karl the conservative. And Martha was looking up old friends. Were we old friends? I carried a bottle of burgundy as our contribution to dinner. We could walk to Martha's apartment. We were warmly dressed against the evening chill. Candy wrappers, bits of newspaper, lost brown paper bags, blew past us. It was only eight blocks away, one block off Broadway. It was already getting dark, the sky settling into bands of darkness. I knew that we would take the bus home.

We found the building, gray stone, fading graffiti. No good slogans to remember. Just names and numbers—James 125, Pete 176. There was a doorman, but he was reading the newspaper. We did not interest him. Possibly we didn't look dangerous.

Shirley checked the buzzer names. "Third floor," she whispered.

We rode the elevator in silence.

"Welcome," Martha said and opened her door as soon as the bell sounded. She was a short, thin brunette. The prettiest thing about her was her black hair which she wore hanging down in two thick braids like a child.

"For God's sake," Martha said and kissed both of us on the lips. "Ages, just ages."

Martha took the bottle of burgundy, but there wasn't going to be any spaghetti after all. "For the three of us," Martha said, "I decided what the hell. We're old friends. I got Kentucky Fried."

Shirley gave me a quick look.

"All right," I said. "Fine."

We followed Martha into the living room. It was neat, even smart looking. Chrome and black leather, white rug.

"Karl's stuff," Martha said and waved at the room. "He's in Chicago tonight."

Martha brought a bottle of vodka, a carton of orange juice, and glasses. "Here," she said. We sat down on either side of the glass-topped coffee table.

"How's Karl?" I said.

"The same," Martha said. "Only fatter. Listen, tough about your folks."

I nodded.

"How long have you been back in the city?" Shirley asked.

"Three months," Martha said and tilted her glass. "I left the Coast three months ago. Did you know Elaine—the calligrapher? Anyway, Elaine and I went out to the Coast together last spring. We shared out there. I knew her from our kiddie days—same street, same schools. She was the child who stayed with her parents until they croaked—if you know what I mean. She got everything. Then she married a man from Bolivia. I used to go to their apartment in Washington Heights. He was remote, distant, inhospitable. Elaine's husband would sit in a room in his own house all dressed up in suit, tie—like he was going to a function or something. One day Elaine told me he said that he was returning to Bolivia. New York, he told her, was a place for heathens. Did he expect Elaine to come along? No way, he says. His missionary zeal didn't go that far. Elaine was left behind. Who needs him? she said. Then my Coast deal came up and she went out there with me. She's still there."

"When I graduated college for the first time," Shirley said between sips from her glass, "I lived for a while in New York, and then I went back to the Bronx to stay in my mother's apartment. She didn't ask me to do that, but she was feeling bad again. While I was in college, she had two small nervous breakdowns. They had her for a time in Jacobi Hospital, but she was never actually institutionalized. She had been in love with a man whose wife was very sick. She can't do it anymore, he told my mother. From the neck down all she does, he said, is have the shakes. For five years he promised my mother that she was going to be wife number two. Then his wife finally died, and one month later he married a neighbor, a widow. For the best, he told my mother. Two breakdowns. Then my mother began taking evening courses at CCNY. She met her second husband there. He's in kitchen remodeling. It was incredible, my mother said, that he didn't want a younger woman. Everyone wants a younger woman."

"Let's eat right here," Martha said. "Do you mind eating here at the coffee table?"

Shirley looked through the glass top of the table. "The rug? It's white."

"Just be careful," Martha said. "We'll be careful. Do you mind drinking burgundy with fried chicken?"

"No," I said.

Martha brought the cardboard container with the chicken, the paper napkins, the plastic knives and forks, the wine, the corkscrew, and three very nice crystal glasses.

"Everyone just help yourself," Martha said. "Also I have cole-slaw. Tell me, Alex, how is your father? You know the news-papers."

"In the hospital," I said and reached for a drumstick. The chicken was cold.

"That hole," she said. "Big?"

"Yes."

"What does Karl do these days?" Shirley said quickly.

"The same," Martha said. "Tell me, Alex, is that hole really for an apartment building? I mean was your father really looking for an apartment building?"

"Yes."

"Interesting. I myself have recently become interested in apartment buildings."

"A hobby?"

"Business. At our agency we are promoting a chain of con-dos—stylish condos all over the country, all identical. Saunas, hot tubs, plants. The compleat living environment, if you know what I mean. The works."

Shirley wiped her hands on a napkin and carefully poured burgundy into the glasses. "Here," she said and handed me a glass. "Alex is planning to adopt my Gloria."

Martha rubbed her mouth with a napkin. "Really? Listen, Alex, I'll get right down to it. My client—my agency's client—is one hell of a big real estate corporation. I dreamed up an idea—I'll admit to being proud of it—an advertising campaign featuring your hole. I call it "An Apartment Worth Digging Up"—with pictures of your family digging away, pictures of the hole—hu-morous captions. I think that it's Bingo, Alex."

"Bingo, Martha," I said and spilled a glass of burgundy on the rug.

Shirley apologized to me later, and I accepted her apology. How could she have known?

notes to walter

Walter, did I mention to you that I have made out a will? It wasn't my idea. It was Jack's idea. Jack said that I should have a will. There is something very adult about having a will, I discovered. It was funny, though—I don't have much to bequeath—mostly my life insurance. But nevertheless I happily bequeathed whatever there was. Jack said that you have a will. I didn't ask him. I don't care whether you have a will. Jack said that you made out a will ten, fifteen years ago—a standard will. How did your will come up? Jack got a telephone call. It was from Castleberry and it concerned wills. Jack told him that Simon business wasn't his business. Wills are premature when a man is still alive.

I don't know, Walter, why I make my brother go over and over the night the fountain was found. It doesn't haunt my dreams—no visions of fountains spouting water into the air. Nothing like that. What am I looking for? Another drop in the Hole. Know what I did last week when I knew that Norman was at the hospital with you and Mother?—I drove to the Bayley Farm House. It should have been raining, I should have checked the time; it was essentially a day for spies, for activities that involved strange devices and codes—but the sun shone with a glare that eliminated shadows. Why did I ascribe strange unseasonable weather to the Hole? Why wasn't it winter?

What I did, Dad, was to park my car in the driveway and walk the circumference of that Hole, around and around. Counting my paces, my irregular steps. It's a hike, a real hike. Cautiously, I approached the rim and looked down—a haze obscured the bottom. I had some plans, like a kid with a Dick Tracy Magic Ring. I was going to take soil samples. An amateur geologist at work. Why was I going to take soil samples? Trace elements, heavy stuff. I had prepared little cellophane bags.

What I actually did was to take a shovel. We certainly don't lack for shovels. I took a blunt-nosed bulldog of a shovel. I waved it, testing its balance. I lifted a shovelful of earth from the rim—grainy, pebbly—and I dropped that earth into the Hole. Then I took another shovelful. First thing you know, I working up a sweat throwing dirt back into that Hole. Ten, fifteen shovelsful of earth, going down and sending up echoes of dust. I was doing this, my breath heaving, when after a few moments I thought I saw something. No, not something—someone. I thought I saw a touch of that plaid flannel by the windbreak. Someone either stepped quickly behind the tree or vanished in a crash of bushes. I felt a pain in my chest—deep, non-organic. My arms ached. I dropped the shovel, it hit a rock and made a sound like a bell.

Was that Conlon snooping around? When did we become his responsibility? Dad, what can he hope to find? I mean you dug a hole—that's all. No crime in digging a hole.

Conlon, I yelled, come on out, Conlon. Come on out, you son of a bitch!

No one appeared.

Norman has cleaned up your fountain, Dad. Too bad you can't see it. All the mud is gone, and it sits in the middle of decaying winter grass. It is not beautiful. In truth, it is a hunk of concrete—big, well-proportioned, but plain. And it is totally grey. I suppose it could have been decorated with carvings or scallops or gargoyles. Time and burial could have worn it smooth. I don't know why Norman keeps it.

As a matter of fact, I would rather that Norman spent less time at the Hole. Do you know that he goes down to the bottom of the Hole? Yesterday I received a telephone call from Eileen in L.A. I'm worried, she said. I'm worried about Norman.

I fail to see what there is to worry about Norman. Norman is smart. Truly, truly smart. He can find his way. Still, I make him retell the events of that night. Running in the mud. I try to feel that mud, glide my mind along it. I try to picture it, brown mud in waves hitting the shores of the Hole. Had it been that wet—has it rained since? The mud oozed, slithered. Were you careless, Walter, there at the rim with that thing, that fountain. The fountain was heavy, yet it swayed in the air on a trapeze with no net beneath. Eureka, they say you shouted. I hear that. I see Mother running towards you. Stop, she yells.

At that point I need Norman. I need his presence, his presence there. I need him to tell me exactly what occurred. I make him tell me over and over, all the details.

I think that he is holding back.

One day Mother yelled at me. Come, come, Alexander. We were somewhere. We were in our apartment, one of our apartments. I ran to the sound of her voice. She was in the living room, standing by the window. I went to stand by her side. I was nine, maybe ten. Look, Alex, she said. I looked. It was a poplar tree that she pointed out to me. A tree that I knew. Something to do with the way the shadows were on the leaves. Oh the green, she sighed. Can you believe it, Alex. I stared, I looked, I tried. It was nothing to me, nothing. It was just green, just maybe dark green because of the shadows. I pressed my nose to the glass. What she saw—I do not know. Mother was an artist, and I was not.

Father, I am going to adopt Gloria. Shirley's Gloria. You like her, I know. I think of her already as my child, my heir. Shirley told Gloria once about how she met her daddy—that man Paul. How I met your daddy, she said. In an elevator—it was very romantic. It was the way life went in a Cary Grant film. The elevator got stuck, she said. High up in a building. Just past the twenty-fifth floor. There were four of us in the elevator. A skinny man with surprisingly thick and curly hair. Your daddy. A knock-out of a blonde. And me, Shirley. Ordinarily, Gloria, she said, I wouldn't have a chance against that type of a blonde, a beautiful woman.

The elevator got stuck, shuddered, and then the lights flickered off and on. Off and on. The blonde became upset. Don't worry, Gloria's future daddy said to the blonde. He had stepped back to stand next to her. The lights went off, the blonde screamed. She yelled, high-pitched, a falling bird screech. The skinny man had a lighter. He clicked on a small flame. Everyone had moved to a separate corner except the blonde. She stood right there in the middle of the elevator floor and kept on screaming. She was hysterical. The lights came back on, but that didn't stop the blonde. The sounds she made had contorted her face, destroyed the reality of her appearance. You daddy didn't want to be near her. He was afraid that she might say that he had done something there in the dark. He moved towards me. We're just stalled, he said. Tremendous safety record, elevators. The lights went off again. The sound from the blonde grew louder. The skinny man said, Let us kneel and pray. He knelt, the blonde knelt, both by the light of the cigarette lighter. Your daddy looked at me and I at him. We were giggling. When the elevator moved again and reached the lobby, your daddy asked me to go to the coffee shop with him.

That's what she tells Gloria. That's the story of how Shirley met Paul.

I saw Shirley and fell in love at once, Dad. She stood and was reflected in a window, her brilliantly colored red hair and a dress of green. I thought she looked like a Jewish Christmas Tree. I saw vibrance and no subtlety, and I was fed to the ends with subtlety and with women who argued the points, the semantics of this or all issues. It was of course fitting that the dress was a gift from her daughter purchased in the company of her grandmother but selected by Gloria. It would never have been purchased by Shirley. But I didn't know that and having given my heart—I am forever bound.

Shirley and I spoke about Norman last night. We were in bed, Shirley and I, tumbled together, soft beneath the blanket.

Norman, Norman, Norman, Shirley raged. Say something

else to me. He's there in that house with that weird semi-wife of his. Can you bear it? And how did he get power of attorney, I'd like to know. Has Walter cognizance enough to give it?

A joint decision, I said.

I waited until she was asleep, then I let myself become a Peeping Tom and shyly lifted the edge of her gown. I stared at her body in the grey night light as if it were new to me. I did not touch her, the lightest touch and she would wake up. So I just looked at her body, the swelling lines, the legs straight and together, and I took an inventory.

Walter, here is an article that Eileen sent to me from the Coast. You wouldn't believe what they emphasize in this one. It's from a Santa Barbara newspaper—a weekly. It's about athletic strength—really. Listen, Dad.

> *Look at the Hole! This was dug single-handedly by Walter Simon who lives in Upstate New York. Mr. Simon, a man somewhere in his fifties, trained for six months before attempting this stupendous dig. When interviewed, Mr. Simon stated that he had added to his diet the following: wheat germ, lecithin, activated yeast, and kelp. Mr. Simon says that good nutrition makes anything possible.*

Mother said that they made this stuff up. Mother said that she did not permit these people access to the house. Dad, they never interviewed you, did they?

Walter, will your hair turn completely grey? Yes, of course, it will. I wonder though if it will go slower for you now. Your skin grows smoother and lines leave it every day. When I touch your hand, I know that it is different. Bit by bit life is sloughed off. Your hand slips across mine like glass. Someone cuts your hair, shaves your face. I would do that for you.

. . .

Pop, I am going to make a deal with you—I want you to make a sign to me. Make the slightest movement on request, any movement will do. And I will keep the secret, I will not speak about it to anyone. You can stay here as long as you want. All right, on the count of two either flutter an eyelid, move a hand, yawn, or stretch a leg.

TWO

I received a telephone call today from a voice that cracked like dry toast.

"Alexander," he said, "do you know who this is?"

"Yes," I said.

"Who?"

"Eric DeLeuce." A wild guess.

"Good boy. Trying to reach your family. Has your father's telephone in God-forsaken-land been turned off?"

"No," I said, "the number is unlisted."

"Your father is still alive?"

"Yes," I said.

"Alexander, you always seemed to be a bright boy to me, skinny, but all right. I am thinking of offering you a position in one of my organizations."

"I don't need one," I said.

"Man must have a future. How's your mother?"

"Fine."

"Can you get a message to her?"

"Yes."

"Tell her Fanny's kicked the bucket. You remember that?"

"Fanny's kicked the bucket."

"Good boy."

I hung up the telephone.

"What did he want?" Shirley said.

"He was just inquiring about everyone's health."

I went into our bedroom. This was a small apartment where we lived, this was a tiny place, this was what I could afford. On top of the dresser was the newest package from Norman. I knew that it was there like an infected finger throbbing away. It was waiting for me—that badly wrapped parcel with the brown paper folded into lumps at the ends. The post office had no standards. The address, though, was carefully printed. Why did Norman keep besieging me?

Everything has altered. In truth, the family used to be divided differently. Norman was essentially Walter's child, while I cleaved to Mother. The oldest boy filling the father's expectations, the youngest claimed by the mother. A perfectly natural division—now reversed.

I don't just open an envelope from Norman—no matter how speedily delivered. No, I let it sit, let it stew, let it marinate. A lot of those envelopes hold papers to be signed. I scribble my signature as quickly as possible. Thank God, the responsibility is his. Get a lawyer, Shirley advised. How the hell do you know what you're signing? We have a lawyer, I said and invoked the name of Jack R. V. Haight. How do we know whose side he's on? Shirley said.

I receive more mail these days, letters pressed into our box between the catalogues. It is amazing how much mail I get. I receive letters from an advertising agency. Too good a deal to pass up, they say. Think it over, Alexander. A letter came from real estate developers—Come, they urge. We'll fly you and the kiddies to sunny Arizona. I got a request to set up a Hole Exhibit in a gallery. Papier-mâché sculptures with stone—meaning and significance.

"Want to go to the movies?" Shirley called out. "There's a Fellini festival."

"No."

"Mind if I go with Sy and Lee?"

"No."

"Make Gloria go to bed by nine."

"Yes."

The contents of an unopened package did not exist. I tried to hypnotize myself into believing that. Closed my eyes, opened my eyes. Made secret pacts. This package did not exist with its brown paper enlivened by the brightly colored insignia of speedy service.

But I had to open it, because Norman would call. Did you get it? he would ask. How could I lie, arouse his suspicions, plunge deeper his pain. I went to make myself a drink. I could see Gloria in her room reading the *Red Book of Fairy Tales*. She didn't like to be disturbed.

I poured the drink, went back to the bedroom, and waited until I could feel the alcohol, before I opened the package. Big, thick. I ripped the paper and inside was a notebook with firm covers. Scotch-taped to the cover was a note from Norman.

I thought about espionage and betrayal and countries destroyed, dark secrets on back roads where mysterious cars with out-of-state plates met.

Could I read about my mother?

The journal was recent, written in black ink. *A record,* Mother wrote on the first page, *of various events.* A litany, a wife's pain. Things that Walter had done, both past and present, the birthing of the Hole. The problem was—Walter couldn't object, couldn't defend himself.

This and this happened, she wrote.

It wasn't so bad.

Then she stopped. She changed directions, she went from horizontal to vertical. Whatever the original purpose of the journal—it became different.

I am an artist, she wrote. *It is a difficult life to understand. We lived in the city, the children were little, and I worked all day. I came home in the evening to snatch a few hours for my art. Stolen time to treasure. I sat alone in a room with strange unreal light and tried to remember what had crossed my thoughts, the hues, the tones. What had I seen that day? Hard to recapture visions. Colors mellowed and flowed. One Saturday I went to a gallery, looked at paintings, and met my old teacher. Atkins. What the hell happened to you? he said. Didn't I warn you? he said.*

The telephone rang. It was Norman.

"She had an affair with him," he whispered.

"What?"

"Mother and what's-his-name that teacher of hers. They had an affair, we were kids, they met on Saturdays."

"Bull," I said. "We always knew where she was on Saturdays. Dragging us places, to dentists, to relatives."

"I couldn't read the journal," Norman said. "I read only two pages."

"Long ago," I said. "We were kids. Even if it were so—it was years ago. But I don't believe it—I think she wrote it to make Dad angry. He was supposed to find the journal and be mad."

"That's what you think?"

"Yes," I said. "That is absolutely what I think."

We met in his studio, she wrote. *He had stopped teaching, was trying to do what he taught, I guess. It wasn't much of a studio, small, cold. You could have a corner, he said. You could paint here.*

I was delirious with pleasure. I felt colors all that day, I could not use the color green enough, I leaped through the hours. Was there a price? Did it matter? If we made love—if I rejoiced with him—as artists will.

"What's this?" Shirley said. The letter had been left unfolded on the table.

"Just a letter from the DeLeuce Foundation," I said.

"What do they want? You get something from them every week."

Shirley has a code of behavior. Shirley will ask anything, but she would never read someone's mail.

"Old man DeLeuce offered me a job," I said. "Big salary. In this letter he says that I can become a Senior Program Officer. We can operate from the West Coast, if we want. He'll pay our moving expenses out there. The works."

"My God," she said.

.   .   .

"Norman," I said on the telephone, "have you told anyone about this journal?"

"No," he said, "no one. Wait—Mother is walking by."

We were silent.

"She's gone now," Norman said, whispering into the receiver.

"No one," I said. "Don't even tell Eileen."

"I couldn't read it," Norman said.

"Towards the end," I said. "It's short, anyway. But the last entries—the last few entries mention, suggest that she has seen him again."

"Who?"

"The teacher—what's-his-name—Atkins."

"Seen him recently—you mean now?"

"I mean like a few months ago."

"Shit."

"I'm going to look around for him," I said. "See if he's in the city."

"Why?"

"Something that I think I should do. It's Conlon-related."

How did I actually meet Shirley? She moved into my building. I saw her arrive. I was standing by my window, an idle day. Three old women I knew were sitting outside the building on folding chairs, the cheapest chairs with thin webbing of criss-crossed green and white plastic, supermarket chairs. The old women had placed their chairs in a row near the curb facing the building where they could watch the people. It was amazing that no one had chased them away. It was not a street where women sat like that. For some reason they had left the building, and one of them had said "Here"—and they sat. The women all lived with married daughters, everyone waiting until the mothers grew old enough and enfeebled and could be properly put away into one of those nice places with names like Homes for _____ or Daughters of _____ or Children of _____. Meanwhile they sat there, the mothers of married daughters in front of the building. They sat there watching. Three old women wearing thin polyester cardigans on a day when all the young ones passing had bare arms, strapless halters, cool shorts.

"Mother," one of the daughters had said right beneath my window. "Mother, it is hot as hell. How can you stand that sweater?"

An old woman shrugged.

"No matter," the daughter said then and patted that sweater-clad arm. But hadn't the daughter's eyes narrowed? With all that fat, that padding, the old woman ought to feel the heat, the daughter must be thinking. Was the temperature regulating mechanism breaking down? Wearing out?

The three women sat. Joseph the doorman could not make them move. He lacked an authoritative physique. He was short, skinny. He didn't like seeing them there. They gave the building the wrong look, destroyed the effect created by the marquee. The women in turn didn't like Joseph.

The truck pulled up in front of the apartment building. *Let Us Move You Within the City Limits.* That was the truck. Joseph hurried out to the curb. "Ladies," he said. "The truck has got to unload. A new tenant."

He had them all right. They couldn't sit there blocking the passage of goods. Besides, they were afraid of truck drivers. Truck drivers unlike Joseph were not answerable to married daughters.

"All right, all right," one of the women said. She tightened her grip on the handle of her straw purse and slowly stood up. Her legs were thick, firm poles, and she wore beige cotton stockings which blurred purplish-blue bumps. All three women were standing now, folding up the chairs. The truck driver and his helper had already opened the double doors on the side of the truck. The women were directly in the path of those doors. The women might have separated then, it was almost noon, one could have napped. The kitchens were theirs alone at noon—queens of the kitchen.

In a moment the women would have been gone. A taxi pulled up and stopped abruptly behind the truck. The woman who got out was arguing loudly with the taxi driver. "I thought you were going to hit that truck," she was saying. "I thought you were goddamn going to ram that truck. I banged my knee, do you know I banged my knee in your goddamn cab!"

The three women backed up to the two-foot iron railing that protected a few mongrel shrubs from animals. The women were now to the left of the building's entrance, blocking nothing. They reopened their chairs and sat down.

The woman yelling at the taxi driver had red hair, dyed probably to the interior lights of the beauty shop. In daylight the hair was flaming, too-bright red. The woman wore a green dress and a paisley scarf tied around her neck. One of the old women recognized the scarf. "That is," she said, "the twin of my married daughter's scarf. A Liberty scarf. Do you know what those cost?"

"Look at the hair," another said, "like the baby's crayons."

Was the new tenant from the city? The woman with red hair cursing the taxi driver sounded as if she had been educated elsewhere, but none of the listeners were travelled enough to identify the accent or perhaps it was just the distinct pronunciation.

When the woman with the Liberty scarf turned completely to face them, the old women saw that she was the age of their married daughters.

"Unload, unload," the woman ordered the truck driver.

"Not an hourly rate, lady," the driver replied. "It's a flat rate. You got a flat rate. So if we want to take a break, we break."

The old women watched. Would she do anything? Joseph was listening, enjoying, maybe trying to estimate if she was a tipper.

The new tenant came over to where the women sat. "Hi," she said. "My name is Shirley. How's the building?"

"Nice," one woman said.

"Good," said another.

"Which floor?" the third said. The new woman sounded like noise, stereos, loud parties. Sons-in-law were not crazy about noises, they fled, sometimes they moved.

"Eleventh, facing the street," Shirley said.

"Breezes," one of the women said. "You'll have breezes."

"But traffic sounds," said another. And then astonished at her boldness—it came from another time—she asked, "How many in your family?" New tenants were never available for questions. Not if they were of the age of married daughters.

"Two—me and a child, a little girl."

"Your husband?"

"He's gone to California."

The woman asking the question nodded. Her daughter had friends with husbands who had also gone west.

Shirley waved at the women. "Watch the truck," she joked. "Don't let them bounce the stereo more than once."

She went over to Joseph. "Here," she said to Joseph. She gave him five dollars. "Watch the stuff."

"Yes," Joseph said. "Yes, ma'am."

As far as I know, those women never spoke to Shirley again nor she to them. Maybe they were warned. Don't mix too much with the neighbors. I officially met Shirley the day she moved into the building. After the adoption, I plan to recount this meeting to Gloria. Maybe I'll change it.

One Saturday an ambulance came to the building and took one of the old women away. Her daughter followed the stretcher all the way to the curb. "It's all right," she kept saying. "It's all right."

noTes To walter

Flesh, Dad, soft flesh. I think you should try to zero in on flesh.
Never mind the philosophical, the shadowy. No one ever had a
good time that way. Think of appetites. Think of the long sexual
life of man.

Don't cut it short, Dad.

Sex, Walter. You must miss sex? What the body has once
known, can it freely give up? Just think, Dad, confined as you
are, even the cutest nurse can't be seen, appreciated. And I swear
to you, there are sights to be seen even here. Can you bear it,
Walter, not to fuck anymore, to deny your body? I know that you
were a looker, a viewer of tight asses, well-adjusted boobs. Walter,
surely you do not want to give this up in the very middle of your
life cycle. Tender yearnings gone to waste. Just remember—
whatever you haven't done—can still be done.

Believe me, Pop, I couldn't just lie there like some goddamn
stone. Would I give up a life of loving that easily? Listen, when
I was thirteen I was already a bad kid. I went after a neighborhood
girl—did I go after the three who chased my friends? No way, I
said. Easy bear, I thought. I went for a virgin queen named Lila.
The engineer's daughter two floors down. I was way past looking
up skirts, I was into deflowering. And it wasn't easy—where
could we go? There was no car—even when I was older. There
was no car, no back seat, not even an unmoving backseat. Lila
had a full house—parents, two kid sisters, babysitters. Someone
always in the apartment. They encouraged me, the parents. Lila
is young to have a boyfriend, they said. But such a nice boy, they
slurped. And he lives in the same building too.

Sweetie puss, Lila said, no cock tease. Find someplace.

At thirteen, Dad—where?

I did the inevitable, Pops, I brought her home. Honest. Home
to foggy bottom. In our very own apartment. There you were—
a burglar could have attacked—Mother painting in the corner,
you with Tchaikovsky blaring.

Hush, I said to Lila's splendid brunette charms. If you giggle, we are lost. Lila pressed her training-bra boobs against me. Later I knew that I was wrong—they were all they should have been. We couldn't tiptoe down that corridor, because if seen we were in search of books, papers—if unseen, we were on special business. I marched my girl proudly down the hall. Unseen. We made it to my bedroom. I had no lock, but I wedged a chair under the door. I like this, Lila whispered. This is crazy. We stripped. I unhitched my corduroy trousers. Preliminaries kept to a minimum. I went at her, Dad, with the ferocious tenacity of a young cat. Did I deflower her? I wasn't skillful enough to know.

That was not my last tryst in the family halls. I had discovered that it was possible to bring a girl down the hall under everyone's eyes. It permitted a comfortable evening's fucking on clean sheets without any great danger. Until I acquired Lucy. Lucy was the daughter of an obstetrician, a man who could not call his time his own. Her mother had migraines. At Lucy's suggestion we even reversed the process. I went on occasion down her hall. This scene however was filled with too many unknowns for me; at Lucy's apartment I was very nearly impotent and at a mere fifteen. I heard noises, I jumped. Once her father stood outside our door and called—"Lucy, are you home?" My naked body shivered. Could I jump from a twelfth-floor window? We hung together breathless. No whispers, no answers.

Hell, I said, this is not for me.

Lucy wanted to spend an entire night with me. Fuck, fuck, fuck, she said. That I assured her was asking for trouble. Even my family's apartment at night was quiet, sounds would be heard. Lucy was a moaner. I can do it, Lucy said. I'll wait until my father gets a certain type of call, the two in the morning call. Then after he goes, I leave, walk two buildings, and you meet me. What if he comes home early? I asked. He's not going to look in my room for Christ's sake, she said. He'll fall into bed cursing, that's all. In the morning I'll go back home. We can't do it, I said. If not you, Lucy shrugged, then someone else.

. . .

Dad, we could exchange confidences. Why not?

I set myself the task of learning the parts of the female body,
a bar mitzvah speech of growing up. This preceded the period
when I collected tales that I heard from other boys. Collected
and wrote them down—breast stories, genital feeling-up stories.
exposure stories, the art of getting it. Some of the boys could be
goaded into giving names, some not. I would use those names
in the accounts I wrote—true life, you see. Later I wondered
whether it was so, if what they said had actually happened. When
certain names recurred, I would seek out that girl—not to involve
myself, but just to observe, to wonder if indeed she had allowed
the softest, deepest pinks of her body to be opened to inspection
by strange, rude fingers. If indeed the easily hardened penis of
that stranger had entered her. You wouldn't believe the details
that I craved to learn about these girls. Sometimes, I befriended
them, became a confidante. They could trust me, they could talk
to me. But the names of wild girls rarely appeared on my lists.
Their availability was the problem—they seemed without mystery, these girls.

Walter, things happened. I had no idea about protection,
about diseases—there was a dry spell when I was sixteen. I was
weary of masturbation. I went with Salvo to a certain woman
pointed out by Salvo's brother. She used her apartment. She was
a middle-aged woman, neat, soft-spoken.

I got something, Dad. I caught a disease in my stupidity. I
was frightened, ashamed. I didn't know who to tell. Should I
confess to Norman? He was lofty, he was clean. Stupid, I imagined he would say. You are defiled. You are sick. What I did,
Dad, was to go downstairs to Dr. Shapira. I saw him alone. I
asked him to see me. Look, I said. Dumb kid, he said. Come on,
come on—drop your pants. He treated me. He did it without
money, without telling anyone. I was grateful. Later, I learned
more things. I learned to be careful. I learned an entire list of
names, disorders of the genitals, flutterings of the spirit.

I left home at an early age, Walter. I moved out mostly for

women, never mind what I said at the time. I moved out for an endless, non-stop array of women. They constituted my ambition. So I went on a marathon fucking spree. In my one and one-half rooms. I went through all those I might have missed first time around. And surely all the expected events happened—I got diseased again, I got beaten up once by someone's boyfriend, once by a brother. For stealing what was stolen or for what, I was not certain. I received threats.

I also read dirty books, Dad. At one time, Walter, I had a truly large, truly impressive collection of books on filth. Some off the racks of girlie book collections, but some rare and honorable volumes of erotica. I plunged myself into my collection, rooting around in search of treasures. I still have these books. They are in a locked glass cabinet, because Gloria is in the apartment. They are under lock and key.

Dad, I am willing to read dirty books to you, willing to describe in detail sessions of sex—in complete detail. You just name the type and age of girl, and I will tell you what happened. All this, Dad, I am willing to do—just move one goddamn finger. Also, Walter, I have in my possession a journal that I could read to you. A graphically descriptive journal. You won't like it, I mean you will not want to hear this—this journal was written by Mother, by your wife—but yes, I will read it to you if necessary. It will definitely make you angry, livid, furious. This is a warning.

THree

Norman called me at the library. I don't think that he had ever called me there before. When I heard his voice, identified it on the telephone, I was sick, I expected the worst.

"What happened?" I said.

"I had a fight," Norman said.

I listened to the rattle of his breathing. "A fight?" I whispered. "You mean a physical fight."

"Nearly," Norman said.

"Nearly? How nearly?"

"I pushed him," Norman said. "He wouldn't leave—it's our property. He didn't fall down, but I distinctly pushed him. He yelled about lawyers, about physical assault—he lost his temper."

"You pushed him," I said. "You pushed Conlon."

"What? Not Conlon. Why would I push Conlon? I pushed Castleberry."

"Why?"

"He appeared here," Norman said. "It was unexpected. I was in the Hole. I heard him calling my name. I looked up. I thought he had come back for the money—changed his mind and wanted the twelve thousand back. But it wasn't that. I want you to stop digging in the Hole, he said. Leave the Hole alone. I grabbed my rope and climbed up. Who do you think you're talking to? I said. I want my Hole undisturbed, Castleberry said."

"Norman," I said, "how could he say that? *My* Hole?"

"He said Walter made a new will. He said that Walter was leaving Bayley Farm House to him."

"Hell!"

"So I pushed him. Furthermore, he said that the motel was to go to Stopwood—this added after the push." Norman paused, cleared his throat. "Alex, do you believe that there's a new will?"

"No," I said, "of course not."

"The man's a skunk, Alex, a pure skunk."

"Norman," I said, "did Mother ever mention a will—a new will?"

"No, why would she? Walter handled all that stuff through Jack. Jack never said anything about a new will."

"Because there isn't one," I said.

On Wednesday, I decided to go to Bayley Farm House. It was spur of the moment. Should I have told Shirley? That would have meant explanations, reasons, a purpose. I left as if going to work—I called in sick. I had twenty-three sick-leave days left at the library. They were rapidly vanishing. I knew the way to Walter's house, the curves in the road, the best gas stations. The map stayed folded in the glove compartment. I held different views than Walter, I kept a car in the city. The country air did not soothe me, it was disquieting. Leaves rasped across the ground, unknown vegetation sprouted. The sky was clear, the air vaguely moist.

In my pocket flat against my chest was another letter from Eric DeLeuce. Why, he inquired, had my mother never telephoned him or written? Had I told my mother about his calls? About Fanny?

Never, Mr. DeLeuce.

Also the letter contained another offer. *With me*, DeLeuce had written, *you have a future. I have no sons*, he added.

The man had started a siege, an attack, a blitzkreig.

How much? Shirley asked when the last letter came. This one she didn't know about. This one, I felt, was one I wouldn't just leave around.

I wasn't going directly to the Bayley Farm House. First, I'd detour to Shilton and stop at the Cheese Shoppe for a piece of Port Salut. Mother was partial to Port Salut, I thought. How often had I driven to Shilton? Not often. I generally avoided the town. But I knew where the cheese store was—next to the railroad station, tied into a bunch of new stores constructed with phony antique bricks to impersonate the past.

As I drove down the primary artery—the Main Street that should have been almost deserted at eleven a.m.—something was different, something signalled wrong. I knew that the day was not ordinary. Maybe normally I would have seen a quick sprinter from car to cleaners. But look—people! This morning there were clots of people on the street. Three here. Two there. Four farther down. Solemn folks dressed in up-country plain. I slowed the car to a crawl.

In the window of the Cheese Shoppe was a sign with large red letters—CLOSED. I turned around in the railroad station parking lot. No cheese. Maybe I'd stop in a market and bring apples. This was the apple season.

What I noticed then was that the next four stores that I passed were all closed. The hardware store, the produce market, the meat market, the drug store. Was it a holiday? No holiday that I knew about. A town holiday perhaps—a celebration of the founding fathers. At any minute I expected men with cornstarch in their hair and dressed as colonial musketeers with knickers and ruffles to appear, march two-abreast, and do battle.

Curiosity conquered. I parked the car easily, just pulled it to the curb, but I got out cautiously. There was a woman standing nearby on the sidewalk. A dour, pale woman. "Excuse me," I said to her. "What's up?"

She looked at me, I thought she smelled of glue. "A tragedy," she said. "Someone is missing—a man is missing."

A man is missing.

The scene that came to mind in the blast of morning light was that a black stretched limousine had glided mysteriously down the street, this very street, stopped, and men with fierce manner and uncompassionate eyes had leaped from the car and had grabbed someone, snatched a struggling man from the bosom of the town and driven off with him.

"How missing?" I asked.

The woman grunted. "If we knew," she said. "Terrible thing."

Go, I told myself. Better to move onward, questioning nothing, learning nothing.

"Who was it?" I asked desperately.

"One of our leading citizens," she said. "Prentice Castleberry." She sighed. "They'll find him. You can bet on that."

It was Castleberry.

How had he disappeared? Packed up his clothes, chose a lightweight airplane suitcase, cleaned out his bank accounts. He had vanished that way? I envisioned a blonde—sweet, petite, greedy.

"Gone in a flash," the woman said.

Tell me no more, I would have said. I nodded mutely. I went back to my car. The man had gone—that's all—happened all the time. Castleberry had skipped.

However, I no longer felt like going to the Bayley Farm House. Not that I actually had known Castleberry. No, it was just that his loss was becoming unbearable. It tightened my chest, it pinched. I drove back to the city—I couldn't go to work, I couldn't go home.

I had begun to keep a list of tasks, this was a new habit, there was much to do these days. I took out my list, I kept it on the back of a library check-out card, carried it with me at all times. *Atkins*—I had written that.

I drove back to my neighborhood, parked the car, skirted the shoppers, and sticking close to buildings made it to the subway station unnoticed. I pulled out a folded sheet of paper from my wallet. I had done some prior looking, some homework. There was no shortage of the Atkinses—they were invasive. I had cross-referenced the name to an artists' directory. By first name, there was one in this city, two in San Francisco. I wasn't going to San Francisco. The Atkinses weren't famous—I couldn't find their biographies, see who fit the circumstances.

I knew that I should call up the *local* Atkins. Do you know my mother? Could I say that? My mother's teacher. Hell, my mother's lover. I decided not to call him. I would arrive unannounced, unheralded. Why not? I couldn't go back to the Bayley Farm House.

This Atkins—the local one—lived in Soho. I rode the subway. I wondered if Mother knew this new place where he lived? Did she have easel space here? It was almost one o'clock. I was hungry by the time I got to Spring Street. I thought about lunch.

But I decided to find Atkins. Should such a meeting be conducted hungry?

I smelled food as I walked down the street, checking addresses. Pizza, frying fish, Greek delights. It was an artists' neighborhood, lots of people looked the part. I found the right place, an old building where Atkins lived, with halls that smelled of urine and stale, forgotten air. Splintery wood and plaster-colored walls heavy with insignias, slogans, dated messages. There were doorbells, though. Mailboxes. *Atkins*, one said, white letters on black plastic. I pressed the corresponding button. Someone buzzed back, but the outer door had not been locked.

I walked up the stairs, met no one, creaking my way upward, announcing my passage. I had four flights to walk. Someone looked down at me from the stairwell. White hair, waving arms, an old man.

"If you've come to collect for something," said the man, "save your feet, buster. No cash here."

"No," I called out. "No collection."

Atkins was old, but not as old as Eric DeLeuce. But Atkins was easily past seventy. He did not look like a man in good condition.

"Who the hell are you?" he said when I had reached his level.

"I'm Alexander Simon," I said. "Sara Simon's son."

"Who?"

"Sara Bromfield—used to be your student."

He stared at me. "You aren't *my* son, are you?"

"No."

"Good. You never can tell. A lot of this kind of thing happening today—kids in search of long lost fathers. A crock!"

"No," I said. "I am not your son."

"How is she—what's-her-name—Sara?"

"Fine," I said. I tried to look past him into the apartment. I couldn't see anything, the door was only partially opened.

"Do you still paint?" I asked.

"What kind of dumb fool question is that? Of course I paint. An artist is an artist. What did you say her name was?"

"Sara—Sara Bromfield Simon."

"Yes," he said. "My student."

I realized that I wasn't going to be invited in. We were going to stand there in the hall, assailed by smells, by dust, by the curious. Didn't I hear the latch on the nearest door slide free?

"Maybe we could talk. Lunch? Would you like some lunch?" I asked.

"Certainly," Atkins said. "Poverty is not character building. Wait until I get my hat."

He went back into the apartment, closed the door behind him. Whatever was there, I wouldn't see. I waited in the hall until Atkins came back. He carefully locked his door. We went down the stairs together slowly. He wore a plaid woolen shirt, a knitted cap. Up close he smelled of linseed oil, of turpentine. He seemed a decent enough old man.

"Where shall we go?" I asked. "It's not my neighborhood."

"Ribs," the old man said. "I crave ribs and a glass of gin." He looked closely at me. "On the other hand, I wouldn't be averse to a hamburger and coffee. It depends."

"I can afford ribs," I said. "And gin."

"Good. This way. Won't talk, though. Emphysema—can't talk and walk."

I followed the old man for two blocks. It was a small restaurant he chose, and the odors were good.

"Now," he said when we were seated. "You're her son."

I thought perhaps he had forgotten the name.

"Yes, Sara's son."

"She had talent," he said abruptly. "I seldom got a student with talent—almost never. I mean one who was an artist. Like her. But nothing came of it, did it?"

"No," I said.

"Now me," he said. He paused for the drinks that the waiter put down. "Me," he said, "I've talent. Nothing came of it either."

"You don't," I said, "think it's strange—my coming here, do you? You don't wonder why?"

"No," the old man said.

"My mother must have thought highly of you—as a teacher."

"Who knows? Could I have another glass?"

I nodded.

"When did you last see her?" I asked.

"Who?"

"My mother—Sara."

"Who the hell knows—I don't keep a calendar. My student, eh?"

"Yes."

I saw someone else here, someone else asking questions. Mr. Atkins, that person would say, how well did you know Sara Bromfield Simon? When did you last see her, Mr. Atkins?

"To tell you the truth, boy—I don't exactly remember her face—I remember the name—I think," Atkins said. "I remember knowing that she had talent. Don't marry, I advised her. Go for it, I said."

I drank my gin.

"Your lover."

"Who?"

"My mother."

"When?"

"Years ago—and recently."

"Hell, not recently. Recently, I would remember. Hardly anything, recently. Are you sure about years ago? Are you sure you're not my son? Had a daughter show up here eight or nine years ago. It didn't help her, it won't help you."

"No," I said, "I am not your son."

"If you want to know if Sara was my mistress—lover—the truth is I don't know. How long were we together? Once—a week?—a month?"

I shook my head.

"I really meant to be an artist," the old man said. "Had one student when I was teaching upstate—real talent. Don't marry, I told her. Paint! Don't listen to what they say—devote yourself."

"But," I said, "you haven't seen her recently then—my mother?"

"Is she lost? Are you tracing Sara?"

"No."

"Well then, no. I haven't seen her recently."

"Suppose I showed you a picture?"

"Show me a picture."

I pulled out the photograph from my pocket and put it in front of Atkins.

He wiped the grease from the ribs off his hands and picked up the picture. He bent close and studied it.

"She hasn't aged a bit," he said.

"God," Shirley said, when I unlocked the door to our apartment. "Where have you been?"

"Why?"

"Terrible, Alex! Just terrible! That man has been reported missing."

"Who?"

"Castleberry. It's just an item in the *Times*—but I saw it. What does it mean, Alex?"

"Possibly," I said, "that Castleberry is missing."

She stepped closer, her nose wrinkled. "You've been drinking?"

"Yes."

"I don't want to know," she said. "Don't tell me. You heard about it, didn't you?"

"Yes," I said.

"That made you drink—this early."

"Yes."

"We are in this together," Shirley said and squeezed my hand. "Eileen called from the Coast. How did she find out? I told her nothing, though. I told her you were at work. If there was anything to worry about, I told her, then you would not be at work."

"Nothing to worry about," I said. I went to wash up.

Gloria was in the hall.

"Hi," I said.

"Hi, Pa," she said.

Shirley had clearly labored over the dinner. We had a leg of lamb that had been butterflied and tied and filled with her special stuffing of herbs and mushrooms and finely ground almonds. In the center of the table in a vase were six anemones, violently tropical. "I could feast on the sight of those alone," Shirley said.

"Can I read at the table?" Gloria asked.

"No," Shirley said.

"I'm at a good part."

"You heard me!"

"Daddy, can I?"

I almost said yes—but legal adoption took a long time.

"No," I said.

After dinner I went into the bathroom. I turned on the faucet to let the running water hide the sounds. I lifted the toilet seat. I put my finger down my throat as far as I could and made those horrible gagging sounds that I remembered from childhood. I wobbled and saw only a red blurred world, uncertain how that happened. Yet I saw redness and felt rushing and pounding in my ears. I took away my hand and food splashed into the toilet bowl. I flushed it all away, taking care to wipe the rim of the bowl with tissue.

I straightened up and opened the window, pushing it up as high as it would go. Anyone who came into the room would know what happened. I opened the door to the medicine cabinet. There was a large bottle of 4711 cologne. I unscrewed the lid and sprinkled cologne generously on the floor. I brushed my teeth.

noTes To waLTer

Walter, it doesn't just come down to money and getting along. I didn't always know this, Dad. I just realized it now—I think. Here I am and what do I feel? I'm looking at you. I love you.

My God, it's true.

Walter, I love you. Father, I love you. Dad, I love you. Pop, I love you. Do you love me? I am certain that you love me too. You are a caring father. I have no complaints.

I have fought off basic emotions, Dad. I am big on banter. Sometime I will tell you how I proposed to Shirley. I don't remember whether it was different when I was a kid. No, I don't believe that even then I often said the word *love*. But Walter, I love you.

I am overwhelmed with love for you—love fills me with warmth and well-being. And Dad, I want nothing from you.

Norman sent me a small snapshot. It's a picture of the Shilton Historical Society membership. At least that's what is printed in ball-point ink on the back. You are standing in the front row, Dad. The whole front row have their arms around each other's shoulders—a standard comradeship ploy. Also on the back is an arrow directly behind your picture and initials printed—*W.S. & P.C.* I have put my finger over *P.C.* and turned the picture over. Is that Castleberry next to you, Dad? I can just make out his features. I think the picture must have been taken at Bayley Farm House. I recognize a tree in the background. You and *P.C.* have shovels—and you're resting your hands on them as if they were walking sticks.

Dad, Shirley told me that she was asked at her office whether the Hole had a purpose. These people asked her, approaching her like a delegation. They meant a purpose that was not written about in the newspapers. For instance, did you find an old map? I know that they were thinking about buried treasure. No, Shirley told them. No map, no treasure. But she asked me, Dad.

What do you think, Alex? Do you think that perhaps—just maybe—he had some such paper?

No, I did not.

I've been reading about Upstate New York, Dad. I've been searching for some clues, but they had a history just like everyone else. I've avoided asking Norman for his Lazarre file. I mean architecture has a minimal hold on me. I like Bauhaus. I like Frank Lloyd Wright. By the way, did I ever tell you my Frank Lloyd Wright story?

I was just a kid—maybe fifteen—we were riding on a bus in the Village. I was with a girl. Her name was Sandra. She was the daughter of that man who owned the Happy Appliances Store. We were on this bus, at five p.m., an almost deserted bus.

Jesus, I whispered to her. Look there.

What? she said.

There, and I pointed.

We stared. The man wore a grey-blue suit, a broad-brimmed hat. With him was a woman of his own age.

God, Sandra said. It's him.

You bet, I said. When the bus reached Eighth Street, they got up to leave. We got up to leave. Frank Lloyd Wright exchanged a look of extreme annoyance with his companion. He thought that we were following them. But it was our stop too. They ducked into a doorway. Sandra and I walked past.

Walter, guess who called me yesterday? You'll never guess. It was old Half-Uncle Cyrus.

What did he want? He wanted nothing good, I'll tell you that. Al, kid, he says. Get the names straight, I tell him. It's Alexander. You and your mama are sure causing an uproar, Al-ex-an-der, he says. Every night I thank God we got different last names. To this, Dad, I wisely answer nothing. What I'm calling about, says this little piglet, is that *my* father is worrying about your mama. Yeah, I said. He tried to call her, but I guess you didn't pay the bill—because he couldn't get through. Yes, I say. Well, have your mama call him before the old man has palpitations. All day he tells me—she shouldn't have married Walter, she shouldn't have married him. I say—Pa, it's too late. She made her bed, she spilled her milk.

I have chopped off the branch of the family tree from which Cyrus clings. Hate, Dad, can be a cleansing feeling. I remember when you told me that. Sometimes, you said, it's all right to hate. Why not? you said.

When I was a little kid, one day this guy turned up. I remember I came home from school. It must have been spring, because the rooms were cool and dark. I came into the apartment, and I heard voices from the living room. I couldn't make out any words. I went in, and there you were, Dad, sitting on the couch. You had come home too early for a school day. I only had to walk a few blocks, but you had to take the subway from Queens. Also sitting in the living room on the chair with the prickly grey covering was this man, this strange man.

Alex, you called. Come meet your other grandfather.

I trotted farther into the room. Now to my knowledge I had to date only one grandfather. He was a man who lived in a really nice place in the city. A difficult man to know. Be a businessman, he always said to me. Make a future for yourself. Once in a while he gave a quarter, but not too often. Now sitting in my living room holding a glass was Grandfather Number Two.

Hello, I said but from a distance.

Babe, this grandfather said. You are the spitting image of me. Here, kiddo.

He was handing me a dollar.

What did you do? Norman asked me later.

I took it.

Who needs him? Norman said.

But the deal had been made—he was my favorite grandfather and I was his favorite grandchild.

Once he asked me what I wanted to be when I grew up.

I don't know.

That's all right, he said. A man has a lot of options.

The second time I saw him, that grandfather took me for a walk. It was a Sunday afternoon. A car coming down the street—a flat level street loaded with sunlight—hit a tree at the corner. It did no damage to the tree except for some bark scraped away in sheets as if intentionally whittled. The car however had collapsed at once, a pugnosed injury. A lot of neighborhood people ran to the scene of the accident, we ran too. The driver got out of the car, shaky but apparently all right.

If that car had been made before 1939, a woman standing near us said, it would have been the tree that would have gone.

You bet, Grandfather said.

My late husband had a '38 Dodge, the woman continued. God, if I only had it today. We never changed the oil. Had the car through '59 and never changed the oil. Wish I still had it, but the husband and daughters nagged. Didn't want to be seen in a jalopy.

Grandfather smiled at the woman. He gave me a dollar. Can you find your way home? he asked.

What do you think I am? I told him.

The third time we met occurred in the evening—no, in the night—and I wasn't actually included. I was listening unobserved, hiding behind the door. It was past midnight, but maybe I was mistaken. They were not pleased with him, my father and mother. A lot of yelling. Norman must have been a heavy sleeper. You idiot, my mother was shouting. Get the hell out of here.

Wait, my father said. I've got fifty bucks on me. I don't have any more right now.

Out, Mother was saying. You are more than a disgrace.

A mistake, Grandfather said. Listen, Sara baby, a mistake.

. . .

Walter, I was disturbed by yesterday's occurrence. What do I mean disturbed? Disturbed isn't even slightly close. I was scared enough to piss there on the spot. I drove back to the city at top speed.

Walter, Castleberry has vanished, disappeared, skipped.

I have at some pains managed to purchase a copy of the local, the one and only *Shilton Daily*. *Local Historian Vanishes* was the headline. The only words not used were *foul play*. Christ, Dad, he has been missing more than forty-eight hours. Does a man with regular habits just vamoose? Clothes in closet, suitcases on shelf. Money—nothing missing from the regular account. Just twelve thousand big ones. The account that was searched was that of P. and F. Castleberry.

What I think: I think he has money elsewhere—in Orckin's safe maybe. I believe that a man who plans to take off has moola stashed somewhere. He can't just pick up the blonde and run. He has to have money in hand. That's what I think.

What do you think, Dad?

I believe that you must know about the money. I mean according to Jack R. V. Haight you were the biggest contributor to the Historical Society—spell that Castleberry. Where's that money gone? Didn't you ever wonder about that, Dad? I try to think about why you gave so much, but nothing comes. You were a man of practical knowledge, you could add one and one.

Other woman comes immediately to mind. Castleberry's other woman. Wife is a lump, an indoor mother-wife. Didn't Castleberry yearn for excitement? Didn't he meet the right young lady who enticed him away from his regular duties. Young, pretty, undomestic—a woman in search of thrills.

When did the good people of Shilton notice that old Castleberry was not in place?

When Wife Faith reported that he did not come home to dinner—pot roast, mashed potatoes, new peas. Did he vanish with the daily proceeds from five stores? No, he made a trip to the night depository. This is recorded. Somewhere between the night depository and Faith's bed, he skedaddled.

The car, Walter, is important. It is significant that Castleberry has his car. I mean he does not have clothes but he has his car. He has transportation. First of all, the clothes he had were country clothes, reeking of small town—not travelling clothes. I think along with the cash our Castleberry had a complete wardrobe hanging. This is what I think.

I know you, Walter. You are a man of perceptions, tastes, fun-loving. How did you get to know this character? This small-town charlatan, mountebank, lover of history. What did Castleberry have to offer?

Norman is worried, Dad. He fears a genetic pattern of disruption is lodged in our loins. When he hears about my plans to adopt Gloria, his fears will mount. You know something, he will demand. Dad has confided in you.

You never confided, Walter. I knew that Mother was an artist—but about you I only know the simple facts.

Do you know what is going on right now? I suspect that all of Shilton is hunting through the countryside for Castleberry. I see groups of men walking in the woods, beating bushes with sticks, calling his name, poking into piles of leftover leaves. Castleberry! Castleberry! A small man, narrow of physique—the snapshot Castleberry.

Castleberry didn't drive a new car. I think he owned a brown one. Norman said that. Castleberry parked in front of our house in a brown car, the color of wet mud, a well-shined brown car, glistening from care.

Dad, yesterday about nine p.m. the telephone rang. Shirley answered. She yelled to me. "Alex, Alex, pick it up."

It was Mother. Mother on the telephone.

"My God," I said.

"Be quiet and listen," Mother said. "Norman is in the yard. When he comes in, I must hang up."

"Yes," I said, whispering at my end.

"Lousy connection," she said. "Be attentive, Alex. I was called an hour ago by what's-his-name—the local cop."

"Conlon."

"Yes."

"He called you?"

"You bet. He asked me if I could account for Norman's whereabouts for the last two days. Of course I knew where Norman was every minute. Sitting in this house. He has been sitting in this house for two days, I said. All yesterday. He has been my constant companion since Mrs. Sorbitol went away. Although I hear that she may return now that our company has departed."

"Why?" I asked. "Why was he asking about Norman?"

"I think it has something to do with Castleberry. I hear he is gone, reported missing."

"Yes," I said. "How did Conlon sound?"

"He is always calm," Mother said. "Nevertheless, I want you to tell Jack everything."

Dad, at this moment it would be expedient for you to answer a question. You were a familiar of Castleberry. Where would he go? Should we look locally or in Argentina?

Four

How much could a man do? A wife, a child, a job. There were almost more items on my list of things than I could handle. Shirley was also keeping a numbered accounting of telephone calls that I must return. It was no use ignoring them—someone always called back.

"What I think," Jack was saying to me on the telephone, "is that you should speak to my friend Peter."

"Why?"

"He's an excellent lawyer," Jack said. "I wouldn't steer you wrong."

"You're a lawyer."

"This Castleberry disappearance," Jack said, "has got to be considered, Alex."

"We are not involved."

"Alex, I am unable to discuss this with Norman. Norman just clams up. He keeps saying that he hasn't seen Castleberry since Castleberry delivered the soup. What the hell does that mean, Alex?"

"I don't know."

"I think that Norman has been out at the house too long. Can't you find someone to relieve him—he needs some time to himself."

"They have a woman. She's coming back, I hear."

"Good," Jack said. "Now, Alex, write the name and telephone number of my friend Peter. I smell trouble."

I wrote down the name and telephone number of Peter.

But I dialed a different number.

Mother answered. She sounded surprised. I don't think that telephone in Walter's room had rung before.

"Can you talk?" I asked.

She hesitated. "I guess so," she said. "I'm here alone with Walter."

"Where's Norman?"

"He went for a ride. He can't sit inside all day."

"I understand. Mother, this Castleberry thing—this disappearance—does Norman talk about it?"

"I think he's upset, Alex. Look, we knew Castleberry. But if he's gone—then he's gone."

"Has Conlon come to the house? Has he spoken directly to Norman?"

"You figure it out, Alex. Do you want me to do everything?"

"Mother, just tell me this—has anyone said anything about what happened when Norman pushed Castleberry?"

"I haven't heard a word about that," Mother said. "But they made a lot of noise—woke me up. A loud argument, then the fight began."

"Fight? Norman just pushed him—pushing isn't exactly a fight."

"Pushed him? You heard incorrectly, Alex. He punched him—not pushed. Possibly Norman even bloodied his nose. I'll get you, Castleberry said. I'll get you. He was on the ground at the time."

I held my breath. "My God, Mother, we have to get another lawyer. I'll call Jack's friend."

"Wait," Mother said. "Norman was obviously provoked. And Castleberry is gone. I think he's gone. Castleberry appears to have made a clean getaway."

"Mother—"

"Wait, I hear Norman. He's talking to a nurse in the hall. He's coming now. Goodbye."

"The prognosis is not good," Dr. Herschl said. "After a time one must face facts."

"Explain," I said.

"Not a catatonic stupor. Unnatural position, extensor rigidity."

"What do you mean unnatural position?"

"He looks uncomfortable."

"He does not."

"Wrong. Anyway, and I address you as the spokesman for the family, Mr. Simon, your father is not showing any improvement. We cannot accommodate such cases. He will have to be moved to a chronic care hospital or a nursing home."

"When?"

"Within the week. We never keep chronic care—we are not equipped. Social Services will give you a list, assist in placement."

The word *placement* made me sick. I wasn't going to call anyone else. Let them call me.

"Where do you suppose a man like Castleberry would go?" Shirley said.

"Who knows. I don't know him."

"I mean just suppose he wanted to hide—for whatever reason. Where? The city? The West Coast?"

"Anywhere, everywhere," I said. "Especially if he had money. Plenty of money."

"All right," Shirley said, "I didn't mean to upset you. Gloria, go do your homework."

I sat up reading a work about the history of the Catskills. But Castleberry was on my mind. I saw him walking the streets of distant villages, I saw him wearing new fashionable clothes, I saw him leaving enormous tips.

I told Social Services that I would take my father back to the city when he left their hospital. They dealt locally, they said, but nevertheless they had contacts. The influence of the city was pervasive. Was money an object? I called Norman, and he checked the receipts in the Stopwood Motel savings account. No, money was not an object.

Social Services found two possibilities for me. I could visit the places, check them out, make a choice. I can't do it, Norman said. Go yourself. I have no opinions in this matter. So I made an appointment with the first one on the list.

Children of _____ was a grey brick building with no grounds. They handled severe cases. Was Walter a severe case? Just walking into the building I felt psychic discomfort, monumental thirst.

My appointment was with a Mrs. Topple. Reception sent me straight to her office. "Mr. Simon," she said, "you came highly recommended."

Mrs. Topple was a tiny, skinny woman all dressed in grey. Her office was a room done in shades of pale yellow with couches and chairs sized for the short.

"Thank you," I said. I had to shake her hand, I couldn't just stand there while her hand pawed the air.

She had a dozen framed photographs on her desk, all slanted to face the visitor. Adults—both singly and in groups—and solemn, unsmiling children.

"Your family?"

"Why yes," Mrs. Topple said. "A lot of people think they are photographs of the patients. This one." She pointed. "My brother—a brilliant man. Died in the war in the full bloom of his youth."

I clucked.

"We'll take a tour," Mrs. Topple said, "and then I'll show you my statistics. It's my own innovation. My books will show you that we have the lowest percentage of bedsores in the area. Our patients are turned."

I nodded.

There are some buildings that you descend into, this was one of those. I suppose it was a matter of function. Sometimes when you go somewhere you think you've dreamed the place, anticipate every corner. This was not like that. The walls were white, a slick clean white. The floors a checkerboard of tile. Lots of drains. I imagined men with hoses washing down everything in sight. Overlaying the quiet was the sound of voices, laughter, nurses,

attendants, being normal. I found that I squinted in all that clean-
liness, in the presence of so much shine.

The rooms were silent, the shapes minus a lot of hair. Hairless
lumps with low incidence of bedsores. Tubes, tanks, trays, rail-
ings.

It was easy to make my decision. I had Walter's welfare in
my hands.

"Mrs. Topple," I said enthusiastically, "my father already has
bedsores. His presence here would louse up your statistics and
bring down the batting average."

"You're an ass," Shirley said, but she was crying.

She went to The Daughters of _____ for me.

"Grass," she reported back. "Some people get well. The rooms
aren't white. I must tell you also that I smelled urine, and down
certain corridors a stale odor of frying food."

"All right," I said.

I drove out to Bayley Farm House, arriving about ten p.m. There
was just one light on downstairs. Mother must be asleep. I used
my key, I didn't ring the doorbell. The dog came running. Norman was behind her.

"You," Norman said. "I wondered why Chaminade was silent."

"Norman," I said. "Let's drink."

"Sure," he said. "Scotch?"

"Gin."

"All right."

I followed him into the kitchen. We'd sit and drink there. I
waited while Norman poured the drinks. He looked tired, thin.
The glasses he wore for reading were on the table on top of some
pamphlets.

"Norman," I said, "do I know everything about the night Dad
fell into the Hole?"

"Yes."

"About what you saw, the sounds you heard, the wetness of the mud?"

"The whole fucking thing."

"Norman, when I parked my car in the driveway—I saw some kind of shape in the yard. A hump."

"I've been piling up the bricks I found—I didn't know what else to do with them—I've been piling them up like a wall."

"How many?"

"About three hundred and twelve, sixteen pieces of tile. Nothing else, though."

"I think we should sell this place, Norman. Mother probably doesn't want to hang around. And Walter will be in the city."

"I'll take it under advisement."

"What the hell does that mean?"

"I've got power of attorney."

notes to walter

What I tried yesterday—I won't do that again. It was just that I
wanted to rouse you, Pop. I was thinking about liquor, the beneficial, the startling results of whisky. Golden brews, the blush
of amber, select malts. I bought a fifth. I planned it all out, Walter.
I put the bottle in my pocket. I wore a loose jacket, unbuttoned.
I was going to pour the whisky down your throat. I had a trial
run. I lifted your head a good three inches off the bed, a reasonable incline. I supported your head in my hands. You felt warm,
solid, substantial. I was careful not to tangle the tubes. The head,
I believe, contains the soul. I tested your lips—they moved, they
were pliable. I spilled the whisky—more in your direction than
down your throat. I thought for a moment you would not swallow.
I thought I must call out for help, but the whisky went down.
What happened, Dad? There was nothing from you—not the sign
I wanted. Not even a gasp, a choke, the smacking of lips. The
nurse came in. She sniffed in the room. I imagine they just finished an alcohol rub, I said.

Dad, guess who telephoned me? You won't be able to guess. It
was Louise. You know the wife of your friend from high school.
What does she want? First, she wants to meet me for a drink.
Why? Older woman meets younger man? I arranged a tryst in
one of those small anonymous East Side hotels that still have red
leather banquettes. We had drinks. She ordered a gimlet. I've
never been with anyone before who ordered a gimlet. I have no
idea what could be in it. It arrived in a stemmed glass. Louise
was attractive, very pale, dressed like a mystery woman all in
black. She told me that she and her husband are kaput. A confession, I thought. Do you know what her purpose was? She wanted
me to tell you, Walter. You and Mother, I suggested. No, she
didn't give a damn if Mother knew. Mother was not in that ball
park. Walter, she wanted to talk about you. It was *you*, Dad, to
whom she wished to convey this piece of news.

You know, if you were interested, I could manage to sneak Louise into the hospital. She definitely is hot for you. Alex, she said to me, you are an adult. You are no longer a child. My husband, she said, was having an adulterous relationship. The wife of another friend.

Louise is pretty, Walter. I thought she was pretty. Terrific legs. She is also fun to be around. Could you imagine her here in your room? Her hand under the covers, sliding into that peek-a-boo hospital gown. I would stand out in the hall and guard the door, Pop. It would be our secret. Just say the word.

Last night, Norman told me that while he was asleep someone came into the yard—the yard of Bayley Farm House—and knocked his wall down. Chaminade, he says, has given up on night noises. Norman is building a wall, Dad. The bricks aren't cemented in place, just balanced on top of one another. A damn fool way to build a wall. It was an animal, I told him. Deer, probably. That is definitely an area for deer.

Were any bricks missing? I asked.

No, he says, none missing.

Any thrown through a window?

He shook his head.

It was an animal, I said.

Dad, if you would just pull yourself together, Norman could go back to California where he has a very secure job waiting for him. Consider that, Walter. You are standing in your son's way.

My mail, Pop, is getting bad. I had a request to hold a revival meeting on the grounds of Bayley Farm House. What I don't understand is how they got my address. I mean how did they hook me up in the city with the upstate Simons. Shirley, I said, does anyone call and ask if we are related to those Simons? Don't be foolish, she says. You think I would tell them. Gloria, I said,

did anyone ever ask you on the telephone about us and the Hole?
No, Pa, she says.

We supply the tent, the letter said. We clean up afterwards.
This is a well-patrolled meeting, no wild shenanigans. Depending
on the collections, they said, we split on reasonable terms, less
expenses.

Walter, I heard that Faith Castleberry has employed a medium.
A genuine psychic from London, currently here in the States on
tour. I read about this in the *Shilton Daily*. The article was sent
to me anonymously. I certainly don't subscribe to that newspaper.
Mrs. Castleberry, it says, believes that the mystic will lead her
to her husband—alive or dead.

There is a picture of Faith in the newspaper. Her eyes stare
out at you, a matrix of little grey dots.

I have never once considered the possibility that Castleberry
could be dead, Dad. I have imagined him in a multitude of dis-
guises and hiding in remote areas, but never dead. Why should
Faith be so lacking in hope? She is, I understand, a devoted
mother, a devoted wife. But tell me, Walter, wasn't she involved?
Part of the scheme? Castleberry vanishes. The family bank account intact. Sounds like he left of his own accord.

The medium came highly recommended, says the *Shilton
Daily*. Many people located. The medium is known to the police.
This medium, one S. T. Joles of Lancastershire, does not use any
paraphernalia. What? No crystal ball? S. T. Joles will merely sit
at the last scene. The word *last* is misused. Last implies no more,
and Castleberry has more. This Joles (female or male) will then
get a vision. I see this vision, Walter, as a cartoon cloud appearing
above the medium's head—with words inside. Such as: *P. Castleberry is in Buenos Aires.*

What the hell can a medium do? Sniff Castleberry's clothes?
Chaminade could sniff out his clothes—for free. I have never
been to a medium. Shirley told me that once she and three friends
went to a tea room. It was up a flight of stairs. They always seem
to be up a flight of stairs, she says. Closer to heavenly vapors, I

guess. There was a gypsy—a phony gypsy with the standard gold earrings, red gauze skirt. Shirley says that the woman had on a heavy coating of pancake makeup to make her skin look swarthy. Anyway, she does the cup turning bit—three times. Abracadabra. You will marry a tall, thin blonde man from a northern country, she told Shirley. That I assure you left out Paul and me. It's also trips they predict, Shirley says. You will travel extensively in the Orient, the tea leaf reader says. Standard fare—that's what they all say you'll do. Then she started in on my friends, Shirley said.

Truthfully, Dad, I see no reason for anyone to assume that Castleberry is dead. I have been thinking about Castleberry ever since Shirley asked me where he might have gone. I have attempted to reconstruct that night. I see Castleberry closing up his Cheese Shoppe, fingering his whiskers, and redolent with cheesy odors counting the day's take. Then bank deposit bag in hand, he drives down the street. Four times he stops, business booming, he has to take his loot from store after store, counting, entering all on the deposit slip. He has to be careful. This is not the night for an innocent error—a wrongly added column. Nothing must show nervousness, point the way. He says hello to everyone he knows. Maybe a little small talk. How you doing, George? How's the wife, the kids, the mistress? Are his hands shaking, his expression anxious? I vote no, Dad. Definitely no. This is what he planned for, waited for. He has put aside all the money he needs. Hence tonight's deposit. Greed will undo you, he thinks. This is not a night for greed.

Now, Dad, we come to where will Castleberry go. Which direction? Of course, he can just drive his brown car to the city. But you and I know, Walter, that people are found in the city. Great international spies are picked up as they prepare to down roast beef sandwiches. The police would check the airlines, trains, bus terminals. What I say is this—he did not go away. Castleberry hid somewhere in the environs of Shilton. Maybe he's gone by now. I can't be certain.

Maybe not.

notes to walter

They were going to feed me dinner at Bayley Farm House. I maneuvered the invitation, Dad. I believe that Shirley suspected. But this wasn't really a social visit. Mother was cooking. She does that once in a while, Norman had told me. We were having veal parmesan, linguini with garlic and oil, and endive salad. They were waiting for me—Mother and Norman. They looked freshly scrubbed. The kitchen table was set — some white flowers in the center—and two bottles of chianti breathing on the counter.

"Alexander," Mother said and kissed my cheek. "Come and sit down."

"She's been worried," Norman said. "About the food spoiling."

"I'm on time," I said.

"Yes," Mother said.

We waited while she served and filled our plates. Norman poured the wine. I couldn't remember when the three of us had last sat down to a meal.

"Next week," Mother said, "I would like to go into the city."

"Absolutely," Norman said.

"Why?" I asked.

"Galleries," she said. "I want to look around and then check out a framer I've read about."

Mother smiled at me, and I smiled back. I was trying to relax, Pop. I waited right through the sorbet and the cups of cappuccino.

"Did Dad have any dealings with a local lawyer?" I asked.

Mother frowned and looked at Norman who shrugged. "Not that I ever heard about," Mother said. "Just Jack."

"Could he," and my voice was croaking, "have made out a will—locally?"

"Walter?"

"Yes."

"No—why should he? We made our wills a long time ago," Mother said.

"If there was a new will—just suppose—do you think it would be here at the house?"

Both of them shook their heads, Dad.

I believed them.

Walter, I haven't been to see you for a few days—I've been embarrassed. The consensus is that at the very least I made an ass of myself. The cops were involved, Dad. And there was no way that I could prove what I suspected. Walter, I want you to hear this first from me. It's about Castleberry.

Let's consider Castleberry's disappearance, Walter. He took you for a lot of cash. Maybe more than we know. He has it stashed somewhere, and he runs off—before Jack R. V. Haight can get it back. Or suppose he believed this nonsense about a will—you know with him as one of the beneficiaries, and Stopwood as another. Suppose he thinks there is such a will—but he doesn't know where it is. Could he benefit by temporarily vanishing? Flush out the will? And where would he go?

Castleberry in hiding. I couldn't stop thinking about this—it was in my system like when you see some actor in the movies and you can't remember his name, but you can't stop thinking about him. Castleberry was doing that to me.

I made a list of possible categorical hiding places—then I toured the area around Shilton. There's a lot of building going on in the county. First I looked for deserted houses, seasonally abandoned summer homes. But midway in the search, I stopped. Conlon is not dumb. Conlon would have thought of that.

But what wouldn't Conlon think of?

I'll tell you.

The Stopwood Motel.

How shall I describe it, Pop?

The Stopwood Motel Caper.

What I should have done was to get Norman. Why I didn't, I don't know. Actually, it was a reasonable idea. We knew about the close ties between the Stopwoods and Castleberry. What better place to hide than in a motel with special night services. Who was going to break in there? He could have stayed one night, two nights, a whole week. He could still be there. And the cars park around back in a field, they are unseen. Eileen told me all about this. A brown car blending into a field, cozying up to other cars, a Stonehenge in the night.

By the time I got this idea, Walter, it was six o'clock on a Friday evening. I telephoned Shirley. I want to do something at the Bayley Farm House, I said. I lied.

There are ideas—basically good ideas—that come to you at the wrong moment. By the time I drove to the motel, it was past ten. The moon was at the quarter phase. I should have waited— but I was thinking Castleberry was there. He hadn't been spotted anywhere else.

I went down that dark back-country road. I pulled into the driveway and stopped the car in front of the motel at the left end. What I noticed first was that all the window shades were pulled down tight so that only cracks of light around the edges could be seen. Now there seemed to be a gleam peeking from all the windows—but no cars, no cars out front.

I parked in front of the small red neon sign that identified the office. A man came out of that room, letting the glass storm door slam behind him. Stopwood, I figured, but I wasn't sure. I had never met him. The night air was cold, but he was only in his shirt-sleeves.

He looked me over. "Yes," he said. "Can I help you?"

"Room," I said.

"All filled," the man said.

All filled—here?

We stared at each other.

"Simon," I said. "Simon sent me. Norman."

The short man still didn't smile. "Why didn't you say that right away? Pull your car around back, walk through the passageway. I'll meet you."

.   .   .

Just like that, Dad. Obviously, I had used the right password. I got back into my car and dove off the narrow paved parking area into the field next to the motel. It was bumpy, rutted. I turned behind the building. It was very dark back there. Lots of cars huddled together. What did they do when it rained? I imagined that it must be hell trying to maneuver your car in the rain through that mud and with all that high grass slipping beneath your wheels. Someone should take a scythe to that grass.

I pulled next to a long, sleek car. I didn't know whose. I could see the passageway bisecting the motel, lit by twenty-five watts, a soda machine, a coughing ice machine. The ground was dry, but still I just moved cautiously through the grass towards that parsimonious illumination. Stopwood was waiting there for me. He didn't seem to be shivering.

"Need someone?" he asked.

"No," I said. "I'm waiting for a person."

"This isn't Grand Central Station—you pay for waiting time here."

"Sure," I said. "No problem."

"Hours? Night?"

"Full night," I said.

We settled on a price. It was high. I said that I had my own supplies. Stopwood has a fair amount of stuff for rental. The man produced a key.

"Room twelve," he said. "Who will the person ask for?"

"Alex," I said.

Stopwood nodded.

Minus luggage I walked past the doors until I came to the one with black painted numbers—12. I unlocked that door. Now at this point I realized my basic lack of planning past initial contact. What next? I was there—in the motel—I was checked into my room. What I had been thinking about was a better place, quality-type surroundings. I had been thinking there would be an inner corridor connecting the rooms, maybe I could listen unobserved at the doors. But this motel had no inner workings. Each room had its own door leading directly to the empty parking area.

The overhead light was already turned on in my room. There was no lamp. I sat down on the bed. No bedspread but clean-looking blanket and linen. A neatly made bed. The room was done in shades of green. The mattress—and I bounced—sagged. As a matter of fact, much in the room had a concave appearance. Even the ceiling had a definite curve, the plaster holding to a reckless line. Norman should have Stopwood check the roof. No television in the room either.

What should I have done, Dad? You weren't there to ask for advice.

I was on my own.

I opened the door to the room and smelled that damp chilled night air. I was right next to the passageway, the beverage machine clicking and humming, the ice machine clearing its throat again. I did what I had to do.

"Raid!" I yelled. "This is a raid! Everyone out!"

I yelled this maybe two, maybe three times. I was not discreet. The doors opened very fast. I hardly had time to position myself. This motel did not have any back entrance. I stood in the parking area facing the building. The men came tumbling out, tripping as they ran. Were they dressed? At least four came out carrying both their pants and their shorts—bodies pale and shivering. Some women came on the run too. Flesh was everywhere—hairy legs, dangling plump penises, thighs, a belly or two.

As to the women—I was surprised how attractive some of the women were and young. One of them, a brunette, running down towards the field, had a pair of grapefruit on her, Dad. Wow!

In artificial light, cold light, everyone acquired a slightly greenish glow. Sometimes more than one man came from a room. One fat man had wrapped himself in a sheet, a percale toga. I ran up and down in front of the doors trying to find Castleberry, examining the runners, looking for the image in the snapshot.

The men just left doors open when they ran, and many women were still in bed, spraddled on those sagging mattresses. The disruption of these rooms was incredible. The strange thing is, Dad, I had the feeling I knew a few of the men. One thing, though, they all looked frightened—fear is contagious.

A parade of cars began from the field, motors soaring. Automobiles moved like carnival bump-cars, shaking and bouncing all the way up to the road, undersides banging. No one yielded right of way.

Everyone hadn't left, when Stopwood came racing out of his office. "What?" he was yelling. "What?"

There was a fair amount of noise, Walter. Shouts, curses, cries of where's my bra?

"You," Stopwood said and came towards me.

He was strong for a little man. I mean he must be a practitioner of some exotic martial art, because suddenly I was on my stomach in the little paved parking area, tasting stones, feeling gravel being embedded in my neck. Stopwood was twisting my arms behind me.

"A mistake," he shouted at the fleeing.

But you know how it is when you are stopped in mid–flagrante delicto. They couldn't get started again.

At this point I was on the ground, Walter. All I could see were ankles, both bare and with socks.

"Wait!" Stopwood was saying. "Wait! It's all right!"

He wasn't talking to me.

Walter, that little man had hands of steel, I couldn't move. He pulled me towards the office, slid me across the parking area. He had a helper inside the office. From the ankles, I could tell that it was a woman.

"Telephone," he ordered her.

That's when they called the cops, Dad.

Walter, you want to know if Castleberry was there? I don't know. At least a dozen men got away from the time Stopwood pinned me and I stood up again.

· · ·

Yes, the general impression was that I had made a fool of myself. It was in the *Shilton Daily* and I think the Gannett chain also picked it up. What did the headlines say?—*Disturbance in Stopwood Motel.*

Norman had to get me out of jail.

He didn't ask for an explanation. I don't want to know, he said. I would have told him. I have nothing to hide.

Stopwood was not apologetic. I didn't know he was your brother, was all he said to Norman.

I went back to the motel the next day to find my car. The sides had been dented. Was it intentional? I can't be certain. In all that confusion of stopping and starting, it might have been hit accidentally. It was dark back there. Anything could have happened.

Now the way it stands, Dad. If Castleberry had been hiding there—he has since taken off. I fumbled it. I should have gotten back into my car, locked the doors, and driven to the front parking area before yelling—Raid! That way I could have overseen the escapes. But too late.

Five

It was Saturday, a time that Shirley used for polishing off the week's leftovers. She was sitting at the white Formica table that we used as a desk. She was filling out forms, a large pile of forms, and cards—putting in numbers, names, addresses. Many of the details that she needed had been provided by Jack. I watched her struggle, nibbling her nails, twirling her hair, trying to erase ball-point ink. The papers concerned Walter's removal from the hospital to the place of chronic care.

"I'm grateful," I told her. I meant it.

"Grateful? Why should you be grateful? I'm your wife. I should do this for you. You want to know what I've arranged?" she asked.

"Yes," I said.

"The man at the home said don't take a private room. He said a private room is important only if there is some consciousness. With no consciousness, he said, take a room for four, unless the family is big. We're not big. I took a room for four."

"All right," I said. "Do they massage the limbs?"

"What?"

"Do they massage the limbs?" My voice was a bit testy.

"I didn't ask. You didn't mention that," Shirley said.

"I want the limbs massaged," I said, my voice growing louder. "I don't want him to atrophy."

Shirley began to cry. She was not a person for crying, so the sobs sounded large in the room combined with her gulps for air. Gloria came running from her bedroom, dropping her book. She misunderstood. "I hate you," she yelled at me. "Alex, I hate you."

With my hand I swept the forms from desktop to floor, the papers scattered across the rug. It didn't matter. It altered nothing. I didn't even feel good about having done it. I knew that Walter's removal was scheduled for Wednesday, and it would happen unless Walter stopped it.

The doorbell rang.

They stared at me—Shirley and Gloria. No one was able to respond, so I went to the door.

A delivery man stood there. "Simon," he said. "Alex."

I signed for the box. It was for me, anyway.

"What?" Shirley said, wiping her eyes with the sleeve of her sweater.

"A florist's box," I said.

Shirley and Gloria stood by silently while I opened the long white box. I pushed aside the crisp green tissue, underneath were one dozen scentless white roses.

"What the hell?" Shirley said.

I read the agency card out loud. *Alex, sweetheart, we got off on a wrong foot. I was tasteless—considering your father was in the hospital. Furthermore, I gave a really poor pitch. I am a professional—I know better. The money, Alex, will be worth it. As always, Martha.*

Jack said, "You didn't call my friend Peter, did you?"

"No," I said.

"I thought not. I did it for you. I did it because Norman told me that twice Conlon has been to the house within the last week. Twice Conlon has questioned Norman about Castleberry. Who knows what Norman said? I don't like that at all."

"I didn't know about Conlon asking questions. Norman didn't tell me. What kind of questions?" I asked.

"When did Norman see Castleberry last—what went on. Conlon went to the Hole," I was told.

"Everyone goes to the Hole. You can't go to the house without going to the Hole."

"At any rate—I spoke to my friend Peter. We have to be prepared."

"Yes," I said.

I hung up the telephone. Why hadn't Norman told me about Conlon? Actually Norman has scarcely spoken to me since the Stopwood Raid. Could Norman take care of himself?

. . .

I telephoned the Bayley Farm House. Wednesday, I wanted to tell them. On Wednesday an ambulance would return Walter to the city. But it was eleven o'clock, and Norman must have driven Mother to the hospital already. I had a key to my parents' house. Why wouldn't I have a key?

No one would be in the house. The house would be deserted. No one would return until later in the afternoon. This was not like the raid, this time I thought it through.

"Shirley," I said. "I'm going out."

She came hurrying into the hall from the kitchen. "Where?" She was frowning, looked anxious. She had been unable to wash away all signs of her tears.

"A ride," I said. "Just a ride."

I drove that morning through the world's longest autumn. I drove to the Bayley Farm House. After Walter returned to the city, there would be no reason to keep the house. I'd speak to Jack. Could we revoke power of attorney?

I'd write the advertisement for the newspapers myself—*Bayley Farm House for Sale*. Last week I had called Mother. "How did the house get its name?" I asked. "Was it named after the original settlers?"

"No," Mother said. "The real estate man couldn't tell us, but the mailman did. The mailman has lived in the area since 1921. The Bayleys bought the house in 1938 from a widow's estate. The widow's children were in California—sell, they told a local man. The Bayleys moved in—a father, mother, three children. He was in insurance or something. Then in 1941, the Bayley man enlisted in the navy. He was shipped overseas, and the woman and the children lived in the house. Then in '44, she put the house up for sale. Strange, everyone thought, the war not being over. Hardly anyone selling. Up the house went and was bought just like that. The Bayleys packed their possessions and

left. Later someone found out that they had been divorced ever
since '42. The house afterwards was called the Bayley Farm
House. No other Bayleys living around here. The children never
came back."

I was right, the house was deserted. For a moment though,
I was worried. Man caught burglarizing house. I stopped that
thought. I had a key, a legitimate key. I had picked the right
time. Norman and Mother were at the hospital. First, I rang the
doorbell. Made the dog bark. Then with the true caution of a
thief, I silently turned the key and opened the door. The dog
greeted me wildly, passionately, leaping at my body, surrounding
me.

"Cham," I said. "Good dog." I moved into the hall. "Hello!" I
called. The house creaked in response to the sun that heated and
cooled it as the earth moved. "Hello!" I called again. No one was
there. It was quiet.

"Well, old dog," I said. "Just you and me."

Why had I come to the house? I came because I couldn't
forget what Eileen had said when she called me that day before
she left to return to the Coast. I'm getting out of here, she had
said. Your mother must be nuts, she said. There I was looking
at some paintings when she comes on like a lady wrestler. She
twisted my arm, Alex. She grabbed me. She dragged me down
the stairs.

Norman had never taken this matter up. Perhaps he hadn't
heard the details. Hadn't noticed. Mother had always been an
artist. I knew that. Never mind that nothing satisfied her. Never
mind that there were no paintings for me to show to friends.
Eileen had been looking at paintings. But they didn't have to be
Mother's.

I went up the stairs quietly—the cat burglar never slips from
his role. The dog accompanied me, delirious with company, twirling between my legs. I slipped twice. On the second floor, I
paused. Again I called out. "Mother!" In the silence I knocked

on her closed door—opened it, turning the knob with oily grace. She was not there.

The dog came with me on the climb to the third floor. I had been up to that floor only once that I could remember. In the main attic room was Mother's typical setup. I recognized the neat precision of it. An artist's cell with its careful placement of colors. I walked around. Carefully inspected a pile of paper. All blank. No pictures here—it was as I suspected. Mother saved nothing.

There I was looking at some paintings, Eileen had said, when she comes on like a lady wrestler.

I went into one of the tiny bedrooms. They were depressing rooms, empty, rain-stained rooms. I opened the closet door. I could see paper on the shelves, stretched canvases stacked against the wall. I could not blink them away.

I started with the large papers first. I took those papers from the shelf. "My mother did that," I whispered. She had signed everything. I was staring at the Hole. Pictures of the Hole—the Hole in charcoal, the Hole sketched in pencil, watercolors of the Hole. The Hole peopled by scores of unknown souls—having picnics, orgies, tea parties. I was shocked. The Hole in various seasons—incredible colors. Walter was not to be found in any of these pictures. I thought one shadow might be Chaminade.

I pulled down the stretched canvases—the oil paintings. They dazzled me—more colors—deep blues, light greys, pale greens, pure whites. The Hole was everywhere. But in the oils, the Hole became ominous, brooding, beckoning. "Mother," I whispered. She was an artist, she had painted all of these.

I went into the second bedroom, tried that closet, found more paintings. An entire collection of Hole paintings. There was a shadow in the bottom of one Hole—of something or someone, I was uncertain.

How many pictures? I was afraid to count them. I put all the pictures back into the closets—hoping everything was exactly the way I had found it—closed the doors.

I decided to risk a telephone call before I left the house. I called from the downstairs hall.

"Jack," I said, "she's been painting the Hole."

"Painting the Hole? Who?"

"Mother," I said. "Pictures."

"I didn't know she kept any pictures."

"She kept these."

"Alex, don't tell anyone. Who knows?"

"Eileen."

"Hell. How much did she see?"

"Not much. She didn't mention the Hole to me."

"Listen, Alex—your mother doesn't have a painting of Walter at the bottom of the Hole, does she?"

"No."

"Thank God for that."

notes to walter

Norman cannot be fathomed, Pop. Norman is weird, impossible, unrealistic. Know what he wants to do now? He wants to paint the house. He wants to paint the outside of Bayley Farm House. Why in heaven's name? I asked him. Shabby, he says. All the houses around here are spruced up. The words are his, Dad. Spruced up. This from a person who always claimed that God made the cities for a purpose—for people to stay there. Away from country houses that must be spruced up. What did I do, Dad? Norman, I said, that is a damn fool idea. We are not going to keep the house. What? he says. The house is going, I said. Who will live in the house, Norman? Will Mother live there all alone? Without Walter—absolutely not, no way. Let the new owner paint the house.

My decision, Walter, was sensible. I must tell you that I feel less and less like the younger son—and I am not putting Norman down. It's just that the more advice I give, the older I feel—by all accounts I am currently ancient.

Hey, Dad, I bet you are surprised to see me here this way—not part of the regular schedule—no, it isn't. Why am I here now?—because it is necessary, that's why. There's no more time. Walter, you have got to take charge right now. It's your turn, Dad.

Walter, I am capable of the worst possible actions. Take my word for it, Walter. I will, given the opportunity, do almost anything. Exploitation doesn't bother me in the slightest. You are in no condition to stop me. Are you? You can't deny that. Guess what I'm going to do? I'll tell you. I am going to sign a contract with an advertising agency. Yes, I am. Dad, I am going to let some half-wits take pictures of your beloved Hole for an advertising campaign. What are they selling? Apartments, Dad. They will be selling apartments. A complete living package—saunas, whirlpools, plastic all-season grass. They will take pictures, Pop. Pictures of Mother digging. Pictures of Norman with a shovel. Pictures of Chaminade crapping in the Hole. They will even superimpose a picture of you digging away. Yes, I will give them permission to do that. Then, Dad, for a final coup de grace—a photograph of you here in this very bed. Yes, indeed. A picture of Walter now incapacitated—why? The caption will read: *Walter needs a new place to live.*

Think about it, Dad. A picture of you flat on your back in this bed—powerless to stop them, to stop me. Walter as advertising symbol. Great, huh? You think I'm joking, you think I'm kidding, you figure he'd never do that. Try me, Walter. I am unstoppable.

Mother and Norman are in the hall, Dad. Mother does not look well. Maybe I shouldn't tell you that. But she looks lousy, skeletal, distracted, We fear for her. She cannot really cope, Walter. Hers was not the generation of women who can cope. Also, I think that Conlon may be harassing her.

He's a real character, Dad. Our Conlon is a peach. Doesn't he own a change of clothes? For a while I said to myself this man is off the wall, he is bonkers, but then I thought it through. We are his big case. I mean we are his moment of glory, his trial by fire. How can he leave us alone?—he can't. Read the *Shilton Daily.* What's there? Speeders, minor vandalism, drunken and disorderly. I did some looking myself. In the past—the recent past—say fifteen years—what's happened? I'll tell you. One guy cut up his wife in little fleshy bits and dropped her down his well, some guy shot his brother-in-law deliberately, and two lovers had a nasty time of it. That's it, Pop. The total sum of the trouble in these environs. I know you will say that was just what got into the newspaper—but what else can we go on—hearsay dies with the speakers. We must rely on the written record.

You understand, Walter, Conlon cannot abandon us. We will make him news, give him a purpose. And where is Castleberry? Do we *know*? Does Norman know? Mother?

Did someone hit you, Walter?

.   .   .

DIGS

Dad, I guess you are curious about why I have appeared this way late at night or rather early morning. It's past three in the morning. I came in response to a telephone call from a doctor whose name I do not recognize. Walter, they have cancelled the move. That's why I am here—this is off-hours. Pay attention, Dad. They are leaving you here. Did you arrange that?

They say that you are failing—that you have moved from chronic to acute.

Those are false tidings.

Failing from where to where?

Dad, it's just an apartment house down there.

But, Walter, if you want, I will help with the Hole.

Me and Norman.

Say the word, Dad.

But you better speak up quickly, because in a few minutes they are coming in here to hook you up to more devices than you ever imagined.

You will not like that.

Believe me.

LETTER TO CONLON AND LAST NOTES

LeTTer To ConLon

What's been happening around here, Conlon? I'll tell you. I believe that you should know, so I am sending you this as soon as possible. Never you mind who I am—I'm not getting myself into any trouble, thank you. I am only doing my duty and bringing certain facts to your attention.

How do I know these things?

Easy—I'll tell you. I follow the stars. Astronomy as a hobby. But when all this uproar, this business started—hell, I said to myself, the area has got to be protected. I will use my telescope.

I have from time to time watched the Hole.

Don't think that you can trace me by my admitting to having a telescope. You wouldn't believe how many telescopes there are around here. I know.

Tuesday night, past midnight it was when I started hearing noises. I went to look outside, but nothing. It was dark, and I could see nothing. What kind of noises? Trucks. I heard truck noise—then silence—then a definite rumbling of a truck.

Call you?—what good would that have done? I know what you would have said. From the highway, you would have said. You are just hearing noises from the highway. Wind conditions, a peculiar echo effect. No law against trucks riding down the highway at night.

Nor do I think there should be such a law. Trucks have got to deliver their products. But I knew that wasn't the source of my noise. I mean once in a blue moon we hear truck noises from the highway. But that's a single rumble—maybe a very heavy eight-axle job. This was as I said—truck noise—silence—truck noise.

I said to myself, a truck is coming and going. That is a reasonable assumption, Conlon. Now it was past three in the morning—I was dead for sleep—but no sooner than I seemed about to drift off—when wham, rumble, rumble, brakes squeak—the truck again. I'm thinking smugglers, bootleggers. On Oglethorpe Road, you would have said.

I knew damn well that's what you would have said. Me—I'd have come off as four kinds of an idiot. So every time I picked up the telephone receiver—I said to myself—No.

I was completely out a night's sleep, Conlon.

One lousy telephone call could have stopped everything.

If you think I didn't mutter Bayley Farm House, you're crazy. Of course I did. But it was the middle of the night—not even a full moon. I didn't know what the hell to do. I just sat up in a chair and maybe got a little sleep.

When I woke up it was half-past seven, and I had a stiff neck from that chair. It was daylight. I went and looked out the window. Trucks or no trucks, everything looked the same. I had breakfast. Shows you how influenced we are by other people's explanations—I was already convincing myself that it had been trucks on the highway. But somewhere tucked away in the farthest corner of my mind—I was thinking the Bayley Farm House.

After breakfast, feeling jumpy from not enough sleep and the coffee, I decided to have a look. This was I might add in the nature of preserving the peace of the area. Just so you don't get the wrong idea. I do not look into windows.

I knew just where to position the telescope for a look-see at the Hole.

I focused and almost leaped backwards. What did I see? I saw a large dump truck parked out there. My truck noises—now you understand. But that's not the marvel of it—the marvel of it, Conlon, was the Hole.

No Hole, Conlon.

They had filled that Hole up with dirt. Must have driven that truck back and forth all night. Who? I'll tell you—one of those brothers—Norman and Alexander—the ones in the newspapers. It shows you, doesn't it, who gets publicity in this world.

The Hole was gone, Conlon. I could hardly believe it. I'm still looking through my telescope, improving the focus, when one of those brothers comes out into the yard. I had an A-one view of him. He did not look happy, Conlon. Near the site of that former Hole is one big pile of twigs, branches, and other stuff.

What is he going to do? My God, Conlon, he pours from a can onto the wood. He lights a match. A fire, Conlon. He was burning that wood. I wanted to call you, but I'm afraid to leave my telescope and good thing too. He was bringing things from the house—paper, maybe some pictures. Threw all that on the fire. Then that one—who knows which one?—he's got some kind of a notebook and ripping the pieces of paper and also tossing them on the flames.

I tell you, Conlon, I was jumping up and down with excitement. When the other brother suddenly comes running from the house. He's yelling, I think, and waving his arms. He goes over and punches his brother, then he runs around and around where the Hole used to be. Then I saw those brothers get into a car and drive off. There was a point when looking through the telescope, I thought they might be crying—the brothers. But the criminal mind is devious.

What I did then was dangerous—I'll grant you that—deadly dangerous. I went there, Conlon. I raced over to the Bayley Farm House. I was able by using a long pole to save from the fire two half sheets of paper with writing on them and a fragment of what looks like an oil painting.

I enclose these in the envelope for your use, Conlon. And God bless you.

Last note to Conlon

Conlon, I will arrange to have this note smuggled to you. I'm in Connecticut in a place called a rest home—but letters don't go either in or out. Am I in need of rest? For a long time I would have said yes. But now—no.

When did I first know that the pictures were gone? Would you believe that I sensed it. An overwhelming primitive knowledge of loss. My *pictures* were gone. Conlon, I was filled with blackness—past despair—there was nothing. They had destroyed me. They had destroyed the artist.

That, of course, was ego, Conlon. It was me that was destroyed. How could I give up the sense of me. Recreate the pictures? No, Conlon, I could not do that. They were painted just once—they existed.

Do you understand? They *existed.* I closed my eyes—I searched my mind—my soul—the pictures were there.

I am an artist.

I created those pictures.

I need do nothing else.

That's a relief, Conlon. I thank you for your time and attention.

Listen, I have done nothing for you.

Is there some way that I can help you?

Would you like me to say something? I'll oblige. If it would be to your advantage—a promotion or a raise or something.

Since I have fulfilled my life's purpose, I would be glad to give you a confession.

Just say the word.

I'll confess to anything.

Hitting Walter on the head.

Knowing where Castleberry is.

The matter of the wills.

Last note to alexander

Alexander, brother mine, I am sorry about the fight in court. I really believe that we could have settled this between us. I blame Jack for instigating everything. I am also sorry that you lost.

But kiddo, I am staying here. That is that. The Bayley Farm House is where I am staying. I like it here, Alex. Perhaps I'll travel someday—come and see you.

But right now I am busy—the sides of the Hole have to be shored up. I am also looking into the rental of a large tent. If the Hole were covered in winter, then work could continue. What have I found recently? The following:

    674 bricks, pink tone
    145 pieces of blue tile
    1   stone fountain
    26 pieces of copper flashing
    misc. bits of ornamental stone, nails, left side of a mantel

The work goes on, Alex.

By the way, Jack gave me your address—reluctantly. He wanted to forward the letter—but I would have no go-between. I want to approach my brother directly. Are you living permanently in Italy? I hope you are well, Alex—you and Shirley and Gloria.

I am enclosing a newspaper clipping. Ignore the article, pay attention to the picture. It's a picture of the directors of the country's leading foundations at their annual meeting in California. I have circled a figure in this photograph with a red pen. Look closely, Alex. Isn't that Castleberry? I am almost certain that he is out there.

Last note to walter

This is the last time I will address you, Walter. You are dead and buried. Then too this is the last time you will be here alone. Tomorrow, we place Mother by your side. You disrupted the world, Dad. None of us are the same. Mother's paintings are gone. Castleberry also. If there were crimes, Conlon cannot solve them. In case you are interested, the Hole remains. Not because I wanted it to exist—you should know that I did everything that I could to destroy it. Immediately after you died, I filled in that Hole—completely filled it in—thought that would be the end of it. I was wrong. Norman is digging it out again.

I cannot stop him.

I knew that after the reading of the will.

We fought over the money, Dad.

It all comes down to money, doesn't it?

We wept, though.

A NOTE ON THE TYPE

The text of this book was set in a digitized version of Primer, designed by Rudolph Ruzicka, who was earlier responsible for the design of Fairfield and Fairfield Medium, faces whose virtues have for some time now been accorded wide recognition.

The complete range of sizes of Primer was first made available in 1954, although the pilot size of 12-point was ready as early as 1951. The design of the face makes general reference to Linotype Century—long a serviceable type, totally lacking in manner or frills of any kind—but brilliantly corrects its characterless quality.

Composed by Maryland Composition Company, Inc.,
Glen Burnie, Maryland
Printed and bound by The Haddon Craftsmen, Inc., Scranton, Pennsylvania
Designed by Virginia Tan